PRAISE FOR ROBIN CAI

"CAROLL HAS COMBINED MURDER AND SUSPENSE WITH VIVID DESCRIPTIONS AND EXCELLENT CHARACTER DEVELOPMENT."

— CBA RETAILERS + RESOURCES

"THIS FAST-PACED FAITH-BASED THRILLER COMES WITH UNIQUE ELEMENTS NOT NORMALLY COVERED BY CHRISTIAN FICTION....CAROLL'S NOVEL WILL GO DOWN EASY FOR FANS OF ROMANTIC SUSPENSE."

— PUBLISHER'S WEEKLY

"CAROLL'S LATEST TALE FOR ROMANTIC SUSPENSE FANS, ESPECIALLY THOSE WHO LIKE A BIT OF WESTERN FLAVOR AND LORE MIXED IN WITH THEIR THRILLS."

— LIBRARY JOURNAL

SNARES OF DEATH

ROBIN CAROLL

RC PRODUCTIONS, INC

© 2021 by Robin Caroll

No part of this book may be reproduced, distributed or transmitted in any form or by any means, including photocopying, recording, or other electronic or mechanical methods, without the prior written permission of the publisher, except in the case of brief quotations embodied in critical reviews and certain other noncommercial uses permitted by copyright law. For permission requests, write to the author at: www.robincaroll.com

Publisher's Note: This is a work of fiction. Names, characters, places, and incidents are a product of the author's imagination. Locales and public names are sometimes used for atmospheric purposes. Any resemblance to actual people, living or dead, or to businesses, companies, events, institutions, or locales is completely coincidental.

Scripture quotations and paraphrases are from The Holy Bible, English Standard Version®, copyright © 2001 by Crossway Bibles, a publishing ministry of Good News Publishers. Used by permission. All rights reserved.

Printed in the United States of America by RC Productions, Incorporated.

ALSO BY ROBIN CAROLL

Stratagem

Darkwater Inn Series

Darkwater Secrets

Darkwater Lies

Darkwater Truth

Recipes from the Darkwater Inn (companion cookbook)

The Evil Series

Deliver Us from Evil

Fear No Evil

In the Shadow of Evil

Hidden in the Stars

Torrents of Destruction

Weaver's Needle

The Bayou Series

Bayou Justice

Bayou Corruption

Bayou Judgment

Bayou Paradox

Bayou Betrayal

Bayou Blackmail

Dead Air

Justice Seeker Series
Injustice for All
To Write a Wrong
Strand of Deception
The Christmas Bell Tolls

For Middle Grade/YA Readers
Samantha Sanderson At the Movies
Samantha Sanderson On the Scene
Samantha Sanderson Off the Record
Samantha Sanderson Without A Trace

*In memory of my son-in-law, Robert Keith Fotioo II.
You brightened all of our lives with your sense of humor, love of history, gift with all things electronic, and patience with children.
You are so missed.*

"The cords of death encompassed me; the torrents of destruction assailed me. The cords of Sheol entangled around me; the snares of death confronted me. In my distress I called upon the Lord; to my God I cried for help. From his temple he heard my voice, and my cry reached his ears."

— Psalm 18:4-6 ESV

PROLOGUE

Some calls were hard to make. This was going to be worse than hard.

Over the car's voice-activated Bluetooth, he ordered his cell to dial the number he'd acquired before leaving his office. Waiting for the ringing to come through the car's speakers, he steered out of the city and onto US Highway 19, heading home.

The call went to voicemail, the beep bouncing off the leather interior of the car hugging the contours of the road.

"Christian, it's Henry." He downshifted the Porsche 911 into fifth gear as he sped south toward the Gauley River communities. The setting sun streaked the West Virginia sky with a brilliant orange, like creepy fingers of fire. "I know this is a little out of the blue, but I didn't know who else to talk about this with."

Wasn't that just the understatement of the decade?

Henry Wolfe gripped the steering wheel a little tighter as he navigated the set of curves of the familiar road. "I owe you a huge apology. Well, much more than an apology, but..." No sense muddying the waters. "But, anyway, you were right, and I need your help."

He pressed in the clutch and shifted back into sixth as he gained speed on the short straightaway of the road on his way home from

Summersville. "I found something today at the office that's concerning, to say the least." The report he'd uncovered...Henry shook his head even though he was alone in the car. He shifted into seventh, gaining speed despite heading toward the next set of tight curves. No biggie—he'd grown up driving on this road.

"I really want to talk to you in person if you're willing to meet me. Show you what I found and make sure I'm reading it right." Although it would be impossible for him to not understand the gist of what the report clearly reflected. "I'd like for you to advise me what steps to take next."

Henry had a good idea what he should do—what he needed to do, and that's what had him tied up in knots. "Anyway, if you could give me a call as soon as possible, that'd be great. It doesn't matter what time it is. I really need to talk to you."

Henry moved his finger to push the button to disconnect the call, and took a tight turn to the left—at the same time, lights split through dusk's darkening hue. Everything happened at once—

A car rushed toward him, in his lane.

"Get out of my lane!" He instinctively jerked the steering wheel to the right.

The speedster's tires slid on the loose gravel.

The fender crashed into the metal guardrail.

Time seemed to move in slow motion.

...

Henry's seatbelt dug into his shoulder as the car flipped...

...

Rolled...

...

Time stopped as pain hammered against his body.

Crash!

...

Glass spilled everywhere, like heavy raindrops from a driving downpour.

...

Henry's sides caved as if a heavyweight boxer pounded his body.

His neck popped, the sound echoing against the pulse pulverizing his temples. The back of his head slammed into the headrest with a resounding *thunk*.

Bam! Bam! Bam!

Boom! The airbag punched him in the nose. White powder filled the Porsche.

He couldn't breathe. The air hissed from the airbag, allowing oxygen to fill his lungs with an echoing wheeze.

Red-hot agony seared his face. He couldn't feel his legs. His arms wouldn't respond to his demands that they move.

A metallic-coppery taste filled his mouth. He coughed, then spit—sprays of crimson shot onto the cream-colored leather dash.

An agonizing wail echoed in his ears. Who screamed? He was the only one in the car. Had he shouted?

His vision blurred. Henry closed his eyes.

Images filled his mind: Harper…his dad…his mom. Oh, his mom. He could almost hear her voice at the moment.

Henry, honey.

No, that couldn't be right. She was dead—had died his last year of law school.

What was happening to him?

He struggled to open his eyes. A familiar stench filled the air, sharp and pungent, like by fuel pumps.

He exhaled. The side of his head smashed against the doorframe.

Black coldness overtook every part of his body.

Kaboom!

1

Grief came in starts and stops. It pervaded every space of her being, especially wherever her love for him hid at any given moment.

Harper Wolfe gripped his pillow close to her chest. Closed her eyes and inhaled deeply. His unique scent—a mix of his woodsy shampoo-bodywash combo and his familiar cologne, flooded her senses. Her raw throat tightened while the ever-present tears burned her eyes.

No, she couldn't just keep crying continually. She pushed to her feet.

She set his pillow back on its place on the bed, pausing to stare at the framed photo on the nightstand. Harper lifted it, running a single finger down the cold glass. They had been so happy. She remembered so clearly the day they'd taken the selfie. They had gone out to celebrate both of them passing the bar. While Father had wanted to take them out to dinner, they'd chosen to go alone to meet with the friends they'd made in law school. It was probably the last time Harper could remember being truly happy and carefree.

Sighing, she returned the frame to its place on the nightstand. While she would go through his belongings later, now wasn't the time. Harper moved to the living room and stared at the two fishbowls sitting side-by-side on the credenza. The two male beta fish, Republican and Democrat, seemed to be standing off against one another.

She opened the food container and dusted a pinch of food in each bowl. What was she going to do with them? She didn't like fish, especially not two that were too aggressive to even be in the same bowl together. Strangely enough, Henry had loved the two betas.

How was she going to go on without him?

Fresh sobs rose from her chest. She braced herself against the smooth walnut of the antique piece of furniture.

A key rattled in the kitchen door to the garage.

Harper's heart jumped to pound at the base of her throat. She glanced around. What could she use for a weapon?

The door opened. Nell, the sweet, elderly housekeeper, shut the door. "Oh, Harper. I didn't realize you were here." She set her purse and keys on the kitchen counter and smiled at Harper. "If you need me to come back later, that's no problem."

Harper swallowed against a dry mouth. It had slipped her mind that Nell came to clean the house on Fridays. Nell didn't know about Henry yet. Then again, how could she?

"Harper?" The older woman was nurturing to both Henry and Harper, so much more than just a housekeeper. A member of the family. How could Harper have forgotten to call her and break the news to her sooner?

"Nell, let's sit down." Harper gripped the back of the chair at the table in the little nook in the kitchen.

The older woman lost her smile. "What's wrong?"

"It's Henry." Each word...every syllable took enormous effort for Harper to get out of her mouth. "He was in an accident Wednesday night." Was it just two nights ago?

Nell made the sign of the cross over her chest. "Oh, merciful heavens, is he all right?"

Harper slowly shook her head. She could no longer deny the tears. They escaped and raced down her cheeks.

"No...no...no." Nell's eyes filled with moisture and spilled over, too. She reached and pulled Harper into her arms, alternating between rubbing Harper's back and patting her.

Harper clung to her and let the sobs loose. Nell's shaking seemed to act in tandem with Harper's, but Harper couldn't move out of the embrace if she'd wanted to...it felt so nice to have someone to just hug her. To hold her. To let her cry.

"Oh, baby girl, I'm so sorry." Nell's gentle rubbing soothed the nerves Harper felt were zapping just under the surface of her skin. "I heard nothing about this on the news."

No wonder. Harper dabbed at her eyes and reluctantly eased out of the warmth of Nell's comfort. "Father has kept the press at bay, delaying any announcement of Henry's death until the police's initial investigation and coroner's report has been concluded. The initial results came in today, so it'll likely hit the news cycle this evening." How her father had managed such a feat, Harper didn't know. Even her own status as an Assistant Prosecuting Attorney for the county didn't yield her that much power.

At least not yet.

Nell nodded. "Can you tell me what happened?"

Harper forced air into her lungs. "A car accident. On Highway 19." She shook her head and swiped her eyes with the back of her hand.

Nell sucked in air and pressed her fingers against her mouth.

Harper repeated the details, reciting almost in a monotone as if reading aloud instead of sharing details of an event that was literally ripping her heart to shreds. She had to use her *lawyer voice,* as she and Henry had laughingly dubbed it years ago. She wasn't laughing now. "No one else was involved. The police think he took the turn too fast and lost control of the car when he tried to stop." They'd analyzed the skid marks and concluded just this morning that he'd tried to stop, but the loose gravel that lined along the edge of the road had only spun the little sportscar out of control.

Balling both her hands into fists at her sides, Harper struggled to even her breathing. If only Father hadn't bought Henry that stupid

Porsche as a gift when he joined the company. But Henry had loved that car.

Now it served as his coffin.

Harper sniffed and focused on Nell. "His car went through the guardrail and over the side." It was hard to see through the moisture in her eyes. "The coroner said he never had a chance and that he was most likely dead before the car exploded into flames." She clung to the hope they were right about that.

Nell began mumbling under her breath, and gripped the cross necklace she always wore. "Oh, Harper, I'm so sorry. So, so sorry." She gave Harper another tight hug, then stepped back again with a gentle squeeze of her upper arm. "What can I do for you? How can I help?"

Harper gave a slight shake of her head. "I don't even know where to start. We'll have a memorial, of course. Sometime next week. I just don't know more than that right now."

"What about your father?"

Harper shrugged. "He's in denial. I don't think he can come to terms yet that Henry's gone." He'd been on autopilot the last day or so, just going through the motions. Harper understood—she was having quite the time wrapping her mind and heart around the loss herself. "I guess we should start with planning a memorial. I'll need to set a date and let our friends know. Probably Wednesday. That's a good day for a memorial service, right?" Her education kicked in. "I'll have to look over his will." They'd drawn up each other's when they were studying for that portion of the bar exam.

Nell reached out and gave her upper arm a rub. "Just take it one step at a time." She frowned. "You shouldn't have to handle all of this yourself."

Without Henry, Harper felt more alone than ever. As if part of her was missing.

Because it was.

Nell's voice broke through her heartbreak. "Let me handle the memorial service. I'll call your church and get everything set. You can pick out the personal touches once the pastor lets me know what he needs."

Harper practically flung herself into Nell's arms. "Oh, thank you." She hadn't had any idea how she was going to go through the motions of planning his memorial. "That would mean so much to me. Thank you." The last person she wanted to talk to right now was Pastor Ford.

Or God.

"Of course, honey." She shook her head. "I'll also put a call out to the ladies' group. They'll want to schedule delivering meals for you and your father."

"That's not really necessary, Nell. You know Father's staff can handle meals."

"Of course it isn't, but it's what we do. I'm sure your father will have plenty for the staff to do in the wake of such a tragedy. They can take over running your Father's house without direction." She smoothed Harper's hair hanging down her back. "Most importantly, you need to concentrate on grieving. You were the person closest to Henry. He loved you with everything he was. There was no denying the special bond between the two of you."

The boulder in the back of Harper's throat returned. "And I love him more than anything. I always will." The hole in her heart would never heal. Its darkness would forever linger, growing bigger and wider until it swallowed her entirely.

"I'm going to go talk to your pastor, then I'll be in touch." Nell lifted her purse. "You take the time here to feel Henry…to remember the love you two shared." She gave Harper a quick kiss on the cheek. "I'm only a phone call away. Don't be afraid to call me any time. Day or night. Anything you need."

Harper nodded. "Thanks, Nell. I just…" Her throat tightened again, her new normal, apparently.

"No words are needed, honey." With a final pat to Harper's shoulder, Nell headed out the kitchen door into the garage.

Alone again, Harper glanced around the kitchen. Memories assaulted her, like the time they tried out that recipe for spicy pork loin and the end results were so much of a disaster that a pizza order was the only way they were able to eat that night. Or the time they'd tried to recreate a lasagna they'd seen on a cooking show. She was pretty sure there had to be tomato sauce still hiding somewhere after the pot boiled over and the lasagna sauce exploded everywhere. Oh, the laughter they'd shared in this kitchen.

How could you have left me all alone, Henry?

She moved back to the living room, letting the grief wash over her once more. More remembrances came to mind. Loving Henry wasn't always easy. The arguments they'd had about their career paths after graduation. The quarrels over him going to work with Father, and of her accepting the position with the Nicholas County Prosecuting Attorney's Office. He was proud of her, of course, but couldn't understand why she didn't push Father to go to work with him at Wolfe Mining.

Everywhere she looked, memories of Henry accosted her. His laughter. His slightly crooked grin. The faint scar just above his lip from his attempts at riding a motorcycle just before being accepted into law school. He always had been the daring one...the one who wasn't afraid to take risks. And now he was gone.

She pushed back the onslaught of memories. Henry's presence filled every nook and cranny of the house. She would have to put the house on the market. No way could she ever be in this house and not feel Henry's presence, and that was something she couldn't take. Probably never would.

Bam! Bam! Bam!

Harper jumped. She turned and stared at the front door, as if she would magically know who was on the other side.

But magic didn't exist. She crossed the room.

Bam! Ba—

Harper jerked open the door, glare firmly burning her face.

"Oh. Sorry. I'm looking for Henry." Christian Gallagher, in all his bad-boy aloofness, stood on the stoop, his thumbs stuck at angles in the front pockets of his well-worn jeans. A totally relaxed posture that models struck on the covers of men's magazines, but most men couldn't pull off. Yet Christian seemed naturally born into the pose.

Harper pushed the observance away. "Now's not a good time."

She moved to shut the door, but Christian moved faster, pushing his hand against the door.

"I need to talk to Henry. Is he here?"

A scream built in her chest. She inhaled deeply, pulling her emotions into check. "No, now will you please let go of the door?"

But he didn't. "Is he at the office? I can go there if I have to. His voicemail said to call him ASAP, but he hasn't been answering his phone all morning. It sounded important before the call was cut off."

She froze, hand on the doorknob. "He left you a voicemail? When?"

Christian's intense stare locked on her face. "Wednesday."

The day he died. Harper's heart hiccupped. She opened the door wider and waved him inside. "Maybe you should come in."

He gave her a sideways look, but crossed over the threshold into the foyer. "Now I'm worried. Henry's message sounded really cryptic, and now you're suddenly being congenial...what in the world is going on with you two?"

"Please, have a seat." She shut the door behind him and motioned to the couch.

Sitting, he pushed his long legs out in front of him and crossed his arms over his chest. "So, what's going on?"

"What time did he call you on Wednesday?" She eased herself onto the chair adjacent to the couch. Her heart pounded against her ribcage.

He pulled out his cell phone and scrolled. "Seven forty-two. I was on a job, then went straight to an overnight guiding trip, so didn't get his voice mail until today." His gaze met hers. "Now, what's going on?"

That was in the time frame the coroner and police had set for Henry's time of death. The time of his accident. Her heart caught even as her stomach churned. "Do you still have the voicemail? Can you play it for me?"

He held up a hand. "Whoa, there. I'm not telling you anything more until you tell me what's the deal with Henry."

How many times would she have to repeat the same story that ripped open her pain? No wonder the victims in her cases sounded emotionless after retelling their story for the umpteenth time. She swallowed. Once.

Twice.

A third time.

"Henry was in a car accident Wednesday evening." She licked her lips and blinked. Hard. "His car went over the guardrail and he...he died."

~

Henry...dead?

No way. He had to have misheard or misunderstood. "I didn't hear anything about this on the news." He'd listened to the radio all the way over. The story of his dying would be a top story in the Gauley River area, but he'd heard no mention of Henry's accident.

"Father kept it out of the media. The news will break tonight or tomorrow—that's as long as they agreed to hold off the report."

This had to be a mistake, but as Christian stared at Harper, he knew it was true.

"What happened?" Christian could barely push out the question.

Harper took a moment, squaring her posture, her light red hair slinging over her shoulder, before telling him about the car wreck. "So, you see," she wound down her explanation, "whatever voicemail you have is most likely the last thing Henry said just before he died."

Now the sounds at the end of the voicemail made sense. He'd actually heard the crash. As he glanced at Harper, he hesitated. That ending wasn't likely something she should hear. It was basically the death of her twin.

"Christian?" Her tone was so much softer than her usual tone when she spoke to him, as if she were broken on the inside. She probably was. Her probing eyes held his stare, glistening with so many clear emotions.

What if it were a recording of his sister's final moments alive? No matter what, he'd want to hear. He'd want to know what happened to Katie-cat.

He tugged his cell from his pocket, pulled up the voicemail, then played it on speaker.

Tears flowed from Harper's deep green eyes as Henry's voice seemed to boom inside his living room. The recording seemed to go on forever, which had to be agony for her. She pressed her fingers to her mouth as the message drew to a close, then finally ended.

Silently, Christian held his cell.

Harper pinched her eyes closed, keeping her fingers against her mouth.

How could he comfort her? Were there any words that would bring him solace at such a time if their roles were reversed?

There were none, so he sat in silence.

She cleared her throat and shuddered as she opened her eyes. Harper blinked, then cleared her throat again. She held his gaze. "That was the wreck."

He nodded, not sure what he could say.

"What did Henry mean in his message? What were you right about?" she asked.

Christian shook his head. "I have no idea. I haven't talked to Henry in weeks." He ran his hand over his face, the stubble pricking against his skin. "I've been out with a group on the Gauley, but as soon as I got back in, I checked my phone and heard his message. It sounded pretty important, so I tried calling multiple times and when I couldn't reach him, I drove over here."

"Can you play it again, please?"

He hesitated. "Are you sure?" It was hard to hear, even for Christian. He couldn't imagine how Harper had to feel listening to the death of her twin brother.

She nodded.

He started the recording again, almost dreading the ending.

"Get out of my lane!"

"Stop it." Her perfect posture straightened even more, if that was possible.

He tapped his cell and glanced across the coffee table at Harper. "I'm so sorry. I can only imag—"

"No," she cut him off. "Did you catch what he said? He said to get out of his lane. Someone had to have been coming toward him in his lane."

"Well, yeah. I guess." People who didn't know the road well sometimes did drift out of their lane in curves.

Harper sat forward. "But that's what caused the wreck. It had to have been." She shook her head. "Someone was in his lane and that caused him to wreck. They didn't even stop, either. He went over the side of the road and crashed."

"Maybe, but we can't know for sure." He resisted adding that it didn't matter. None of it would bring Henry back. Maybe Harper needed to believe something—anything had caused her brother's death. She had to blame something...someone other than Henry. He could understand that. He'd probably feel the same way if it were Gabe or Katie.

"But we can try." She stood. "We can take the recording to the site. Estimate what happened."

"Can't you find out what the police determined? I mean, because of your job and all." She was, after all, an Assistant Prosecuting Attorney for the county.

Her face scrunched up. "The detectives who conducted the investigation determined it was an accident, but they didn't have this as evidence that someone else was responsible. That recording clearly shows someone else was responsible for Henry going off the side of the road. Then they left the scene. That's a crime."

Christian pushed to his feet and looked down at her. "But you going there might not be the best idea."

"As an officer of the court, I'm obligated to report crimes." Her eyes shimmered with moisture. "I need to know what happened. I've felt it inside that this wasn't a random accident. Call it a twin thing or wishful thinking, I don't care, but I just can't accept that Henry himself caused this accident. And now you have the proof that it wasn't." Her gulp was audible between them.

He let out a slow breath and pocketed his cell. "Even if we can show someone else was at fault, that won't bring Henry back." He used the softest tone he could and stared right into her eyes as he spoke. He felt as much sympathy for her as he ever had another person.

She swiped at her eyes. "I know it won't bring Henry back. Nothing will." Her tone came out snappy and sharp. "It can make a difference, legally and in his reputation, in how his death is categorized. And someone, intentionally or not, caused the accident and then left the scene. That's a crime and they need to answer for it."

Christian hesitated. He wasn't sure about the legalities, but he wasn't a lawyer...she was. That aside, he understood all too well about a reputation. To have it reported that Henry Wolfe, son of Elliott Wolfe of Wolfe Mining carried a lot of stigma itself in the region. Add to it that he was speeding and lost control of his pretty little sportscar and died...those opposed to Wolfe Mining's methods would say Henry got what he deserved. *That* would keep Harper's wound of grief open wide. Every comment would be like pouring alcohol into it. Over and over again.

"If you don't want to go, don't want to get involved, I understand." Her voice lost its edge. "You can just forward me that voicemail and I'll go myself."

He stared at her for a moment. Harper Wolfe had made no bones that she didn't like Christian. She'd told Henry many times that he was a bad influence. She'd even blamed Christian when Henry had wrecked his motorcycle. Even when Henry had dated Andrea, who'd used every trick in the book to try and get Henry to the altar, that was Christian's fault in her eyes because Christian had introduced the two of them.

She shifted her weight and fisted a single hand on her hip. Christian would be desperate for the truth if he was in her position, too. Christian owed it to his friend to find out the truth, and also what had prompted Henry to call him in the first place. What had Henry found at the office that was so important?

Christian shook his head. "No, I'll go with you."

2

The yellow poplar and sycamore trees lined the road as Christian drove toward US Highway 19. Harper hadn't even hesitated to jump in the passenger seat of the Dodge Challenger. That spoke volumes of the emotional mess she was because he was practically certain she normally wouldn't be caught dead in his car. He regretted his choice of words, even as he thought them. Thank goodness he hadn't said them aloud.

"You really have no idea what he found that he wanted to discuss with you?" Her words sliced through the silence.

"No idea. His call was out of the blue, so you know as much as I do."

"What had you been talking about the last time you spoke?" She turned her attention to his profile.

"I can't even remember." Man, but he wished he could.

She shot him a skeptical look. "You can't remember? It had to have been important for him to have called and said he owed you an apology and that you were right. Whatever it was, it had to be paramount, just by his tone and the sense of urgency in his voice."

"Look, it's been months since Henry and I had spoken. I honestly can't recall." He slowed to a stop, before turning left.

Harper persisted. "He said he had something he wanted you to look at and see if he read it right. That would indicate a document of some kind, wouldn't you say? Something he wanted you to read?"

"Maybe." Christian slowed to turn right at the next road.

"Maybe?"

He lifted a single shoulder, but kept his hands on the wheel. "Sometimes, guys use the word *read* not meaning actually reading. Sometimes it's like asking a buddy for their take on how something is. A perception. That may have been what Henry meant."

"Hmm." She stared out her window, but Christian could almost see her thoughts racing around in her head.

He had questions of his own. "Do you know of anything at the office that might have caused Henry to have such a concern?" He eased across the line to pass the car in front of him. "As you said, he had a sense of urgency to his tone."

She let out a heavy breath. "I wish I could tell you, but I have no idea what he could have meant. I don't work for Father. I have no idea what goes on at Wolfe Mining."

"Yeah, I figured." That seemed to take her aback for the moment. He risked a sideways look at her.

Harper Wolfe had always been pretty, but as she'd grown up into an adult, she'd become absolutely stunning. It'd been some time since he'd seen her, but he'd know her anywhere. Her hair that was kissed by fire, hung in wavy thickness down to the middle of her back. Those green eyes of hers...well, no wonder they said she could pull the truth from a witness on the stand. Those eyes could see almost directly into your soul.

She was tall, maybe five-nine or five-ten, but she certainly wasn't scrawny. Her build was more...hmm...graceful. Yeah, that was it, graceful. Her posture was always proper, just like the way she walked. Dignified. His brother-in-law, Hunter, was an FBI agent and called people who carried themselves like that refined or rich or well-taught. Harper Wolfe was a combination of all three of those.

She stared out the front windshield. "The way he said he owed you an apology and that you'd been right...sounds almost like you two had an argument about something." Her tone, on the other hand, could come across as nice or haughty as all get-out. Guess it served her well when cross-examining a witness.

Christian chose to ignore the accusation hanging in her words. She was grieving and probably still a little in shock. And looking for deserved answers. He just didn't have any to give her. "I'm as clueless as you are. Like I said, we hadn't talked in some time, and even then, we didn't have an argument that I can remember."

"Did you have a discussion about something that you two disagreed on?"

He chuckled, despite the situation. "Come on, Harper, when *didn't* we disagree on something? We've been on opposite sides of most contentious issues for years." Christian was a freelance Wetland/Environmental consultant and river guide in his family business while her family's business was mining, for Pete's sake. How could they *not* disagree on most every issue?

"Why would he need you to advise him on next steps to take about whatever her found? He's a lawyer, he's the one usually advising others."

"I don't know." Christian slowly turned onto US Highway 19. That had been bugging him as well. It had to be something that had to do with Christian's particular knowledge base. It had to involve the Gauley River or the area's environmental status, or both.

"Why didn't he talk to me about whatever it was? I'm a lawyer, too, and his twin." The hurt hung heavy in her words.

He felt for her. Nobody should have to endure such pain. Especially not when she'd already gone through so much before. "I don't know, Harper, I really don't. If I knew anything, I promise, I'd tell you." Acting purely on instinct, he reached across the console and took her hand, gently squeezing it.

She went rigid, then jerked her hand free. "We're almost to the site of the wreck."

Christian gripped the steering wheel with both hands, straight at the ten and two position. He slowed even more as he approached the big curve. Of course, this would be where Henry had wrecked. Not only the tight curve, but the steepest drop loomed below on the whole stretch of highway.

They approached almost at a crawl. Right in the middle of the curve, four of the metal guard rails on the opposite side of the road, nearest to the drop-off, were gone. A bent and mangled one stood alone.

"This is it." Harper dug her fingers into the console until her knuckles were white.

He eased the Dodge off the road onto the inner shoulder and parked. There were no cars in either lane as he stepped onto the gravel of the shoulder. There wasn't any tell-tale yellow police tape, either. Oh, the power of the Wolfe name in this county.

Harper slammed her door shut and walked around to the front of the car. She hesitated as her stare locked onto the gap in the guardrails.

Again, Christian ached for her loss. "You don't have to go over there. I'll take a quick look and see what I notice."

"No, I need to go. I need to see." She set her chin, swallowed, then looked both ways before she crossed the street. The slightest tremble of her hands hanging by her sides could barely be noticed as she walked.

But Christian noticed. He hurried to move beside her.

She knelt at the curve's shoulder, staring at the deep tired marks in the gravel. Their exact outline was hard to determine as there was a lot of scattered and moved gravel. Probably from the tow truck and the police investigators

Christian stood beside her and looked at the road just before the mess of the gravel on the shoulder. Two skid marks clearly defined where the Porsche had braked before skidding off the road. They were just before the curve.

Harper stood beside him. "Play the message again, please."

He did as she requested. As soon as Henry said something about a car in his lane, she asked him to stop the recording and she pointed at the skid marks. "Right there is where he sees a car in his lane."

Christian turned and looked over his shoulder, forcing himself to render a mental image of what his friend would have seen, heard, and done. "For Henry to have noticed the car from there," he pivoted and pointed to where his car was parked, "the oncoming car would've had to have been about there."

He looked back to the skid marks. "He sees the car and applies his brakes, realizes it's not going to move, and tries to get out of its way by moving onto the shoulder."

"Play the recording from there."

He did as she asked. At the sound of the first crash, they both looked at the gap in the guardrails. The recording ended.

Harper shivered. Christian understood as he felt the eerie chill pushing the hairs on the back of his neck to attention as well. He looked back to where his car sat. "If this played out like we're thinking, then you're right—the other car would've had time to move."

She nodded. "Even if they didn't, they clearly would've known Henry went over the side. They could have called for help. Maybe even went down themselves to try and help Henry."

Without a word, Christian moved to the last guardrail before the gaping hole and looked down. There were parts of metal strown all the way down to the bottom. Glass glistened under the midday September sun of West Virginia. A tire sat lonely off to one side of the cleared path. The bottom of the area was singed dark black where the car had caught fire and burned.

Beside him, Harper gasped. "No mistaking he was down there." She looked up at Christian, fisting her hands on her hips. He could just about feel her trembling over the few feet between them. "Either someone is a totally heartless person and just left him to die down there, or this wasn't an accident. This was murder."

∼

SOMEONE KILLED HER TWIN.

Every fiber of Harper's being activated, like someone had plugged her into an electrical socket. Seeing this spot...knowing that someone had made the decision to either leave Henry alone in his final moments or they had acted on purpose filled her with a rage she hadn't imagined possible.

"Let's not jump the gun and go right to murder. Whoever was driving the car could have been scared." Christian's voice carried on the gentle breeze.

"Scared? Are you serious?" Surely he didn't mean that.

"Think about it, Harper."

"Think about what? That someone left Henry here to die all alone?" Tears welled in her eyes, stinging and blurring her vision. "He died a fiery death down there. He had to feel all alone. Scared? I imagine he was frightened out of his mind. Terrified. Especially if..." Her words trailed off as sobs took over.

Christian cleared his throat. "What if it was some kid? Heck, Henry and I had some wild times driving like maniacs on this road when we were teenagers. If a kid made the curve and was in Henry's lane, saw Henry skid off the road and down the drop-off, that would have scared him out of his mind."

"Even as a teen, Henry would've stopped. He wouldn't have left." She let her gaze travel to lock stares with him. "I suspect even you would have as well."

He slightly tilted his head, acknowledging her barb. "What if the kid wasn't supposed to be on the road? Maybe he wasn't even supposed to be driving." He shook his head. "Maybe he wasn't even old enough to drive. Any of the scenarios could've scared the kid spitless. He would know the police would come. He didn't want to get in trouble. Especially if he wasn't supposed to be here, or if he'd been drinking or something."

That was all logical, but none of that excused what had happened. This was *Henry*. Her brother. Her twin. The kindest person she'd ever known. "Of course that makes sense, but someone caused his death, and no matter the reason, they should have to own up to what they did." They deserved to pay. She glared at him. "Especially if he'd been drinking. We already know they were driving recklessly. They were in Henry's lane."

"When the news hits, someone might come forward, Harper."

"After learning that the person they left here died and they could be charged with several crimes? I doubt that very seriously." While she wanted to believe the people around the Gauley River were honest and would come forward, the fact that they'd left the scene didn't bode well for them coming forward now.

It was more likely the person was some type of tourist, the Gauley River rafting season had opened, and they were probably unfamiliar with the roads. They'd probably gotten out of West Virginia as soon as they could. Or, if this was intentional, then the police needed to investigate it as a homicide.

Homicide. Henry.

Just when she'd thought all the tears she'd had inside of her were gone, fresh ones burned her eyes.

"You're probably right." Christian's voice was soft...smooth. "I'm so sorry, Harper."

She could feel him move closer to her rather than see him. "I don't know what to say or what you need. Tell me." His voice cracked.

Harper let out a long breath and willed the tears back. "We need to take the voicemail to the police."

"Won't that just confirm it was an accident?"

"It proves someone was in Henry's lane. It proves that it wasn't an accident and it wasn't Henry's fault. It rules out any question of suicide or driving while texting or being under the influence."

Christian gently took hold of her arm and turned her to face him. "They thought he committed suicide or was drinking and driving? Henry?" His eyes grew wider and wider. How had she forgotten how intense his stare was?

She shrugged. "Both were mentioned. I was kind of in a daze, so I'm not sure they weren't just throwing out possible scenarios. That voice mail removes any question of either of those inciting incidents and brings into play possible homicide."

Before Christian could reply, a car rounded the curve and came to a stop behind Christian's Challenger. Gravel dust danced in the air. Janet slammed the door to her dented, economy sedan and rushed to them. She flung herself into Harper.

Clinging to Harper, Janet sobbed. "I just can't believe it. I can't believe he's really dead." She wailed loudly. "He's gone."

Harper caught her breath and stepped back out of Janet's grip, her heart clenching for the young woman who Henry had been seeing. "I know. It's hard to believe." She noticed Christian's single raised eyebrow. "Christian Gallagher, this is Janet Meyers, Henry's assistant and girlfriend."

"And you are who, exactly, Christian?" She offered her hand, even as she blinked rapidly and sniffed.

"He's an old friend of ours. One we grew up with," Harper interrupted. "He and Henry were the best of childhood friends."

Janet crossed her arms over her chest and slowly nodded. "Yeah, I think I heard Hanky mention you a few times."

"Henry." Harper considered maybe this was the reason she'd never really warmed up to Henry's girlfriend—she insisted on calling him by such a ridiculous nickname. Hank was bad enough, but Hanky? It made Harper want to grind her teeth.

"I'm sorry. I forgot you didn't like my nickname for him." Janet lifted her gaze to stare at Christian. "He loved his pet name."

Harper remained silent. She had no idea how Henry had felt about the nickname, and it wasn't fair of her to judge. She studied Janet, trying to see her through her twin's eyes. She was curvy and normally had a bright smile. She wore her nondescript brown and curly hair short. She was attractive, so Harper could easily see why Henry had been attracted to her.

Now that Harper thought about it, really, the only problem she had with Janet was that the woman seemed to have moved into Henry's life at super speed. Barely a month or two passed after mentioning he'd hired her as a new assistant until he was bringing her home as his girlfriend. It rubbed Harper the wrong way, but it wasn't exactly Janet herself, but more that Henry had always been impulsive. He often didn't consider that people didn't feel the same intensity—or lack thereof, as he did.

Despite Janet's pointed stare at Christian, he didn't seem impressed or intimidated. His stock just rose in Harper's estimation.

"Janet...I hope it's okay that I call you Janet?" Yet, charm practically oozed from his tone.

"Of course. Any friend of Hank—er, Henry's, is a friend of mine." Janet smiled as she slipped a side glance at Harper.

"So, Janet, what are you doing here?" he asked.

"Wh-What do you mean?" All façade of politeness and coyness fled her face.

"What are you doing here? On the side of the road?" He cut his eyes to Harper, and for the second time in her life, she could just hug him.

"I...well, I just felt compelled to come to where my Hanky had died." The tears came again. "I needed to see for myself." She looked at Harper. "I guess the same reason you're here?"

Harper straightened. She wished she could cry...could mourn, but Wolfes didn't display such emotions publicly. "Actually, we're here because Henry was on the phone with Christian when he went over the edge."

Janet's eyes widened as she looked back to Christian. "Oh?"

"He left a voicemail."

She licked her lips. "May I hear it? Please? I just need to...well, I just want to hear his voice."

A twinge of understanding nudged Harper and in that moment, she wanted to sob for Janet. No matter if she was a gold-digger or whatever her reasons for going after Henry, she had cared about him.

Christian looked at Harper and barely lifted a shoulder.

She nodded and Christian began playing the voice message that Harper had memorized now. It didn't take away the sting though. Harper pressed her lips together as the recording ended.

Janet trembled and put her hand over her mouth. She shook her head and turned her back to them.

Harper moved and laid her hand on Janet's shoulder. She'd better get used to reaching out to others because in the coming days, she was going to have to comfort people, even though all she wanted was to be comforted herself.

Turning, Janet hugged Harper again. Tighter than before. This time, Harper returned the embrace. She held it for a moment, then released Janet. "We have to be strong. It's what Henry would have wanted."

"Yes. Of course." Janet swiped at her face. "What did he find at the office that was so concerning?"

"We don't know."

Janet squished her brows together. She turned to Christian. "What was he talking about? What were you right about that he would need to apologize for?"

Christian shook his head. "I have no idea." He paused for a moment. "Maybe you could tell us."

"What? I don't know what you mean."

"You were his assistant, right? Surely you have some idea what he'd found at the office that would have been concerning." Christian slipped his thumbs in his front jeans' pockets, assuming that model pose.

"I have no idea. He never mentioned to me anything that worried him."

"Well, what had he been working on the last couple of weeks?" Harper nodded. Christian was right in his implication—if anybody knew what Henry was working on at the office, it'd be Janet.

"Really, I have no idea. He'd just been catching up on stuff of your dad's. P&Ls, reports, open cases...just normal stuff like that."

Janet's words deflated any hope hiding in Harper like a pin stuck into a balloon. Harper had been hoping that maybe Janet would have some idea. Something, anything that made sense of why Henry was dead.

Now she had nothing.

3

Law enforcement in the area was about as helpful as a broken paddle.

Harper and Christian had been taken back to the officer who filed the police report on Henry's accident, but even though she was an Assistant Prosecuting Attorney for Nicholas county, she hadn't gained much traction. The cop had Christian send a copy of the voice mail and had told Harper that the matter would be looked into, but he didn't seem overly interested in checking out something that had to do with a closed case.

Christian could feel the frustration rolling off her in waves as they got back into his car.

"That was a total waste of time." The tone of her voice echoed the vibes emitting off of her like the Gauley in March—deep and deadly. "Thanks for driving me anyway." She snapped her seatbelt with the force of a class-five rapid.

He started the car and secured his own seatbelt. "Of course." He shifted in his seat to look at her. Devastation tugged at the corners of her mouth. "At least they have a copy of the message now. Who knows? That cop may have just acted nonchalant because of you, but he really plans on checking things out thoroughly. A real investigation into the matter."

"Me? Why would he act any certain way because of me?"

"Because you can intimidate the daylights out of guys."

Her eyes widened. Why did he say that?

"Do I intimidate you, Christian?" She smiled, for the first time that he'd seen today.

He smiled back. "No, but I'm not in law enforcement facing you as a lawyer with the prosecuting attorney's office." He left out the part that her beauty and brains could intimidate any man, cop or otherwise.

She tilted her head. "Well, I guess there is that."

Christian backed the car out of the parking space of the Nicholas County Sheriff's Office. "So, don't discount an investigation by that one officer's attitude. You can always follow up in a couple of weeks and see if anything's been done."

"Yeah. Good idea." Harper paused. "Thank you, Christian, for everything today. I'm not thinking as clearly as usual, so you being here for me...well, it's really appreciated."

Heat crawled across the back of his neck. "Of course." It was his turn to pause. "Look, I can't say I understand how you feel, but I did lose my mom so I know loss." He turned, putting Summersville in the rearview mirror. "I was also Henry's friend, and despite our differences, we could always end up laughing together. I will miss him. A lot."

"Me, too."

They drove a few miles in silence. "You know..." Maybe he should keep his advice to himself. What he was about to suggest might disrupt their shaky kind-of-friendship.

"What?"

Christian made the turn onto Highway 19 and began to pick up speed. "Whatever he'd found and wanted me to look at is probably in his office."

Harper nodded. "Most likely."

"If it was as big of a deal as we think, where would he put it to keep it safe?"

She let out a long breath. "I don't really know. It's been a while since I was in the office. Henry's office. I don't even know if he has a safe, but I'm guessing he probably does. I can always look, I suppose. It shouldn't be hard to get into his office."

"Maybe you could ask Janet?"

A shadow fell over her face and Christian knew he'd read their relationship correctly. "I'm not sure much help Janet would be. For an assistant, she's not even a paralegal or a legal secretary. Actually, I'm not quite sure what she's capable of doing other than cater to Henry."

He kept his eyes on the road. "I take it you aren't fond of her." It was more of a statement than a question.

"I don't dislike her as a person. I just feel like she put a move on Henry from the get-go, and seemed determined to do everything she could to get under his skin, in a good way. I just don't know her motives." She sighed. "Guess that makes me sound like a judgmental twin—that no one would ever be good enough for Henry."

"No, not at all."

"Did you find her ingenuine?"

It was Christian's experience that snap judgments weren't always dead-on. "I just met her, so it's not really fair for me to form an opinion of her. Especially during a time of shock, sorrow, and grief."

"True. Now I really sound like an awful person."

"No, you don't. You know Janet without all the emotional load of what's going on right now. You're smart and savvy and knew Henry better than anybody, so I would say to trust your gut instincts."

"I just don't trust her, I guess." She hated to admit that to herself, much less aloud, but it was true. "Then again, I haven't had much opportunity to need to trust her."

"Then don't trust her, but you *can* use her to try and figure out what Henry was talking about in his message."

Harper nodded as he turned toward Henry's neighborhood. "Would you help me?"

"Help you?"

"I'm going to need to bring you things and see if it's possibly something you two might have argued about before. Something that he would tell you he was sorry for, and that you were right. Anything that might seem like he'd bring it to you."

"Without hesitation, yes. I want to know what he was talking about, too. For him to call me...leave such a message...and admit I was right? It had to be something we'd discussed before and disagreed on. I'd like answers." Christian eased the car into Henry's driveway, right behind the later model Mercedes SUV, and put the car in PARK.

"Thanks. I'll look through his office here at his house, too. Just in case he brought something home and put it in his safe here."

"I'm assuming you have the combination?"

Harper nodded. "We exchanged all that information in case of emergencies." She gave a sad tilt of her head. "I guess it was for instances like this."

"Do you want me to come in and look with you?"

"No. I don't think I'm going to look today. I'm just not up to it. Besides, I have to talk to Father...let him listen to the message."

Christian's heart went out to her. "Please know that I'm here to help in any way. Just let me know. I mean it."

She smiled. "I really appreciate that."

"You have my cell phone number now since I forwarded you the voice mail. I'm one hundred percent serious. Call me anytime. I'll let Gabe and Katie know not to schedule me on overnight raft trips."

"That's sweet."

He hesitated, then took the chance. Christian grabbed hold of her hand. She didn't jerk it away. He ran his thumb over her knuckles. "You don't have to go this alone. I'm here for you. All you have to do is ask." Funny how much he meant that. It even surprised him a little. But she just seemed so lost and alone.

"Thanks." She gently removed her hand and grabbed the door handle. "For everything. I'll be in touch soon." She opened the door and got out of the car.

Christian watched her walk to her SUV and with a final wave, climb inside.

Stop being a nervous nilly and just go in there.

Harper's nerves knotted into a tight ball in the pit of her stomach as she stood outside her father's study doors. Why did he have the continuous ability to make her feel seven years old again—gangly, awkward, and stupid? Maybe because that's how he saw her...at least that's how he treated her.

Enough was enough. She had graduated magna cum laude, had been published multiple times in law review, and was an Assistant Prosecuting Attorney. She faced hardened criminals every day without flinching. She could go against the most cunning and devious defense attorney—and win. She was respected and gaining a reputation for being a top-notch prosecutor.

Yet, when facing Elliott Wolfe, self-made success man, she reverted back to her childhood when she'd been dismissed by him, while Henry had been revered and welcomed. The time-old custom of favoring a son over a daughter.

Harper sucked in a deep breath, squared her shoulders, and knocked sharply on his door before opening it. "Father?"

The study, normally dim because of the dark wood walls and furniture, had become dark. The heavy drapes were drawn over the windows. Only the small lamp on the desk lit the room.

He glanced up from where he sat hunched behind his desk. "Harper. Come in."

She hesitated as she studied the man who'd been both her hero and her tormentor.

The always immaculate man was not the man who sat before her. His silvery-gray hair, usually perfectly styled, was disheveled and unruly. His usual attire was a suit, but his casual wear was also always pressed and coordinated. Right now, he wore a wrinkled, crinkly old shirt that Harper had never seen before. But what stood out the most was the way his eyes looked anchored into dark bags. The crow's feet seemed to spread into his hairline. He was a shell of the man most people held in awe or outright feared.

"Come sit." He waved her toward the couch as he stood.

Harper flipped on the side lamps before taking a seat. He joined her on the couch, and she had to swallow back a gag reflex because of his body odor mixed with alcohol. When was the last time he'd showered? Eaten? As she looked into his eyes, she noticed how bloodshot they were. When was the last time he'd slept?

Maybe this wasn't the best time to let him hear the recording.

"I'm trying to stay home today because the press has already gotten wind of Henry's accident. They'll be camping out on the lawn any minute now." He looked at her as if he finally *saw* her. "You should probably avoid going out, too. They'll be all over the place. We have to be careful and not give them any reason to stir up all the mixed information about the company."

Harper bit the inside side of her cheek. Of course, it was always about the business to him. Even in grief. "Father, I have something you need to hear."

"What is it?"

She couldn't tell if the roughness of his voice was fueled by grief or annoyance. Probably a mix of both. "It's a voicemail Henry made the night he died."

"And?" No mistaking that tone: frustration.

"It's actually *when* the wreck happened."

"He was on the phone?" His eyes widened.

She nodded.

"What was that boy thinking? Talking on the phone while driving. Distracted driver. Good thing the police have already closed out their report." He shook his head, then narrowed his eyes at Harper. "Why didn't you mention this recording before?"

"I just found out about it today. Here, let me play it for you." She pulled out her cell and played the voicemail Christian had sent her.

Her arms pimpled with goosebumps as the recording played until the tragic end. Harper blinked back tears, turned it off, and waited for her father's response.

She didn't have to wait long.

"What in the name of all that's holy is he talking about?" His voice boomed off the walls of the dank room.

There was the man she'd grown up with. So much for hoping Elliott Wolfe could offer any comfort to his own daughter. She forced back the sigh. "I have no idea. I don't work for the company."

"He's your twin! You two are thick as thieves. Surely he said something to you." His face had lost the pallor and now had returned to his ruddy complexion.

Harper's pulse raced faster than the rapids on the Gauley River. "I wish he had, but he didn't, Father."

"Who is he talking to again?"

"Christian Gallagher." She braced for it.

"That tree hugger?" He let loose with an obscenity. "Why in tarnation was he asking that Gallagher boy for input on anything that's related to my company?"

She shook her head. "I have no idea, Father. Janet didn't either."

"That gold-digger has heard this?"

Harper nodded.

Her father snorted. "I'm not even going to ask why you would play that for her."

"Because I thought, as Henry's assistant, she might have an idea of what he was referring to and why he needed to talk to Christian so urgently."

He ran his hands through his greasy hair. "I'll have to get someone to go through his office. Hire a new attorney for the company." He looked at Harper. "But first that worthless assistant of his will have to go."

Harper took a deep breath. "You're missing something vital out of that voice mail, Father." She continued without giving him a chance to respond. "Someone was in his lane and that's why he went off the road. Someone else is responsible for Henry's death. He wasn't under any influence nor was this in any way a possible suicide."

"It doesn't matter. The case is closed, ruled an accident. That's that. We have to move on." He pointed his finger at her. "And don't you be going around telling anybody it wasn't an accident. Don't be stirring up a mess. It's over and handled. Period."

She stood, ready for the battle ahead. "Father, although I'm sure it's slipped your mind, but I'm an Assistant Prosecuting Attorney for Nicholas county. As such, I'm an officer of the court. That means I have a duty to report a crime. Causing an accident and leaving the scene is a crime."

His jaw set and she could hear the faintest grinding of his teeth. "You don't know any such thing." He stood as well. "You have nothing to report."

"Well, I disagree and I've reported it to the sheriff's office."

"You talked to them with this nonsense?" The expression in his eyes was unreadable, but it looked stormy, at best.

"I gave them a copy of the voicemail and requested they look for the person responsible for killing my brother." Heat flushed over her face and chest. She dropped her hands to her sides. "I would think you'd want to know that as well. Henry was your only son, and someone is responsible for his death."

"Don't be snippy with me, Harper." His tone was lighter. "Of course, I want to know what happened and if someone is responsible, to see that they pay." He paused and Harper waited. "I'll talk to the police myself. The ones who headed up the investigation."

Somehow, that didn't reassure Harper, but there was nothing more she could say or do at the moment. Well…except…

She swallowed. Did she really want to do this? Maybe throw away her career? Tarnish her reputation? Would it be worth it? Would she be able to learn the truth?

"You don't worry any more about this…this recording." He waved his hand toward her cell phone. "You can just record it."

She ignored his directive and made a decision. "Father, until you find adequate counsel for Wolfe Mining, why don't you let me fill in?" Right or wrong, she'd bitten the bullet.

He stared at her as if she'd lost her mind.

His expression irritated her. Greatly. "I'm just as qualified as Henry. Probably more since I held a four-point-oh throughout my college years while Henry...well, he did have his struggles." Usually girls or some drinking. Harper suspected there was a time when he tried recreational drugs as well, but that was in the past and he'd never done anything that she knew for fact.

"I can take a leave of absence and some of my vacation time to work for Wolfe Mining, which will give you enough time to find someone permanent." Once said out loud, it didn't sound as bad as she'd originally thought. If she could get her boss to sign off on her leave and time off. "Just temporarily."

Her father gave a slow nod. "I suppose that could work."

She'd won the battle, and felt the surge of pride in standing up to her father. Yet, he hadn't even considered her without her asking or offered her the job permanently. Not that she wanted it—she took a quick inventory of herself and found that much was true. Still, it would have been nice had her father even considered her.

At one time, she wanted nothing more than for her father to want her to come on board the company with Henry, but today, she realized she loved her job and the freedom from her father's controlling ways.

Harper nodded. "Nell is taking care of the memorial arrangements. Do you have any preferences for the service?"

Her father shook his head. "I'd prefer the sooner, the better."

While she understood his wanting to move on, she wanted to linger in her grief just a little longer. Once the memorial service was over, people would forget Henry. Oh, not intentionally, and not all at once, but little by little, day by day, he'd become a distant memory.

Except to her. Losing her twin was like losing pieces of herself.

Ones she'd never get back.

4

"It was a beautiful service, Nell. Thank you for arranging it." Harper's mouth was as dry as her eyes were wet. How she'd managed to make it through Henry's memorial service without breaking was nothing short of a mystery and a miracle. But that's who she was—a Wolfe, and a Wolfe never lost control. It was just a fact ingrained in her since birth by her father., but even stronger after her mother died.

Nell gave her another sideways hug. "Of course, honey. Now, I'm going to go back to your father's house and make sure his staff has everything set up before any of these people get there. The funeral home is delivering the plants and flowers there as we speak." The sweet woman who'd loved on Harper and Henry so much and so often glanced around the small funeral home lobby. "Y'all don't be too long following." She gave Harper a final hug, then bustled off.

Harper gripped the bottle of water tighter as she turned to face yet more platitudes from individuals she didn't even recognize. Some of these people hardly knew Henry, much less were here to pay their respects. Many just wanted to come and see the family in their grief. It was no secret many in the West Virginia, Gauley River area were no fans of Wolfe Mining.

"How're you doing?" The recognizable voice came from behind her, unexpected.

She turned to face Christian, surprising herself with how relieved she was to see his familiar face. "It was a nice service, wasn't it?" The reply was ready on her lips, having been used so many times today.

He nodded. "It was, but that isn't what I asked you." He leaned down, putting his lips to her ear. "How are *you* holding up?" His breath tickled the baby hairs around her earlobe.

Emotions she couldn't yet define clogged the back of her throat. "I'm fin—"

His hand settled on her shoulder...his voice barely a whisper. "You are many things, Harper Wolfe, but today, you are most definitely not fine."

"I have to be." As soon as she got the words out, the reality of her statement settled over her as tight as a wetsuit. She couldn't even grieve at her twin's service. She would mourn him later, alone. Without Henry, she'd never felt so alone.

He gave her shoulder a squeeze, then jerked his head toward her father. "How's your old man doing?"

Elliott Wolfe stood in the middle of a circle of his associates and a few lobbyists, no doubt running his business from his only son's memorial service. "He's...he's Father." Everyone handled grief differently. At least he looked better than he had over the last few days. Coming to grips with the new reality that didn't include Henry.

"While I know what it's like to lose parents, I can't even imagine how it must feel to lose a child."

Harper snorted. "Henry was hardly a child. We are the same age, remember?"

"Yeah, but we're talking about Henry here." Christian let out a small chuckle.

She couldn't help herself, she smiled. "Well, you do have a point."

"Do you remember the time he and I decided we were old enough to handle the river on our own? We snuck one of Dad's best rafts and tackled the Upper Gauley."

"Y'all were what, all of fifteen? Sixteen?"

"I was sixteen and Henry was about to be." He shook his head, grinning.

His smile was infectious. "If memory serves me correct, you two had to be rescued and the raft was destroyed."

He nodded. "Yeah. Dad was mad. I had to clean all the wetsuits and rafts for a month. I couldn't believe Henry got off without any punishment, and it was his idea to begin with."

"Oh, he had repercussions, he just didn't tell you about them."

He raised a single brow. "Do tell."

The lightness dissipated as the memory washed over her. She shrugged. "Father gave Henry a very stern talk, and after that…well, he buckled down and concentrated on getting back on the right track. He also curbed a lot of his zest for fun." Now that she thought about it, Henry had not only been more somber and serious after that, but sadder as well.

"Hmmm." Christian shoved his thumbs into the pockets of his black jeans. "We didn't hang out too much after that. Henry needed to get his grades up, so had to study a lot more. Especially since you two graduated early. Y'all headed off to different colleges. Different lives."

Father threatening Henry to stay away from "that no-good tree hugger who will never amount to anything, just like his father" was probably more of the reason they weren't close after that. Along with their father pushing their mother, who home-schooled them, to have them graduate early. Essentially, stealing part of their childhood. At least all the rites of passage: homecomings, proms, sports…close friends.

Harper swallowed hard. How had she not fully realized how Father controlled Henry, even back then? It shouldn't surprise her— Father had always been able to manipulate her and Henry into doing his will.

Christian shifted his weight beside her. "We might have drifted apart, but we were always there for one another when it mattered." His voice thickened. "I'll miss him."

"Me, too." The myriad of emotions that had filled her since she'd been told about the wreck returned.

Without a word, he took her hand in his and pressed his warmth into her. Before she could process his touch and how it made her feel, Pastor Ford joined them. Harper took his proffered hand. "The service was very nice. Thank you."

His hands were colder than Christian's as he wrapped her hands in his grip. "I'm so sorry for your loss, Harper, but know that Henry is in a better place. He is with your mother now."

The knife in her chest twisted. Now was not the place, nor was it the time to ask Pastor Ford how that was supposed to bring her comfort. Not only losing her mom, but now Harper had to live without her twin. Some *loving* God.

But she knew not to cause a scene. To remain poised and in control when in public.

She gently removed her hands from Pastor Ford's grip and forced a pleasant expression to her face. "Thank you."

A sob from across the small room broke the awkwardness of the moment. Janet wept into a handkerchief as her shoulders shook.

Pastor Ford excused himself to go see about her. Harper let out a sigh of relief as he moved away.

"She's quite distraught." Christian stared as the pastor joined Janet, speaking in low tones.

"I know she has to be grieving." She glanced over to the younger woman. "They hadn't been dating that long. I think maybe she read more into their relationship than Henry did."

Henry had told Harper that it was more a relaxed, fun relationship than one that he could see heading into the future. Janet's sobs switched to sniffles, but still echoed off the walls. Harper chanced a glance at Father amid his friends and associates. The disapproving frown on his face as he stared at Janet said it all.

Janet's days at Wolfe Mining were numbered and she would be out of their lives forever. For that, Harper felt sorry for her. She knew firsthand what it was like to disappoint Elliott Wolfe, and the repercussions that followed.

She spied a group heading her way, people who knew Henry, and genuinely cared that he was gone. She glanced up at Christian. "Please excuse me. Those are friends of ours from law school."

He gave a nod of his head and took a step backward.

"Christian?"

"Yes?"

"There is a repast at the house now, if you'd like to come."

His brows furrowed. "A what?"

"A private reception with family and friends after the service to gather together and mourn."

He paused, studying her face. "Won't your father disapprove?" He gave a slight grin.

Warmth tingled her toes. "All the more reason to come, yes?"

                        ~

"I REALLY NEED you to guide this trip, Christian. It's only the lower. You know it won't take you but four hours, tops." Desperation made Gabe's, the oldest of the Gallagher siblings, voice crack over the phone. "Katie got back last night and is going to watch the shop. I have a group coming in tonight for my morning overnight trip."

Christian eased his car to the intersection stop sign, pushing down on his brakes. "Why did you double book?" He normally wasn't short with his brother, but Christian was on his way to the Wolfe estate.

"We didn't. They're a last-minute request." Gabe sighed, so many emotions coming through the connection. "We need to accept every booking that we can."

"Maybe we should consider hiring someone for the season." The rafting business season on the Gauley River was only September and October. Sure, they hosted fishing trips and quiet retreats in their cabins off-season, but their main vein of business at Gauley Guides by Gallagher was the rafting trips.

"Right now, we can't really afford to add someone. Business is down and the bottom line tight."

Christian swallowed as he turned left. He'd been so caught up with his own work lately that he'd pushed the day-to-day running of the family business to Gabe. Katie tried to do as much as usual, but she also took advantage of every available day off her new husband had to spend time with him. "I didn't realize."

"I wouldn't ask if I didn't need your help, Christian." The worry clearly evident in Gabe's voice now.

No use volunteering to give the company some money, even as an investment. Gabe had made that rule years ago, and he hadn't budged since, despite Christian's multiple offers. As the only sibling that had an *outside* job, Christian could easily help out the family business. Gabe wouldn't hear of it, and that annoyed Christian more than he could describe.

The only thing he could do was work there as his schedule allowed. "Okay, I'll be there. I do have a couple of projects in the works, so please don't count me in for any overnight trips. I can work around watching the store or guiding a day trip, but I need to work on these projects." He'd make it all work, even if that meant working later in the evening or early mornings.

"Thanks, Christian. I'll see you in the morning."

Christian steered his car toward the driveway of the Wolfe estate. The large home was neoclassical architectural, Palladian design. Formidable with its monstrous gargoyles mounted atop the concrete posts on each of the two cement staircases, standing guard with their bared teeth and glowing eyes. Domineering with the brass-adorned dome atop the pinnacle of the roof. Unwelcoming with the six massive columns hiding the ten-foot, solid oak front door.

The guesthouse, now where Harper lived—at least the last Christian knew, barely peeked around the edge of the impressive garden just beyond the koi pond to the right of the main house.

He pulled up into the circular drive behind the other cars already parked alongside the perfectly manicured lawn and turned off the engine. So many memories rafted over him. Back before Mrs. Wolfe died, when they were kids, Christian and Henry were always running through the house. Playing billiards and video games in the basement-turned-gameroom. Running down the stairs from Henry's room to jump off the back balcony into the Olympic-sized pool just outside the back door.

Then Henry's mom had gotten cancer in their freshman year. Or maybe she'd been sick before then, but just not showing symptoms. Or maybe she wanted it hidden. At any rate, once she began chemo treatment, she became so weak and tired, and Christian rarely saw her. He and Henry couldn't run through the house being loud anymore. The invitations to dinner slowed, then finally stopped all together. Everything changed.

A couple walked past Christian's car, yanking him from his stroll down memory lane. He locked the Challenger and followed them up the stairs to the front door. A black wreath draped over the entry that one of Elliott's staff held open for each person, directing them to sign the guestbook on the entry table.

Several pictures of Henry at various ages adorned the table. As Christian bent to scrawl his name, one of the pictures caught his eye: he and Henry sitting on the diving board, wearing sunglasses and smiles. They were probably fourteen.

"I hope you don't mind that I used that picture with you. It reflects happy times in Henry's life." Harper's accent was a little more pronounced here at the home where she'd grown up.

He straightened and smiled, and took a few steps away from the table so others could sign. "I don't mind at all. I was just thinking about all the fun times we had."

Harper smiled back. "You two did seem to be able to have a grand time with whatever you were doing."

He let her lead him toward the buffet set up in the library just off the kitchen and hall. "I always wondered why you never wanted to join us."

Handing him a plate, she shrugged. "I guess I was a little jealous of you."

He froze the spoon full of au gratin potatoes midair. "Jealous of me? You've got to be joking."

"It's true. Henry was *my* twin. *My* friend. Then you come along and he wants to hang out with you, play with you, get in trouble with you." She grabbed them both lemonades and led the way to the back patio where no one else sat. "I would really like a moment of privacy right now, if it's okay with you that we sit out here."

"Of course." He sat down, bowed his head and silently prayed, then took a long swig of the lemonade she'd set on the table. He took in the outdoor kitchen, the drapes flowing from the pergola, and the addition of more rattan seating areas. "It's been updated quite a bit since I was out here last."

"Yeah. Father let me redecorate it when I was redesigning my place."

"Now owner of the guesthouse?" He took a bit of the potatoes. Cheesy goodness with just the right amount of spices tingled on his tongue.

"Yes. Henry had been encouraging me to buy a house in his subdivision so I could have a fence for Atticus, and I'd been looking, but now..."

That melancholy look was returning to her face, and she'd looked more relaxed in the last twenty minutes than she had in days. Best to change the subject. "Atticus?"

"My puppy. He's almost two, and is the sweetest thing." The smile spread across her face.

Good, a subject that truly made her happy. "What kind of dog?" Probably a toy breed or one of those little frou-frou balls of fluff.

"English Mastiff."

He nearly choked on the lemonade he'd just taken a sip of. "That's a big dog." Yeah, he could see that. A big, loyal dog.

"Oh, but he's such a gentle giant." Harper glanced in the direction of the guest house. "He's probably going nuts right now, hearing all the noise but being shut in." She frowned. "That's why Henry was begging me to get a house in his neighborhood. They all have fenced in back yards."

The gloom had settled back over her face. Time for another change of subject. "These potatoes are amazing. You'll have to get the chef to share the recipe."

"Actually, those are one of the casseroles that Nell's church ladies brought."

"Have you tasted these?" She probably hadn't eaten today...maybe not much the last week.

She shook her head, and Christian figured he was right. He scraped a forkful and shoved it at her. "Try them."

"I'm good."

"I said, try them." He waggled his brows and grinned, hoping to amuse her.

It worked. She giggled and took the fork. "Okay." After chewing, she nodded. "You're right, these things are amazing. I'll have to have Nell get me the recipe." She reached to his plate and scooped up another big bite and ate it.

Good. She needed to eat. Everything was probably falling on her since Elliott was most likely moving on, business as usual. That's how he'd been after his wife had died. Took off a day or two, then for the funeral, then back to Wolfe Mining.

"Oh, I talked to Father. I'm going to fill Henry's position until Father can hire a corporate attorney permanently." She cut off a bite of ham from his plate.

Christian noticed she'd also eaten the slice of turkey he'd had, too. "Oh?" Try as he might, he couldn't picture her working for Elliott. Then again, maybe as an attorney she was cold and calculating. That would be right up Elliott's alley.

"Yeah. I start Monday. I'll start going through files and see if I can find anything that might be what Henry was referring to on the voicemail." Her face clouded again. "I still have to clean out Henry's house and handle the terms of his will."

"Take your time. I'm sure there's no major rush. It'll take time to sort things out and if you need to get his house on the market or anything, there's plenty of space here to store things until you can properly assess what to keep and what to give away or throw out." Christian was pretty sure Gabe still had some boxes of their mom's stuff he hadn't gone through, and she'd been gone fifteen years.

"How do you feel about pet fish?" She grinned.

He laughed. "Um, why?"

Before she could answer, the patio door flung open and her father along with four other men stepped onto the smooth pavers. Elliott spied them and glared at Harper. "What are you doing out here, especially with him? We have guests, you should be mingling."

The drained expression dripped down her eyes once more. "I'm just taking a lunch break, Father." She stood, straightening her spine as she did.

Christian stood as well. He'd never really liked Elliott, hated his work ethic and morals, but right now, he just wanted to punch the man for the way he spoke to Harper.

"I see you're mingling for both of us." She gestured to the men around him. Harper didn't need anyone to stand up for her. "We were just finishing up." She pushed in her chair.

Gulping back a chuckle, Christian stood as well.

"Why, hello, Mr. Gallagher." The man directly next to Elliott spoke.

Christin jerked his head. "Mr. Parsons." Vince Parsons. Former member of West Virginia's Department of Environmental Protection, now running for US Congress for the 3rd congressional district of West Virginia. The man who stood for practically everything Christian was against, environmentally. Probably personally, too.

Naturally Elliott Wolfe would support this slime of a man who cared more about a profit margin than protecting their land and wildlife. Scarily enough, the two men were cut from the same cloth.

"Good afternoon, gentlemen." Harper walked alongside Christian into the kitchen.

Christian wondered what Parsons was doing here at Henry's reception, banquet...no, repast? Had there been something regarding the candidate that Henry had found and that's what he was calling about? Christian wracked his memory to see if he and Henry had debated the candidates...wait, they had. Once or twice they'd discussed how they were on opposing sides of even this political race, and they'd each made an argument for what their candidate stood for.

If Henry had uncovered something nefarious that Parsons was up to, that would make his voicemail make sense.

Christian followed Harper into the kitchen and added his lemonade glass to the counter beside hers.

"I'm sorry Father was so rude to you. He hasn't been himself since Henry died."

"It's okay." Christian smiled at her. She had enough on her plate right now. He would wait to be sure Parsons was the reason for the voicemail before he mentioned it to her. No sense stressing her just yet.

Because if Parsons was up to something underhanded or illegal, that would most likely mean her father was involved.

5

The raft lined up perfectly for the *Roller Coaster* wave train.

"All forward!" Christian steered the raft as they slammed against the white water hits.

They pitched and straightened in the rolling, white water. Christian's paddle cut through the frigid water as the raft bounced on the last vestiges of tail waves from the class four rapid.

Christian took stock of the woman sitting in the chicken seat to the right of him. Her knuckles were white as she gripped the paddle. She had lost her color back on *Heaven Help You*, which in fairness, was a class four rapid. She'd stopped paddling on the *Upper* and *Lower M.A.S.H.* rapids, which were class four and five, respectfully. Now, as they approached the last, and most fierce class five rapid of the lower Gauley, Christian realized he'd have to ensure she didn't fall out of the raft, or, heaven forbid, lose her paddle.

He sliced his paddle through the water, steering and guiding while the others checked the straps on their helmets.

This group of three couples, weren't experienced white-water rafters. They were middle aged friends who took an annual vacation together to try something new. Christian didn't think this is what this particular lady had imagined the trip would be like. She looked like she might be sick, something he surely didn't want on his raft. Cleaning the raft later would be more than just a headache.

He didn't have time to think about that right now—he had to concentrate on getting them through the last rapid, a strong class five.

"Paddle hard!" Christian instructed the group in the raft.

The current bent itself around to the left, and Christian fought against the water to avoid them being slung out and hitting the undercut rock or getting caught in the real nasty split to the right.

"Paddle! Paddle!" Christian struggled to keep the raft in the wave train, having little help from the other six people with him.

They punched through the first big wave. "Paddle hard!" Christian did *not* want to have to swim out of this rapid if they flipped the raft.

They slammed through the second wave.

"Come on, keep paddling!" They ripped through the third wave.

"One more. Paddle hard!" Christian braced his feet as they hit the "hell hole."

And with that, they pushed out of *Pure Screaming Hell*. Calmer waters slowed the raft's progress. As usual, Christian let out a relieved sigh. Another successful trip.

The men in the group whooped, hollered, and high-fived with the paddles as if they'd conquered the world, while the women spoke excitedly on top of each other. Even the one from the chicken seat gabbed animatedly. She seemed to have gotten over her fear now that she knew this was the end to the adventure. They were discussing who was buying their video, hoping the photos were good, and how many 'I Survived the Lower Gauley River' t-shirts and tumblers they needed to buy. Gabe would be pleased.

Christian, too, was glad their trip was almost over. Just a little more downstream and Rory would pick them up in the bus and take them back to Gauley Guides by Gallagher. Christian paddled the boat toward where they would meet Rory. As he shook his head hearing the guys discuss how many times they had *almost died*, he stared into the clear water. When the adrenaline rush calmed, they would be exhausted. He hoped Katie or Gabe had dinner ready for all of them—

Wait a minute…was that a candy darter floating near the craggy edge of the river?

About two and a half inches long, several green/blue vertical bars with alternate red bars, and five distinct, black saddles…definitely a male candy darter.

Christian jumped out the raft and studied the little fish. No sign of what caused the fish to be dead, which was problematic. The colorful fish, native only to the Gauley, Greenbrier, and New River watersheds, before the 1990s thrived in their natural habitat of swift-moving boulder substrates, near the riverbed. These particular fish were an important link in healthy, balanced aquatic interdependent food chain by helping to convert and transfer energy in aquatic ecosystems. Candy darters, importantly, also assisted with the reproduction of freshwater mussels, who, in turn, constantly worked to filter out pollutants in the rivers to help keep waterways clean.

Freshwater mussels, declining in rapid numbers, were extremely sensitive to water pollution, so doing everything to help their reproduction, like the candy darters provided, was critical to the lifelong care of the Gauley River.

Since 2018, the candy darters were on the endangered species list, which made an unexplained dead candy darter in the Gauley River a serious problem.

He dug around in his pack and pulled out his empty water bottle. Carefully, he eased the dead fish inside and recapped the glass bottle, then slipped it back into the pack strapped into the raft.

Rory waved, and Christian directed the group where to paddle. Twenty minutes later, they were loaded up in the bus and heading back to Gauley Guides by Gallagher.

Christian's stomach rumbled loudly and Rory looked over at him and chuckled. "Hungry much?"

The older photographer/videographer for the family business, and pickup/drop off person was a longtime friend who Christian respected. "Forgot to grab a snack before we headed out. Do you know if Gabe has lunch ready for these guys?"

Rory laughed again. "Yeah, Katie cooked."

Christian groaned and rolled his eyes. He loved his sister dearly and she was great at many things, but cooking wasn't one of them. "Why do they do this to me?" Oh, Gabe would owe him for this one.

"She's getting better. Hunter even taught her how to sear a steak."

His brother-in-law could cook a mean ribeye. "Is that what she made?"

Rory shook his head. "No such luck. I believe roasted chicken and baked potatoes with corn on the cob and salad was on the menu for tonight."

That didn't sound too bad. Not as hungry as he just realized he was.

Gabe better hope the food was edible.

∽

HENRY HAD LEFT her his house?

Harper read the will again, then flipped through the envelopes scattered over her bed. She found one with 'House' written on the front. She carefully unfolded the papers and read them. His house was free and clear of any mortgages or liens and he'd designated Harper his sole beneficiary. Tears dropped onto her copy of the papers.

Atticus jumped onto the bed and laid his massive head in Harper's lap. Harper absentmindedly rubbed the telling-Mastiff-trait bone at the top of her head.

Harper had just gotten home from the bank to clean out Henry's safety deposit box. She'd just dumped the contents into a bag and left, wanting to sort through everything in the privacy of her own home. There were copies of his birth certificate and his social security card, as well as spare keys to his house and car, a small jewelry box, and five envelopes. The first envelope, marked 'Will,' had contained his updated, certified and filed will, which she went back to reading.

He'd left her everything he had: the house, his car, all the furniture, even his stocks in Wolfe Mining.

Wait. Henry had stocks in the company? She didn't even know there were any stockholders aside from her father. According to this statement of accounts, however, Henry owned approximately twenty-five percent of Wolfe Mining. She flipped through the other envelopes. One was marked 'Company Stock.' She opened it and read, checking the date the stocks were acquired—the day Henry started working for their father.

She read through the stock paperwork. The twenty-five shares had once been in their mother's name, but now they'd been transferred to Henry's. Everything was legal and correct.

Wow. No stocks were ever mentioned to Harper, much less bestowed upon her. The tears dried up, replaced with a hardness gathering in her chest. Well, she owned twenty-five percent of Wolfe Mining now. How would her father feel about that? Hmm. Maybe she'd keep that to herself for a spell.

She moved on to the next items that had been in Henry's safety deposit box.

The small jewelry box held their mother's engagement ring. She smiled sadly as she pulled it out of the velvet lining and slipped it on her finger. She remembered when her mother had told Harper that she was going to give Henry the ring so he could give it to his wife one day. Now...well, now it was hers.

The next envelope had 'Life Insurance' scrawled in Henry's awful penmanship on the outside. She sucked in air as she read the details. She was the sole beneficiary of his life insurance policy that had the value of $500,000.00. Why did he have such a large life insurance policy? She set aside the papers to figure out later what she needed to submit to start the process.

The fifth and final envelope had only 'Harper' written across the front.

Harper worried her top lip between her teeth. Dare she read it now? Her emotions were already so raw...would this be like pouring salt in a wound?

Atticus let out a sigh and stretched out the full length of the queen-sized bed. If he kept growing, Harper would need to upgrade to a king.

At least now she'd have more room. And a backyard.

Curiosity got the better of her and she gently opened the envelope, then pulled the paper out. She unfolded it, smoothing it on her lap. Her breath caught as she read:

H<small>ARPER</small>,

If you're reading this, well...it means I'm gone. I'm hoping that's not the case and you're just being nosy, but we both know that's not you, so that leaves us with something happened to me.

I know you'll be okay—you always were the stronger of the two of us. I'm not sure Father will be all right. Having been working with him, he's still the controlling man we know as a father, and also a shrewd businessman, but he's also starting to show signs of aging. Little-by-little, he's losing the authority and control he once commanded. Losing Mom, then one of us might do him in. Be a little patient with him, Harper, even when he's at his most trying because that's when he's hurting the most.

By now, you'll have seen that I left everything to you. Please don't just give anything away. I know you don't need your big brother looking out for you (hey, four minutes older is still older), but I wanted to set things up so that if something happened to me, you'd be taken care of. It gives me such peace of mind to know that you'll not have to work in a job you hate or for a person whose values don't line up with yours. Don't fight it. I plan to be around long enough to teach your grandchildren all my bad habits, but this is just in case.

One last thing I'd like to ask of you, if I may. Please, Harper, don't let anything that happens to me turn you even further away from your faith. Mom kept hers until death, and know that I have as well. I know I want to see you on the other side, but that's not reason enough for you to embrace your faith again. You'll have to make that choice. All I ask is that you don't let this harden your heart when it comes to accepting how much Jesus loves you. Trust me, He longs for you to run back into his open and waiting arms. Just open your heart to listen for Him is my biggest favor.

Love always and forever,
Your twin from within,
Henry

SHE BURIED her face in Atticus's neck, letting her tears wet his fur. The finality of it all washed over Harper in waves of gut-wrenching grief. She held the Mastiff tighter and cried harder. Everything she'd been holding in since Henry died gushed out.

Sometime later, spent and numb, Harper sat up and put all the papers back in the big bag. She kept her mother's ring on, liking how the cold platinum felt against her skin. The weight of the ring itself somehow bringing comfort, even though that made no sense.

After securing the bag inside her personal wall safe, she fisted her hands on her hips and looked around the guest house she'd set up as a home. Now she could see that it wasn't hers. Not really. While she'd put her touches in the decorating, the place itself would always be her father's guest house.

And that's when she knew she'd move into Henry's house. She'd redecorate it and make it entirely hers, just like he would want her to do.

Atticus lifted his head to stare at her, then barked before lumbering off the bed with a heavy thud.

Harper laughed. "Well, come on. I'll take you for a walk." She grabbed the leash off the hook by the back door and hooked it to Atticus's collar.

They'd barely made it into the garden behind the big house when Harper spied her father sitting under the pergola with Mr. Parsons and another man. Atticus's long tail wagged just before he gave a happy bark.

Her father stood. "Harper, come meet Sammy Johnson."

Her eyes were probably puffy and bloodshot from crying. She

looked rumpled and frumpy from laying on the bed and holding on to Atticus. Yet she had no other choice but to join her father and the two men around the patio. Ambushed while out walking her dog, if that wasn't reason enough to move out, nothing was.

She plastered a smile on her face and locked Atticus's retractable leash and gave him the command to sit so the behemoth wouldn't jump on anyone. "Hello, Mr. Johnson. It's nice to meet you."

"Sammy, this is my daughter, Harper. She'll be sitting in Henry's chair for the company until we can find a worthy replacement."

Harper ground her teeth but kept her smile in place. The implication that she wasn't worthy was all too clear.

"Ms. Wolfe." The man smiled and tilted his head toward her.

He was handsome. Maybe thirty years old, at most, with black hair that curled at the ends just caressing the top of his collar. Big, doe-like brown eyes, and a smile that had probably made a dentist and orthodontist very wealthy.

"Sammy is a lobbyist in D.C." Her father wore the puffed-up look he usually had when introducing Henry as his son, the attorney. "He's a big supporter of coal miners in both here and Kentucky."

No wonder Father was impressed. He'd grown up as a coal miner in Harlan county, Kentucky. Had an office of Wolfe Mining there today. Nostalgia or to prove he made something of himself, Harper never really knew.

"Well, it's always nice to meet someone who understands the importance of fossil fuels." At least, that's what she gathered after listening to her father discuss the topic with Henry on various occasions.

Now her father beamed at *her*. Wow, that felt good. When was the last time he'd praised her in any capacity? "See, told you she was brilliant."

Brilliant? He'd called her brilliant? Heat rushed up the back of her neck and her ears burned. He'd looked proud of her and gave her a compliment?

Would wonders never cease?

But before she let herself be overwhelmed, she remembered his implication. Brilliant, but not good enough to be worthy of workings for Wolfe Mining permanently.

Then again, she was now a twenty-five percent stockholder of the company.

She smiled sweetly as she excused herself and led Attitcus back to the guest house. She would move out, soon. She could redecorate the house while living there. Take it slow...one room at a time, but at least she'd be out from under her father's thumb in a way.

As she let herself and Atticus into the house, she also made a vow that she would use every resource she had to find out who caused Henry's death.

She owed him that much.

6

"I'm still running tests, but so far, I have no clue why the little guy died." Laurie Fisher popped off her Latex gloves and smiled widely at Christian.

That was nothing new. Even first thing in the morning, Laurie always had a ready smile for everyone who visited A-Plus Alliance Labs. It was her extroverted personality that made her nerdy professional less stand-offish to people who just didn't get environmental issues.

Her looks didn't hurt, either. Shoulder-length blondish-brown hair that always smelled like sunshine, and big, brown eyes as warm and inviting as a beloved dog's. She had been Christian's friend for years since so much of their work overlapped.

"Where did you say you found him?"

"At the bottom of the lower, right where the tours usually put out the rafts."

She chewed her bottom lip. "Logically, he would've floated downstream with the current." Laurie lifted her clipboard and read her notes. "His stomach was empty, so he'd not eaten in several hours. I did, however, find high traces of sediment in his stomach."

Christian crossed his arms over his chest and rested his hip against the stainless-steel counter of the lab. "Sediment in his stomach? Don't know that I've ever heard of that with a darter before. You?"

She shook her head. "Can't say that I have. Darters usually have cleaner stomach contents than most fish because of their habitat."

"Right. They need cold, clear, and fast-moving water with clean gravel on the bottom to n lay their eggs."

"So I'm a little baffled as to why this little guy of yours has such a high amount of sediment in his stomach."

"Any ideas?"

"I'll do some checking around and see what I can find out." She shrugged off her lab coat and hung it on a hook behind her. "After I have my breakfast."

"I'm sorry to bother you so early."

She smiled and shook her head. "Don't worry about it. I had to come in and inspect some cultures, so I was here well before daylight anyway."

"I hear you about early mornings. Sometimes, we have a tour group that is scheduled to leave by seven forty-five, which means we have to have them up, ready, and fed before then."

Laurie poured herself a cup of coffee from the pot in the corner. "You can keep that. I'll stay over here in my lab where I can be grouchy until I've had enough caffeine for me to act like a human."

He laughed. "As if you're ever grouchy. Call me if you learn anything else." Christian pushed off the counter. "Thanks, Laurie, I owe you."

"You know what, Christian Gallagher? One day soon, very soon, I'm going to call in all the IOUs I have with you and you're going to have to take me out to a really nice dinner."

"It's a date." He smiled and strode out of the lab. He passed the entry hall and went down the hall, knocking on the open door of his friend's office. "Hey, Pete. About time you showed up to work."

"Ah, the perks of being the manger. What are you doing here?" Grinning, Peter Swisher waved him inside.

Christian plopped down on the seat in front of his friend's desk.

"Needed Laurie to run some tests on a dead candy darter I found. What's up with you?"

"Same old, same old." Peter grinned. No matter what, Peter was always Peter. Two years older than Christian's twenty-four, they'd been buddies back in their college days and stayed friends as they stepped into their similar careers. Peter was the respected environmentalist who managed the lab, focusing on plants in the region.

"Guess you heard about Henry Wolfe." Christian leaned back comfortably in the chair, crossing his legs at the ankles.

"Yeah. I hated to hear that. Odd thing, though, I'd just talked with Henry the day before his accident."

"Really?" Christian didn't realize the two were more than neighborly. Interest piqued, he sat up. "About what?"

"The EPA's latest report that hit last month. Did you read it?"

"Uh, I haven't had time yet." Heat flamed across his face.

Peter chuckled picked up a pen and tapped it against his desk pad. "Yeah, I get it. If I didn't have to read the long, boring reports, I wouldn't either."

"What did Henry have to say about it?" Christian had never known anybody who willingly read the report, certainly not someone who had a vested interest in coal mining.

"Well, there was another article in the report about the damage mountaintop removal mining had on the health of the people in its surrounding communities."

There were articles almost every other report about how lung cancer and other respiratory issues were related to mining dust. Sadly, it was an ongoing issue that was constantly reported on because enough big changes hadn't come through. "But why did Henry contact you? The health correlations to mining isn't the lab's area of expertise."

Peter rolled the pen between his fingers. "No, but something made Henry contact me to ask if our lab had done any research into the damage to the environment that was directly caused by Wolfe Mining."

"What?" Christian widened his eyes.

"I don't know what made him ask, but he did. Trust me, when that call came out of the blue, I was just as surprised as you are right now."

Christian leaned forward, digging his elbows onto the desk. This could be connected to Henry's voicemail to him. "What, exactly, did he say?"

"He just said that he'd read the EPA report and asked if our lab had ever independently done any research into the damage to the environment as a direct result of Wolfe Mining's practices."

"Have you?"

Peter shook his head. "Like I told Henry, we hadn't. He asked if it was possible that someone else in the company had compiled a report."

"And?"

Peter tossed the pen onto the desk and leaned back in his chair. "It's possible. Sometimes our company does send independents to the area to run a specific test if we have a heavy load at the time here in the office. So, yeah, it's not only possible, but it's not uncommon."

"What did Henry say when you told him that?"

"He asked if I would see if I could find out if such research had been done and if so, could he get a copy of the report. I told him I'd look around." Peter shrugged. "I never found any research, testing, or reports in the whole company."

"How did Henry react to that?"

"I never got the chance to tell him. His car accident happened the next day."

Now Christian was sure that whatever Henry had been looking into had to do with the voicemail he'd left. "Wow."

"Yeah. So, getting cozy with the enemy?"

That derailed Christian's train of thought. "What?"

"Wolfe Mining. You've always been opposed to their practices."

Oh. "Henry and I had been friends for a long time, Pete. Even longer than you and I. We were on opposite sides of most everything to do with our passions and professions, but I considered him to be one of my best friends."

"I'm not talking about Henry."

Christian frowned. "Then what are you talking about?"

Peter let out a snort. "You don't read the local paper either, do you?"

"Not usually. I find the important stuff usually finds its way to me. Why?"

Peter laughed. "Consider this one of those times that stuff finds its way to you." He tossed the local morning paper across the desk to Christian.

Front page headline blazed across the newsprint: Wolfe Family Mourning. Underneath, before any article, was a picture of him and Harper sitting on her back porch after the funeral. She was smiling at him, and as far as just this picture went, it looked as cozy as if the two of them were on a date. Definitely not having just had a service for her twin brother.

The article implied pretty much the same thing, too. It cast a very unfavorable light on not just Wolfe Mining, but also on the Wolfe family personally. The implication that the winding roads of the area weren't suited to little sports cars was a dig at Henry's Porsche. The whole tone of the article was mean in spirit.

Most of the locals despised Wolfe Mining because of its practices in mining that everyone believed was bad for their community, and in recent years, they had let their hatred spill over to include the members of the Wolfe family.

Including Harper.

"Looks like you two were cozy." Peter's teasing pulled Christian back to the picture. He hadn't seen a photographer, but with zoom lenses these days…

"I was cheering up an old friend who recently lost her twin, that's all."

But the article implied so much more.

Christian stood. "I've got to run. Let's meet up soon and grab a burger and catch up."

"Sounds good."

Hurrying out of the lab, Christian dug his car keys out of the front pocket of his jeans. He needed to talk to Harper. When she saw the paper, she would have a meltdown. She was very proper in the public's eye. Looking like she was having a date right after Henry's service ripped that image to shreds.

After he talked to her, he was going to find whoever wrote that article and get some type of explanation.

∽

"Janet, it wasn't my decision." Harper helplessly watched the other woman slam her personal effects into a cardboard box.

"Maybe not, but I doubt seriously you did anything to stop your father from firing me."

"I'm sorry."

"Right. I'm so sure you are." Janet added the little fern to the top of the box. "How you could be Henry's twin when you two are so opposite is beyond me. Henry was the sweetest, kindest, most honest man." Tears rolled down her cheeks. "He didn't deserve to die like that. He didn't deserve any of it. But you and your father...you two are just alike, apparently. Caring about no one but yourselves."

"That's not fair."

"Isn't it, Harper?" Janet settled the box against her hip. "Right after Henry's service, at that shindig you had at your big ole' house that I wasn't invited to, you were flirting up with that old friend of Henry's. Looked to me like you were taking care of your own interest. A love interest maybe."

"What? You mean Christian? He's not a love interest for me. He's just an old friend who can understand what I'm feeling right now." Harper was starting to feel less sorry for Janet and more angry. "We weren't flirting."

"Sure you weren't. I could sympathize with you. I loved Henry and he loved me. I wanted to share the mourning of a man we both loved together, but you pushed me away." Tears welled in Janet's eyes.

Harper couldn't argue with her. She had pushed Janet away. She didn't want to mourn with someone who'd only been in his life for a short time. And while she and Christian had reached a point in their relationship where they were heading into a strong friendship, he was no more interested in her romantically than she was him.

Or maybe she was wrong about that, too?

"Yeah, I can see you get it now that you haven't hid your intentions very well." Janet reached over and grabbed a paper and shoved it into Harper's hands. "Pictures don't lie either. Hard to not see what's right there in black and white, right?"

Harper looked down and saw the picture of her and Christian, then the headline. She groaned. "This is taken totally out of context."

"Is it, Harper? Because you two also looked rather cozy when I showed up at the scene of Henry's accident." She hoisted the box higher on her hip. "That's everything of mine. If I accidentally left something, you can just send it to me."

Harper put herself in Janet's shoes and realized she'd probably reach the same conclusion. She'd lost someone she cared about, and her job, all in one fell swoop. "Janet, I'm sorry Father fired you. I'll talk to him about keeping you on."

Janet slammed the box down on what used to be her desk. "Oh, how generous of you, Harper. Aren't you the most self-sacrificing person? You take time away from your precious job in the prosecuting attorney's office to fill at the family business since your twin died. You arranged your brother's service, not even asking me—the woman he loved—if I wanted to say anything or be involved in any way. No, you just took it upon yourself to arrange everything." Janet flung her hands in the air. "And now you'll talk to the boss man about letting me keep my job?" She snorted. "Don't bother. The only good Wolfe is dead."

Harper stepped back as if she'd been slapped, but she actually felt like she'd been punched in the gut. She could understand how Janet felt, but...well, no she couldn't, not really. While they both loved Henry, Harper had loved him all her life...the *twin from within* as they'd coined the phrase as children. Janet had made the choice to love Henry.

And just like that, Harper's anger evaporated. Janet was just lashing out because she was hurting. She softened her tone. "You're right, Janet. I messed up. You should have been included in arranging Henry's service. I was so overwhelmed that when Nell offered to make all the plans, I was so relieved. I couldn't cope. That's on me. I'm sorry."

Janet hesitated, as if gauging if Harper was being sincere or not.

Harper understood. She'd not really given the other woman a chance to trust her. Just like she'd admitted to Christian, she hadn't had an opportunity to trust Janet. "Look, let's start over. I really will talk to my father about keeping you as an employee, but in a different department. Only because whomever he hires as the corporate attorney will usually bring their own assistant and paralegal. If you stay on as my assistant, you'd just be facing the same situation when I leave."

"No, it's okay. I really do understand. It's just so quickly after Henry left. I figured this would be coming, but I thought I'd have a week or two."

"I hear they're always hiring in the marketing department." If Father opted to make a big deal out of that, she'd use the stocks as leverage.

"No, thanks. That's not my cup of tea. I'll just take the severance payment and find something else." Janet smiled, but it was a sad smile. "But I really do appreciate it, so thanks. And I'm sorry about my comment. It wasn't true and was mean and spiteful of me."

"It's okay. I understand. You're hurt and lashing out. I get it. I'm feeling it a lot myself at times as I continually struggle with accepting he's really gone."

Janet nodded, resting her hand on the box. "I keep expecting him to call or text. I just can't believe in one accident, he's gone."

Maybe it was time to come clean. It might help Janet in her acceptance. Or not, but at least there wouldn't be secrets between them. "Janet, Henry's wreck wasn't exactly an accident."

7

"Christian. Hello."

Just hearing her voice made him feel better. And worse. "I'm so sorry about today's paper."

"You didn't orchestrate the article or arrange for the photograph, did you? If you didn't, then it's not your fault." She cleared her throat.

He continued his walk on the gravel road alongside the cabins belonging to Gauley Guides by Gallagher. The fresh, crisp air filled his lungs and cleared his head. "But I can only imagine the fallout you're facing because of it. I bet your father is livid."

She hesitated before answering. "Actually, I haven't seen Father yet this morning. He fired Janet, so I had to speak with her. She's very distraught. She filled me in on what Henry had ongoing that I need to take care of, and she's just as shocked as we are about his wreck not being an accident."

"You told her, too?"

"I did. She deserves to know, and she's willing to help us in any way that she can."

Further down the path, the barks from his sister's dog, Shadow, echoed. "Well, that's good."

At least Harper hadn't seen her father so Elliott hadn't been able to come down on her about the newspaper. Then again, the day was still early. "Did you find anything Henry had open that might relate to the voicemail?"

"Not yet. I've only had time to look over things due this week, and there's nothing here that looks questionable."

He climbed the stairs to his personal cabin and dropped onto one of the large, wooden chairs on the porch that faced the Gauley. "Look specifically for anything that has to do with the most recent EPA report. Particularly, anything that might be connected to the mining practices Wolfe utilizes like the damage mountaintop removal mining has on the health of the people in its surrounding communities."

"Why?" Her voice raised an octave.

"The day before Henry died, he called a friend of mine who manages a lab."

"A medical lab?"

Christian stared out to the trees. A breeze whipped across the river and rustled the fall leaves still clinging to the limbs. "No. This lab tracks the plants in the area, monitors the wildlife, and does testing of environmental elements here."

"So, why would Henry contact them about health concerns that might be connected to an article in an EPA report?"

"I'm not real sure. Maybe because Henry also knew my friend at the lab and felt comfortable asking him or maybe it was because it was disassociated with any organization if Henry wanted to keep his inquiry private, but I can't say for sure. All I know is my friend said Henry asked if his lab had ever conducted research into the damage to the environment here as a direct result of Wolfe Mining's practices."

"Had they?"

"As far as my friend could tell, no."

Harper didn't allow for any pauses. "But?"

Christian filled her in on everything Peter had told him, then remained silent, letting her process the information.

"Do you think it's possible Henry might have contacted other labs and asked the same thing?" Her question implied a good possibility.

"Now that you mention it, I do. I guess we could call around and ask. Not sure they'd tell us much."

"I'll see if Janet will call and do some follow ups. She probably has the contacts from working for Henry and might have a clue which labs he'd consider."

"Good idea."

"I'll call her this afternoon and see if she's willing."

An awkward pause hung over the connection. "Harper, what are you thinking?"

"It's a gut thing. Or a twin thing, I don't really know."

"What?"

He could hear her breathing change. "This is the first step in finding out what Henry was talking about. This report is relevant to whatever had Henry so worked up."

Christian thought so, too. Especially since he'd just called Peter the day before his wreck, and that was when he left the voicemail. "Let me do some digging into the actual article. Maybe there's some sort of connection we're just not seeing here."

"I'd love to know what Henry was thinking. I'll dig around through here, too. I didn't really find anything in his safe here that could be relevant. I'll need to widen my search."

"That sounds good." There really wasn't more to say, but Christian didn't want to hang up. His mind had been going in circles about a couple of things. Seemed like now was the best time to get them out in the open. "Harper, I saw Vince Parsons with your father. Do you know him? Know what he stands for?"

"I know he's a friend of Father's who is running for the congress. I know Father says he's a big supporter of the miners, which is good since coal mining provides for over 500,000 direct jobs from coal mining and around a million plus more indirectly."

She sounded like a commercial. He didn't even really know what to say.

Then, she chuckled. "And I learned all that this morning while reading one of the briefs Henry had been working on."

He let the relief roll over him. It was one of the constant debates he and Henry had argued over the last few years—pro coal mining versus anti-coal mining. Maybe there was still hope for Harper to see the truth. Maybe he should see where she stood with regards to the area's geological environment. "Which is your favorite, the Upper or Lower Gauley?"

"The...wait, what?"

"Which do you prefer to raft, the Upper or Lower?"

"Um, neither." It was a statement, but the way her voice rose at the end, it could be just as easily a question.

"Bad experiences with both?" Henry probably took her and...well, that would've been a mistake. For having grown up in the area, Henry wasn't the best rafter.

"No."

He waited for an explanation. When none came, he asked, "You just don't like white water rafting?"

"Actually, I wouldn't know. I've never been."

"What?" How could she have grown up right here, practically on the Gauley River, and never gone rafting?

"I've never been. You know, there are plenty of people who've never been." Defensiveness had crept into her voice.

He spotted his sister walking along the gravel road, heading his way. "We need to rectify that. What are you doing Saturday morning?"

"Noth—why?"

Katie's Blue Heeler, Shadow, raced toward him, bounding up the stairs to his porch. "Come rafting with me." He bent and scratched the dog's chin. "It'll be fun."

"I don't know, Christian. There's still so much I need to take care of in regards to Henry's business, and I want to dig around to see if I can find any connection to that EPA report." But he could hear the indecisiveness in her voice.

His sister joined him and Shadow on the porch, shooting him a quizzical look as he continued his conversation with Harper. "Come on, it'll be fun. My sister and brother-in-law will be with us."

Katie raised her brows at him as she leaned against the porch rail.

He didn't want to give Harper time to back out. "You should at least go once. The scenery is beautiful and hey, you'll have two of the best guides in the business in the boat with you."

She laughed. "How can I refuse such a deal? What time do I need to be there?"

"How about eight?"

"Okay. I'll see you then."

"It's a date. And Harper..."

"Yeah?"

"I really am sorry for any fallout you get over the paper."

She let out a little sigh. "Yeah, me, too."

He disconnected the call and met his sister's amused stare. "What?"

"Who, pray tell, are you trying to impress?"

"I'm not trying to impress anyone. Just trying to be a friend."

Katie's nose scrunched. "To a female, I'm assuming?"

He nodded despite the heat rushing to his face. "Harper."

"Harper?" Katie's eyes widened and she stood straight. "Henry's twin, Harper? Harper Wolfe of Wolfe Mining?"

"Yes. Can you believe she's never been rafting in her life? Living right here?"

"No, I mean, I guess. I'm more shocked over you asking her out. I thought she didn't like you."

"Thanks, sis." He laughed and rubbed Shadow's belly. "We're working together to figure out why Henry called me that night and what he was talking about." He told her about his conversation with Peter. "So, she's digging around in Henry's office files and Henry's girlfriend is going to call some labs to do some follow up."

His sister nodded. "That's good. Let me know if Hunter or I can do anything to help." She pushed her hands into the pockets of her jeans. "But she is working at Wolfe Mining. That kind of goes against everything you believe in."

"I know, but she's never been involved in the business. She's had her nose stuck in books and criminal law from what Henry told me. It's likely that she hasn't a clue of the company's business practice."

"That may be, but everybody today has to be aware of the hazards of mountaintop removal mining. The health concerns, the fear over what it does to the surrounding areas, the environment, and even the damages incurred from water shedding. All for mining a non-renewable resource." Katie snapped her fingers, and Shadow jumped from his lap and to her side.

"I know, oh, I know. And we've heard all the arguments about how many jobs the mining industry provides and how it's clean energy and in abundant supply and blah, blah, blah. I'm just not sure she understands the complexity of how bad it is." He stood and moved to stand beside his sister, leaning over and resting his elbows on the top rail. "So I want to show her how great rafting and the river is. Let her see for herself what's at risk."

"It didn't matter to Henry."

He shrugged. "Maybe not so much before, but I think he recently had a change of heart and I think he found something that wouldn't let his conscience rest."

She pulled out a piece of candy from her pocket. "Perhaps. But until you figure that part out, you're still an environment nerd freak and she's working at Wolfe Mining."

"Temporarily." His need to defend her surprised him. "She's an Assistant Prosecuting Attorney, and seems to love her job. She's really only at the mining company to have access to Henry's files and papers, trying to figure out what his last words meant."

Katie slipped one of the peppermints she was forever sucking on into her mouth. "Just be careful, Christian. When it all washes out, she's still Elliott Wolfe's daughter."

~

A DATE.

Harper had been staring at her computer screen for almost fifteen minutes, but couldn't tell what even a single word on the brief before her was.

Christian had called the rafting trip tomorrow a date. Had that been just a slip of the tongue, or had there been a real reference as a date behind it? No, that couldn't be. They weren't even attracted to each other!

Well, that wasn't exactly true. She did find him extremely attractive, which was odd now that she thought about it because he was opposite of her 'type.' For one thing, she usually dated men who were clean cut, and Christian Gallagher was anything but with his shoulder-length, dirty blonde hair. It was thick enough to make women either jealous, or their fingers itch to run through it. She wasn't quite sure which category she fell into.

And then there was his laid-back demeanor. Most of the men she'd dated were professional types like fellow lawyers, or the bank officer who had turned out to be a total male chauvinist. Christian didn't fit into that mold. He was college educated and was a Wetland/Environmental Consultant, but he was also a white-water rafting guide. She was more of an indoor type, while he was definitely all about the great outdoors.

They had never really gotten along, even as kids and teens. Most of that was her fault because she was envious of the time Henry spent with him, but he was also daring and adventurous, ready to do just about anything anyone suggested. She was more ambitious in her career, assured she was on track to run for Nicholas County Prosecuting Attorney within the next ten-to-fifteen years. They had only formed this new...friendship because of Henry's death. Moreover, they seemed to be total opposites.

Oh, gracious, I am attracted to him.

The realization almost undid her. As it was, she leaned back in her chair, that creaked in protest.

Was he attracted to her? Had he really meant their rafting trip was a date-date?

No, he was just being nice to her. They'd bonded over grief for Henry. They were both trying to find answers to his death, make it all make sense somehow. Her emotions were all over the place. Understandable, considering the emotional mess of feelings that knotted in her chest.

She reminded herself that once things calmed a bit, when she was thinking more rationally, she would laugh that she ever considered being attracted to Christian Gallagher.

The phone on the desk buzzed, indicating an in-office call. She startled before she answered it. "Hello. This is Harper."

"Ms. Wolfe, your father would like to see you in his office."

Not a request, a demand.

"Let him know I'll be by as soon as I finish up a few things."

"He doesn't like to be kept waiting, Ms. Wolfe." The woman who had been his secretary for years had always been persnickety, but now she sounded downright snippy with the condemnation in her tone.

"Oh, I know my father well, Mrs. Sommers. Just pass along the message please. Thank you." Harper hung up before the older woman could argue anymore.

Focusing on the open response that needed to be filed by the end of the week in regards to an employment claim, Harper dug in to Henry's notes of case law he'd intended to cite. She couldn't help but be impressed with the thoroughness in which he'd laid out the case. A bitter taste stung the back of her tongue. Henry had been a great twin, a good man, and a good lawyer. It wasn't fair he'd been taken. Just like her mother. They were both wonderful people, with many who loved them, and there was no reason for them to be gone. God has just let them die, despite the prayers to heal Mom. Despite how much she needed Henry. Despite it all, God chose not to do a thing to save their lives.

"Harper!"

She looked up to find her father standing in the office doorway, his face flushed with annoyance. She'd seen it many times. She gripped the pen laying on the desk and forced calmness to seep into her very being. "Father."

He flicked the glass door closed. "When I call you, I expect you to come. Not later, but right then." His voice trembled ever-so-slightly.

Harper waved her hand to the computer. "I'm finishing a very in-detail brief, Father, that's due in a few days. I told Mrs. Sommers I'd be there when I could."

"That's not good enough. When I need you to come to my office, I need you to come right then."

She stood, daring her knees to go weak on her at the moment. "Father, I am not a child to be summoned. I am a lawyer, working here on cases for you—for Wolfe Mining. When I am in the middle of something, I can't just drop everything to report to your office like a school girl to the principal's office." Harper gripped the pen so hard that her fingertips hurt. "If it's something very important, you can just call me yourself and ask whatever you need to know."

His face reddened. "Harper, this is my company, the one I built up from scratch. I won't be spoken to disrespectfully."

"I wasn't being disrespectful, Father. I merely replied that I wasn't going to be jumping up and down at your command. I'm here as the company attorney, not a tag-along for *bring your daughter to work* day. I expect the same level of respect." Her heart pounded. What had come over her? She'd never been so defiant toward her father before. It had to be all the messed-up feelings that were tangled up inside of her. "So, what can I help you with?"

He hesitated, his eyes narrowed. He wore the pit-bull growling look that warned her this conversation wasn't going to be forgotten, forgiven, or let go. He would keep on until she either gave in or he felt his point was made. Thankfully, something else was more pressing to him. "Our PR department is working on a statement to do damage control over that article in today's newspaper. What were you thinking, being photographed with that tree-hugger? At my house, too. It looks very bad for business."

She dropped the pen onto the desk and straightened her posture. "I don't see how it's bad for business, Father."

"He's publicly gone after coal mining, stated that coal mining companies were the pilfers of the environment. How can you not see that as bad for business?"

Had Christian really said that? "Look, it was at a repast. We were talking about old times with Henry, which is the whole purpose of a repast. It's unfortunate that some journalist and photographer with a telescopic lens took that out of context, but as with most minor news bits, it'll be forgotten by tomorrow, unless we make a big deal out of it. I don't think we should make a statement of any kind. It's not worth mentioning."

"I have business associates who are very worried about it, Harper. They are mentioning it. Talking about it greatly."

"Then they need to move on to something else. This is really a non-topic."

"These are important people, Harper. You don't just dismiss them. We're talking politicians, lobbyists, others in the business."

She sighed and relaxed her shoulders before she sat back down. "It'll be okay, Father. By tomorrow, there will be something else the news is focused on."

"I hope you're right. You'd better be." He stormed out of the office, almost as frustrated as when he'd entered.

She fisted and relaxed her hands, working on calming her jumble of nerves. If Father thought that photograph and article was bad for business, just wait until he found out she had a rafting date with Christian.

He'd surely come unglued.

8

Harper Wolfe wasn't merely striking…she was breathtakingly beautiful.

She'd gathered her fiery hair into a thick braid that hung down the center of her back. She'd chosen one of the black wetsuits Gauley Guides by Gallagher provided for the customers, and it fit her like a glove. But it was her eyes that truly stuck out. Bright and alert, and taking everything in. Christian found himself feeling strangely toward her, something he couldn't quite explain.

Or maybe it was just the conversation with Katie yesterday that had him all twisted up about her.

"You remember my sister, Katie? This is her husband Hunter." Christian led them toward the couple loading the raft.

"Nice to meet you." Hunter gave her a quick perusal, a habit of his profession.

"You, too."

Katie looked up from securing the pack they always carried in the rafts and smiled. "Hey, Harper. How're you doing?"

Harper smiled back. "Can I tell you after this trip?"

Laughing, Katie nodded. "You're going to be fine. I'm the best guide on this river."

Christian gave his sister a gentle shove. "Hey, I'm a guide here, too."

"I'm just better."

Hunter shook his head and moved to stand beside Harper. "Ignore them. Seems they never outgrew their sibling competitive spirit."

"Oh, he knows I'm the best. Just ask Gabe." Katie slipped a peppermint from her fanny pack.

"Gabe would never take a side." Gabe, the oldest of the three, was serious and intense by nature, but he would never favor one of the siblings over another.

"Maybe not, but we both know which one he knows is the best."

"Children, play nicely." Hunter handed Harper a paddle and grinned. "Like I said, ignore their banter. It's just their love language."

She took the paddle but looked lost as to what to do with it. Before Christian could tell her, Katie addressed her. "The most important thing to remember about white-water rafting is quite simple: don't lose your paddle."

Hunter snickered. "Oh, be prepared to hear that. A lot. From both of them."

Christian recognized the nervousness of her smile. He moved to her side. "Hey, it's going to be fun. We're going to do the Upper Gauley. It's beautiful. All the leaves are bright golds and reds." He gently led her toward the raft.

"It is really beautiful here. I've never been right up to the river."

Christian bit his tongue. How could anyone grow up right in Summersville and not have spent time on the Gauley? Bookworm or not. "Just breathe in." He inhaled right alongside her. The clean, earthy scent carried on the breeze coming across the river.

She exhaled, then inhaled again.

He could practically feel tension leaving her.

"This is really something." She closed her eyes and breathed in. If she only knew how breathtaking she looked at this moment, now that she was in his element...his world. He stared out across the river, committing this moment to memory.

"Janet said she didn't have any idea why Henry would have been checking with labs about Wolfe Mining and reports, but she's left messages at four different labs. I'm guessing if he didn't call any of them, then he only checked at your friend's lab."

And the moment of tranquility was shot. Christian hid his disappointment. Did Harper even know the meaning of relaxing? He smiled and looked at her. She would soon. The rapids didn't give much opportunity to think of anything but them—they were attention-demanding. "Maybe she'll hear back from them on Monday."

"Yeah." She worried her bottom lip.

"What's wrong?"

"Can you recommend a good moving company around here? Someone reliable?"

He tilted his head. "I think Gabe has a friend who owns one. I'll check with him when we get back. Who's moving?"

"I am."

Christian froze. It surprised him how quickly his muscles tensed. "You are?"

She smiled. "Not away. Just out of the guesthouse." She swallowed. "Henry left me his house. It's fully paid for. I have no idea how, but the house is free and clear." Tears welled in her big eyes. "And he left it to me."

He gave her a gentle pat on her shoulder. "You were his twin, Harper. It's natural he would leave you his most important assets."

"He left me everything, Christian." A few tears escaped her eyes and traveled down her face. "Right down to those two stupid beta fish that I can't stand."

Without thinking, he wrapped an arm around her shoulders and gave her a sideways hug.

She relaxed against him, then stiffened as if she remembered she wasn't supposed to lean on him.

Time to lighten the mood. He reluctantly stepped away from her. "You really hate those fish, huh?"

She sniffled, then chuckled. "They are useless pets. I don't understand why Henry had them. He was never a pet person. I used to beg

Father for a dog, but he refused. Henry never asked for a single pet once that I can remember."

"So that English Mastiff you have is partially out of rebellion?"

"I guess. One of my law school girlfriends had one who had puppies. She was selling them and I'd just moved into the guesthouse." She shrugged. "So, I got one. He's one of the best decisions I ever made." The smile that widened across her face affirmed her statement.

"Elliott was okay with that?"

She shook her head. "I didn't ask. I just brought the puppy home. When Father saw him, Atticus was a cute little puppy. He argued and said dogs were too much of a hassle, but I dug in. He probably let it drop because it was the first time I ever really put my foot down." She grinned again. "And he also didn't realize how big Atticus would become."

Christian laughed, trying to picture Elliott's face. "No pets growing up, so you rebel with a Mastiff, and Henry gets meek, mild fish?"

"Oh, you've never met Republican and Democrat. Those two are so mean and vicious that they have to have their own bowls. Democrat tried to eat Republican when Henry had them in the same one." She frowned. "Or maybe it was Republican trying to eat Democrat." She shook her head. "Either way, they bite each other and chase one another. They're horrid."

From the corner of his eye, Christian caught Katie's gesture to come back. He turned them toward the raft. "Henry named his fish after political parties? That's priceless."

"It is, considering he never had any ambition to go into any political arena."

They walked up the path slowly, their steps in sync. "And you? Do you have any ambition to go into politics?" He held his breath. At this point, he didn't know how she felt about protecting the environment versus making a profit. He could only pray she placed more value on human life and the earth being left to generations to come, hopefully, than she did on the almighty dollar.

"I think I'd like to run for Prosecuting Attorney one day in the future. I like to see justice served."

Well, that was somewhat of a relief. "I'm surprised your dad never went into politics. Seems like that would be right up his alley."

She stopped, bent, and pulled a pine needle from her water shoes. "Oh, no. Father much prefers being in control behind the scenes. This is why we always have so many fundraisers and political guests over." Harper let out a long breath. "That's definitely something I won't miss once I move out. I don't enjoy playing hostess."

"Bet Elliott is having a conniption with you leaving the property." They joined Hunter and Katie by the raft.

"He doesn't know yet." She grinned.

Before Christian could ask any more questions or comment about her last reply, Katie finished putting Shadow's harness on the Blue Heeler, then passed a helmet and life jacket to Harper. The four of them secured their safety garments, then climbed into the raft.

Katie did a final demonstration about how to row the boat, then motioned for Harper to sit in what they called the *chicken seat*. Hunter climbed in and took a seat on the opposite side. Christian helped Katie push the raft all the way into the water. The underlying currents of the river shifted the boat. They both jumped into the raft before Katie latched Shadow's harness to the long strap.

They were off. Christian caught the look of expectation and a little fear settling in on Harper's face.

Welcome to my world. This was going to be fun.

∽

WHAT HAD she gotten herself into?

Harper paddled as Katie instructed. Her heart pounded. The river sprayed up on her face as it roared against them. Christian sat right in front of her, Hunter across from him, and Katie in the back beside her. The dog rode the waves like a pro. Well, Shadow *did* have more experience in rafting than Harper.

"Paddle hard." Katie's instruction was louder than the rapid. "This is *First Maneuver*. After this, we'll turn toward *Initiation*, which is a powerful class five."

Shadow barked as the raft wobbled over the ripples, then moved to smoother water.

Harper rolled her shoulders and the tension in her back eased. That wasn't so bad. She took a moment to look around. Another raft filled with people could be seen coming up behind them. But Christian was right, it was absolutely beautiful out here.

"Brace yourself. Get ready. Paddles in the water!" Katie wedged her feet against the back and side of the raft.

Christian glanced over his shoulder at her. "Hold on."

"Paddle hard!"

The water pitched the raft up and down. The four of them sliced their paddles through the water. Christian and Katie crouched forward, pulling and pushing the boat with each strong stroke of their oars.

They passed through the rapid, and Christian turned around and grinned at her. "How're you doing?"

The river raged beneath them, but calmer now.

She gave a nervous laugh. "I survived?"

Hunter gave her a big smile. "Your first class five rapid and you did it like a champ."

The sure-fire blush made her look at Katie. "You and Christian make it look way too easy."

Katie bent and pet Shadow's wet fur. "We grew up doing this. It's in our blood. I kayaked it solo when I was twelve. Led my first tour when I was fourteen."

"Wow." Harper didn't try to hide her impressiveness.

"Look around," Christian said. "The river is a life source all of its own. Close your eyes and feel her breathing."

"Her? The Gauley River is a *her*?" Harper teased.

"Naturally. Temperamental, unpredictable, and extremely volatile. Of course, the Gauley is a female." He chuckled.

"I prefer to think of the river as a her because she's free and wild and amazingly beautiful, even when she's mad as all get-out." Katie grinned at Harper.

"Yes, what my wife said." Hunter winked at Christian.

Katie stuck out her tongue at her brother.

Harper's chest tightened. She and Henry had enjoyed that kind of teasing and banter. Now it was gone forever.

Before she allowed herself to pitch headfirst into grief, Christian interrupted her thoughts. "We're coming up on Collision Creek. It's a nice class three." He looked at Harper. "Just hold your paddle steady and the current will carry us."

"But don't lose your paddle." Katie rested hers across her thighs.

Harper mimicked her, controlling her breathing.

Christian looked back at Harper. "We're entering another class three, French Kiss. Paddle steady."

French Kiss? Her eyes locked with Christian's for a moment before he faced front and paddled. She did as she was instructed, ducking her head so no one would notice the tell-tale blush burning her cheeks.

Water splashed up on her, cooling her face and drawing her concentration until they shot into a calm part of the river.

Hunter leaned over and kissed his wife. Shadow jumped and wiggled between them. The newlyweds parted, laughing, and Katie bent to love on her dog. She smiled up at Harper. "I know you've lived here all your life, but since you've never been rafting, I'm going to ask the question anyway—do you know the history of the Gauley?"

"A little." Harper struggled to pull up what she knew, which, honestly, was nothing but where it was located. The heat rushed to her face again. "Actually, I really don't."

Katie shook her head. "Don't worry about it. Most people here don't, unless they're rafters or in the business." She had the kindest smile. "The US Army Corps of Engineers completed the Summersville Dam project back in 1964. The Summersville Lake Dam sits three hundred and ninety feet above the Gauley River, and has three discharge tubes. When those tubes are released, the average discharge is about 624,000 pounds per second, which is what gives the Gauley its amazing, one-of-a-kind set of rapids in both the Upper and Lower portions."

"Wow." She'd lived here all her life and never knew. It was quite fascinating.

Christian snorted. "Oh, don't let her impress you with her knowledge. Dad made all three of us kids learn the tour guide speech before we were ten."

Katie shoved him. "Smarty pants."

He laughed. "But the best part is the name of our dam."

"Really? Summersville Lake Dam. I thought it was named after the lake. It isn't?" Harper cocked her head.

"It is, but usually the Corps of Engineers name the dams after the closest town. In our case, the closest town when the project was completed was Gad. They considered Gad Dam wasn't exactly the best idea." Christian laughed harder.

"You're joshing with me."

Katie joined in on the laughter. "Nope. He's telling the truth this time."

"This time?" He shoved her foot with his.

Hunter shook his head. "It really is true. I looked it up when I first heard it."

Katie twisted to stare at her husband. "You did?"

He nodded.

Dramatically putting her hand over her heart, Katie frowned. "You didn't believe me? How rude."

He reached over and tugged the end of her single braid that had flipped over her shoulder. "I didn't know you then, sweetheart."

"Yeah, I'm gonna sweet your heart all right."

Their affectionate teasing and obvious love put a lump in the back of Harper's throat about the size of the Summersville Lake Dam. She turned her gaze and met Christian's intense stare.

Her pulse kicked up a notch and she couldn't look away. Her mouth went dry.

A slow smile crossed his lips, then he broke the eye contact.

She exhaled slowly and bent to pet the dog, a great distraction to her sudden, crazy emotions.

Mercy but the man could make her knees go weak when she was already sitting down.

9

God, You made this lady something special, didn't You?

Christian had to force himself to face forward in the raft and not just stare at Harper. How had he missed how beautiful she'd become? He shook his head a little to clear his thinking. He needed to concentrate on the river, who was just as beautiful as Harper, and at the moment, much more demanding of his attention.

"Okay, we're coming up on *Insignificant*, which is anything but." Katie spoke aloud, but she focused mainly on Harper. "It's a five-plus rapid. It has a big dip, then we'll rush down the 'wave train.' *Insignificant* is a shallow rapid, so we'll need to avoid the rocks lining the edge of the river."

Although Christian had heard the spiel so many times—heck, he almost said the same thing verbatim, he felt a charge. He loved this river and being able to be on it as much as he could was a blessing. He knew that, and he appreciated it.

The raft shifted and he instinctively planted his feet. He naturally moved into the ready position and tightened the grip on his paddle. Christian exhaled slowly.

"Remember, don't lose your paddle!" Katie admonished just as the raft lunged under them.

Christian didn't have time to glance behind him to see how Harper was doing. He knew Katie would make sure Harper was okay. His arms shifted and sliced his oar through the river, paddling with the current.

The water splashed up on his face as the current tugged the boat right. More water splashed as the raft twisted left. Christian and Hunter paddled in tandem for about fifteen to twenty seconds, then the raft pitched over the big dip before racing down the trail of continuous rapids.

The raft slowed as their paddling did, and the raging roar of the river was nearly deafening for the next several yards.

Christian's breathing slowed and he turned in his seat to find Harper wearing the biggest grin.

"Ohmygoodness! That was amazing!" Water dripped from the braid hanging out from under her helmet. Drops had settled on her eyelashes, and she blinked rapidly. "I can't believe I never knew what fun this was!" She settled her paddle across her thighs, mimicking his sister. "I think I'm mad Henry never took me."

Katie laughed out loud. "We've created a monster."

Christian joined the rest of them in their gaiety. "Now you see why we're all such nature enthusiasts."

Hunter nodded. "I never was before I met Katie and came to the Gauley the first time. It's addictive."

"I can see that. What class rapid is next?"

Christian grinned. "Only a class two."

"But, right behind that," Katie continued, "is another plus-five one called *Pillow Rock*. Trust me, that one is nothing to play around with. It's one of the ones I told you that you'll need to paddle or die on."

"Set yourselves—it's going to be a bit bumpy." Christian faced front, and they rode out the small class two with a ripple.

The raft shifted, and *Pillow Rock* came into view. Christian and Katie both automatically wedged their feet against the side and bottom of the raft and gripped their paddles. The raft slammed into the inertia wave, the large rock looming in front of them.

"Mild or wild, Harper?" Christian hollered over the furious river rapid.

"Wild!" She didn't hesitate in her response.

Christian grinned as both he and Katie rammed their paddle faces into the river and steered the raft toward the wild side to the left.

The angry five-plus rapid pitched them forward before spinning around backward over the piece of boulder peeking out of the surge of the river. The quick, downward thrust of rushing river caused the raft to go up on its side. The swirling water pushed them free of the rapid amid jostles and bumps. A few smaller waves crested against the raft, causing Hunter and Harper to lose their footing. Hunter recovered instantly, but Harper bumped into Christian.

He turned and steadied her, finding himself holding her a little closer and a little longer than needed.

They locked stares and Christian had to press his lips together and release her before he did something really stupid...like kiss her on her cute little upturned mouth.

She blinked several times as she settled back in her seat.

Katie reached out and gently nudged Harper. "So, what'd you think?"

Harper turned to stare at her. "It was great. I loved it. Is the next one as strong as that?"

Katie chuckled. "Well, we are coming up on *Lost Paddle* in a bit. It's a class five, but our next one is *Hungry Mother*, and she's a class four."

"Oh, good." Harper's smile said it all.

Christian's heart lifted. She was amazing. He'd seen many men balk on their first time on the Upper Gauley, but not Harper. Nope, she was having a great time. He didn't know how to analyze exactly what he was feeling, but it was almost a sense of intoxication. He glanced over to Hunter, who studied him in silence.

The euphoric feeling dissipated. His brother-in-law was an experienced FBI agent, very proficient in profiling and reading people. If he'd just read what Christian was experiencing, and he told Katie... Christian would never hear the end of it.

The raft picked up speed and volume, the rushing river drowning out his own thoughts. He and Katie both set their stance, crouching. They slipped down, carried by the fast current of the wild water forging around the craft.

The boat spun, then slammed against an underwater boulder that kicked the raft back toward the center of the class four rapid.

Christian matched Katie's long, steady strokes. "Paddle hard!"

River water splashed up on them. Shadow barked as he leaned against Katie's leg. The raft rubbed up against *Decision Rock*, pitching and jostling everyone. Then the boat was shoved out of the raging rapid, and slowed.

"Whew, that was a fun one!" Harper's grin seemed to be plastered on her face.

Christian couldn't help but wonder how much fun she would have had if he and Henry had taken her with them when they'd snuck the raft out and rode rapids alone back in their teens. She'd probably have been a blast. She sure was now.

"Well, *Lost Paddle* is right around the next bend, and it's a doozy." Katie scratched under Shadow's chin. "It's that class five I warned you was coming up."

"I'm ready!" By the grin on her face and the determination in her eyes, she was.

"It's pretty amazing, isn't it?" Christian leaned back so she could hear him over the river.

Harper gave a slow shake of her head. "I can't believe I never did this. Now...well, now I don't want to stop. It's more than amazing—it's unreal."

Heart in the back of his throat, Christian nodded. "God really made a masterpiece with this river, no doubt."

The smile slipped off Harper's face and she looked down to pet Katie's dog.

What had he said to cause the sudden change? God? Christian's stomach knotted. Was Harper a non-believer?

Every inch of him went cold. It'd be just like him to find the woman of his dreams only to discover she didn't share his faith. The faith that was so integral to his very being that he couldn't imagine a life with someone who didn't share his beliefs.

Please, God, let her be a believer.

∼

GOD.

Harper followed Katie's and Christian's instructions, paddling hard and keeping a tight grip on her paddle, but her mind reeled. Since when was Christian Gallagher a true believer? Sure, she remembered as kids them all going to church. They were even in the same Sunday school classes, but that's when they were kids and their parents made them go.

Henry and Christian were more interested in running around and getting into trouble than sitting down and coloring their Bible story sheets. Oh, and that time Christian brought in a frog and put it in the poor Sunday school teacher's purse.

Water splashed against her face, the river demanding her full concentration.

"Paddle hard!" Katie fixed her feet wider in the raft.

Harper tried to match Katie and Hunter's stroke-for-stroke, but hers were shorter and choppier. Her muscles tensed into tight masses. She was going to be very sore tomorrow, but it was so worth it today.

The raft pitched and hummed with the river's current. Her feet vibrated with every bump. Water sloshed into the boat and over her wetsuit and shoes. A strong breeze brushed against her face.

"Paddle or die!" Christian crouched in front of her, pulling his paddle through the water easily. His smooth strokes didn't even knot up the muscles outlined under his wetsuit.

Struggling to keep her grip on the paddle tight, Harper rowed as hard as she could. The rush of the river and the focus required held her thoughts captive.

The raft dipped and pitched through the last ripple of *Lost Paddle* before it eased into smoother waters.

"You're doing so great." Katie smiled at Harper. "To be honest, when Christian told me you were coming, I was a little worried we'd have to cut the trip short to take you back."

Harper blinked several times at Christian's sister. "What did he tell you about me?"

"I didn't say anything! Katie, don't mess with her." Christian splashed a little water from the end of his paddle onto his sister.

Katie chuckled. "He really didn't say anything about you, just that you were coming." She splashed water back at Christian. "I just didn't think of you as anything but poised and proper. I didn't expect you to be so much fun. I misjudged, and I'm sorry. You're actually pretty cool." Katie smiled as she scratched her dog's ears.

"Thanks?" Harper didn't quite know what else to say. How to respond to such an admission?

"Please forgive my wife," Hunter said. "She had her tact surgically removed in her years of misspent youth."

Katie shoved her husband. "As if you knew me in my youth." She turned back to Harper. "I am sorry, though, if that came out wrong. I meant you're an attorney and the daughter of Elliott Wolfe. My expectations were wrong. I thought you'd be a little uppity and maybe a bit of a princess."

Harper couldn't stop the snort of laughter. "Oh, you aren't alone in the assumption, trust me. When I came back home and started at the Prosecuting Attorney's Office, so many people treated me like they expected me to bring personal staff."

"But now that I've gotten to know you a little, you are nothing close to condescending or snobby." Katie tilted her head. "I like you."

Harper couldn't take offense to Katie's frankness because it was just so refreshing to have someone so open and honest. "I like you, too."

"Now that we've all established we belong to the group admiration society, we need to concentrate on *Iron Ring* coming up. It's a gnarly class five and we need to pay attention. Paddles at the ready."

Harper rowed as instructed, enjoying the moment because it might not come again. She felt a little pang of grief and guilt. Should she be enjoying herself so soon after losing her twin? Shouldn't she be trying to find out who ran him off the road and to his death? Should she be making friends during such a time?

The river took no consideration of her internal concerns as it dipped once…twice…

"Steady. Steady. Paddle!" Christian leaned almost over the side of the raft. They plunged with the third dip, almost flipping the raft as a massive drop pulled them down the river. They missed the large boulder on the right pushing into the river.

The adrenaline rush made Harper's heart beat faster. Her pulse thrummed. She was exhilarated, and it felt amazing. "That one was fun."

Christian kept his seat but grinned at her over his shoulder. "If you thought that one was fun, wait for the one coming up. *Sweet's Falls* is another class five, but it's tricky."

"I love this so much. Much more than I ever thought I would." Harper couldn't stop the smile.

"Great, we've turned you into an adventure-chaser." Christian shook his head, but there was no denying the pride that crept into his voice.

Pride? Why?

Before she could analyze that train of thought, Katie started giving details about the next rapid. "We're currently at a higher water level, so the ledge hole on the right side of the rapid extends further out into the drop than at lower levels. We'll have to set a hard left slant and punch the hole at the bottom. The channel to the left of the ejector rock will widen and make us a smooth line through the falls."

"Don't panic at how narrow the slip seems or appears. We *can* make it." Christian's stare collided with hers. "Just ride the waves as we head into the channel and let Katie and I do the paddling. We'll steer us right through where we need to go."

"We've done this many times and even if we tip, don't panic. Just hold on to your paddle and swim toward the big rock." Katie unlatched Shadow's harness from the strap. The dog, as if knowing what was coming, pushed behind her master's calf.

For the first time since they'd passed through the first rapid, nerves tightened in the pit of Harper's stomach. She trusted that Christian and Katie knew what they were doing, so she wasn't really scared, but the apprehension swirled in her chest.

Hunter nudged her foot with his. "They got this. Just enjoy the ride until they tell you to paddle."

She nodded.

"And don't lose your paddle." Katie's face was already grim with concentration.

"Here we go!" Christian slammed his paddle into the water just as the first waves hit the raft.

Harper bounced as she was jostled and slammed about. Her feet kept slipping, making her bracing less effective. The raft leapt, dipped, twisted, and did almost a full one-eighty-degree turn. She held the paddle so tight that her hands cramped. Water sluiced over the sides of the raft, soaking all of them. Shadow barked, but kept place behind Katie's open stance.

"Pull us," Katie hollered at Christian as she slowed her intense rowing.

Christian responded by heaving long, straight slices through the river with his paddle. His efforts moved the raft toward the sliver of a space between the two boulders, despite the fury of the river. The muscles in his neck corded as he paddled furiously. "Now, Katie!"

Katie slammed the water with her paddle and matched Christian's rowing. They paddled in sync for several minutes before Katie hollered, "I've got her."

Christian pulled his paddle in and let his sister guide the raft right between the two boulders.

Harper reached out and touched the cold slickness of one of them.

Then, the raft was pushed out into the falls.

"Everybody paddle!" Christian thrust his paddle into the water, as did Hunter. Harper followed suit.

Her strokes weren't as long and smooth as either Christian's or Katie's, or even Hunter's, but she did her best to keep up with them. Sweat formed on her scalp under the helmet. It felt good. Really good. How long had it been since she'd physically worked up a sweat? She and Henry had run at law school, but she'd dropped the habit once they'd gone their separate ways.

The raft eased into smoother waters.

"You good?" Christian twisted to look at her.

The thrill racing through her veins made her smile. "I have to admit, this one really got my heart pumping, but I loved it."

His grin made her heart pump a little harder.

Wait—what?

"Just two more smaller rapids and we'll put out. Rory will be waiting." Katie attached Shadow's harness back to the strap.

"What's for lunch?" Hunter asked. "I'm starving."

"Of course you are." Katie laughed and looked at Harper. "We're going to drop off Shadow at the cabin, then were planning to head into Summersville and grab a burger at the diner. Want to join us?"

She hesitated, only because all her emotions seemed to be jumbled. Not to mention she probably looked a total mess. No, that's what a snobby person would think. She made up her mind in that second. "I'd love to." She glanced at Christian. "If that's okay with you."

His smile was instant and infectious. "I'd like nothing more."

Harper wasn't ready to unpack that statement. Not now.

10

"It's disgraceful the way your family is killing our community. You should be ashamed of yourself." The woman wagged a boudin-like finger at Harper as she approached the diner.

Christian's shoulders squared in response to the woman's attitude to Harper as he joined her on the sidewalk. "Excuse me, ma'am?"

"This...this woman. Her family's mining is killing our land and its inhabitants." The woman gestured toward the mountains in the distance of Summersville. "Look around. I know you, Christian Gallagher. Knew your momma and daddy and always held them in the highest esteem. Have always been proud of you kids for carrying on their legacy. Especially proud of what you do in trying to protect our land." She cut a sideways look at Harper. "And then I saw your picture in the paper with this woman. I'm so disappointed in you."

Before Christian could reply, Harper's hand on his shoulder drew him up short.

"Ma'am, I don't know you and you don't know me. I'm just trying to get a bite to eat. If you have a problem with Wolfe Mining, the office is a block over, so please feel free to go there and file a complaint." Harper's voice was steady and strong.

"You're all murderers over there. Your brother got what he deserved. Be careful, missy, that you aren't next."

Christian felt rather than heard her quick intake of breath.

"Ma'am, that's uncalled for. You should move along now." Hunter's tone left no question to his authority.

The woman didn't appear fazed at all. "I don't know you, young man, but this isn't your business."

"Ma'am, you said you knew my parents and me." Katie's voice held that no-nonsense tone as she took a step toward the woman. "If you know us, then you surely know that Harper was born and raised here." She nodded toward Hunter. "This is my husband, who is an FBI agent. Now, I don't know what your issue is today, but as Harper said, we're going to get a bite to eat, so if you'll kindly move out of the way..."

Christian took Harper's hand and led her around the woman and into the diner. The nerve of her, saying Henry got what he deserved. He trembled with outrage. "I'm sorry, Harper."

She shook her head. "Sadly, I'm used to it."

He led her to a booth in the back, Katie just behind them. The cracked vinyl seat whooshed as they sat.

"That happen often?" Katie slid into the opposite side of the booth.

"Often enough. When your last name is Wolfe in this town, these types of accusations happen." Harper reached for the menus in the slot at the inside end of the booth. Her tone might have sounded calm, but Christian didn't miss the slight tremble of her hands as she passed out the menus.

"I'm sorry for what she said about Henry." Katie's scrutiny didn't miss much, either. Must be a family trait.

Harper lifted a single shoulder. "Thanks." The emotion in her voice belied her composed demeanor.

A young waitress appeared and took their order. Katie ordered for Hunter as well.

"Where's Hunter?" Christian still didn't see his brother-in-law.

"He was collecting her information details." Katie grinned over the menu. "He can be very intimidating when he chooses.

Christian chuckled. "That's the truth." He twisted to smile at Harper, but also took stock of her eyes and how she'd checked her emotions. "Have you heard how I met him?"

She slowly shook her head.

"He was working undercover on a case, and had the misfortune to draw Katie-cat as the guide for the weekend trip. I, of course, had to come along and save their rear-ends."

"Please, as if we needed you to save us. And meeting me was the biggest blessing of his life."

Hunter slid into the booth and kissed Katie's cheek. "It was, truly. God put her directly in my path." He wrapped an arm around her shoulders. "That particular weekend, He put her there several times over."

The waitress dropped off their drinks before moving on to the next booth. The four of them unwrapped their straws and pushed them into their glasses.

As his sister and brother-in-law told details of their big adventure that led to them falling in love with each, Christian watched how Harper absentmindedly twisted the silver ring on her finger. He'd already noted she did that whenever she got lost in thought.

While he knew many in the area felt as he did about destroying the beautiful land for mining purposes, and he'd participated in many protests against mountaintop removal practices, he'd never confront someone just trying to go get something to eat.

He took a sip of his soda and mulled over that thought.

He had ambushed Elliott Wolfe outside of Wolfe Mining a time or two during a peaceful protest to get an answer from him in regards to if he was aware of the damage his company did to the environment. Was that the same thing? He'd never considered how Elliott had felt, but now, after being on the other side of the table, Christian wondered if maybe he should save such questions for press conferences or a more acceptable format.

Harper laughed, pulling him from his own thoughts. "That's a great story to one day be able to pass down to your children."

She had a really nice laugh. Christian couldn't help but grin. "So, honest appraisal, Harper. How did you like white-water rafting?"

"I loved it. Seriously, I could go again right now."

Christian and Katie both started laughing.

"The muscles in your shoulders and arms are going to have your full attention tomorrow morning," Katie replied to the confused look Harper wore.

"You'll find out exactly how strenuous rafting can be. Trust me, your aches will tell you loud and clear tomorrow." Christian smiled at her confused look. "We strongly discourage people who aren't experienced rafters to not schedule an overnight trip because they can barely function in a boat the second day."

"Yeah, it's brutal." Hunter nodded. "Trust me."

The waitress delivered their food, then bounced away without missing a beat.

"Would you like to say grace?" Katie asked Harper.

The color raced off of Harper's face. "Uh, no thank you."

"Okay." Katie shrugged. "Hunter?"

They bowed their heads and Hunter's deep voice offered up grace before ending with a resounding *amen*.

Another indication that Harper wasn't a practicing believer. Sadness wrapped around Christian's heart and weighted it down like a heavy anchor.

"I can't get enough of these things." Hunter wiped his mouth after setting down his burger dripping with greasy goodness. "I can't tell you how many times I want one of these babies when I'm in the field office."

They ate their burgers, fries, and onion rings and in between bites, they visited. Christian was thankful for his sister and brother-in-law's small talk that seemed to have a relaxing effect on Harper. After the woman's confrontation outside before they'd eaten, compiled with just having lost her twin, she needed the easiness.

After paying the bill, Harper said goodbye to Katie and Hunter.

Christian walked Harper to her car. "Thanks for coming with us today."

"Oh, it was so much fun, Christian. Really, I had one of the best times ever." Her smile lit up her entire face.

He grinned. "Then we'll have to do it again soon."

"Yes, please. Just say when."

An awkwardness seemed to settle in the air between them as he didn't know what to say. It wasn't like the end of a date or something where he would normally lean in for a kiss, but he didn't know exactly how to classify the moment. The lightness of the morning's mood had dissipated like the light morning fog.

"Thank Gabe again for the mover's recommendation. I'll call them this afternoon and try and get them scheduled as soon as possible. I'll be over at Henry's house the rest of the weekend, stowing his stuff. I'll keep an eye out for anything that looks suspicious and call you if I find anything."

"Call if you need any help."

"I will." She hesitated another minute, then reached up and gave him a quick hug before she opened the driver's door of her car and slipped behind the wheel. "Thanks again for today. I needed it." Pink flushed her face.

He smiled while she shut the door and started the engine.

She gave a little wave as she drove off the restaurant lot.

Christian had things to do, but he wanted to just be still and remember Harper's hug and smile, and how that blush made her eyes stand out even more.

What?

What was happening to him?

~

HARPER DROVE HOME ALMOST on auto-pilot as she replayed the day in her mind, smiling to herself. Rafting excitement and fun aside, spending time with Christian had been natural. Well, up until the goodbye.

Her hugging him had been impulsive and she couldn't help but regret it. Had she turned their newly-forming friendship into a heap of awkwardness now? She hoped not. The day had been so perfect. Well, except for the God soundbites.

She wove her little Mercedes SUV around another set of curves on the road. Christian, his sister, and apparently her husband were all Christians. It was surprising, but also a little unnerving. She didn't know Hunter's story, but couldn't believe a seasoned FBI agent would be so strong in faith. And Katie and Christian? Everyone knew their mom went missing years ago and that she'd been declared dead. On top of that, losing their dad...how did they reconcile a loving God to losing so much? It didn't make sense. Maybe that was how they coped with their loss—

Boom!

The sound reverberated inside the cabin of the SUV. The vehicle vibrated, then jerked into a fishtail to the left.

Adrenaline pushed everything she knew about how to handle a blowout to the forefront of her mind.

Harper took her foot off the accelerator and gripped the steering wheel tighter at the ten and two positions. The sweat on her palms slicked the leather and she lost her grasp. The SUV pulled stronger to the left. She corrected her grip and struggled to keep the vehicle going straight.

Perspiration glued her shirt to her back as she concentrated on getting to the side of the road. Once her speed dropped to below thirty miles-per-hour, she gently tapped her brakes and fought to steer the Mercedes off the road.

Slower...*correct the steering and ignore the vibrations.* The stench of burnt rubber permeated the cabin of the SUV.

A little slower...*ease off the side of the road.*

She applied the brakes...held the steering wheel tighter to control where the vehicle went off the road. More pressure on the brakes. An inch further.

Finally, the Mercedes came to a shuddering stop. She flipped on the auto's flashers.

Harper let out the breath she hadn't even realized she'd been holding until it rushed out like water from a dam. She released the steering wheel, her hands alternating between cramping and trembling. She could hear her pulse throbbing in her ears. Her heart batted against her ribcage. The tang of metal filled her mouth.

She laid her forehead against the steering wheel.

Seatbelt unlocked, door opened, and on wobbly legs, Harper stepped onto the roadside loose rocks. She walked around the SUV, inspecting the tires. The driver's back tire pushed flat onto the gravel. She squatted to inspect it as she opened the app for her roadside assistance program.

Huh. She didn't see any nail or anything. Might be under the weight of the car.

Before she could access the roadside assistance call, the hum of a Dodge Challenger roared. Christian pulled in behind her Mercedes. His emergency lights flashed in sync with hers.

She closed her app, stood, and shoved her cell into her back pocket.

He rushed to her side. "Hey, are you okay? What happened?"

"I had a blowout."

"You're okay?" His stare made her heart race as much as the blowout had.

"I'm fine. A little rattled, but okay." She nodded at the tire. "I guess I picked up a nail or something."

He squatted and ran his hands over the black rubber. "Tread looks great."

"I just got those tires a couple of months ago."

Standing, he dusted off his hands on his jeans. "At least it blew here rather than a few miles down the road where the curves get more serious." He looked to the side of the shoulder, then back to the road before turning to her. "I'm assuming you have a spare?"

"Of course."

"Then open your back so I can get it out and we'll get it changed right quick."

"You don't have to do that, Christian. I have roadside assistance."

"Of course you do." He chuckled. "I'm quite capable of changing your tire. I got this."

She clicked the fob and the rear hatch opened. Harper realized he was right—less than five miles down the road, and the tight curves popped up. She wasn't sure she would've been able to control the Mercedes if the blowout had happened there. The idea made her blood run cold.

A sickening thought knotted her stomach. Had Henry felt fear like this? Sure, she'd heard his last words, but he would've had to have been just as terrified.

Tears too long denied broke free. She put her face in her hands and cried. Her sobs came in waves.

"Whoa, it's okay." Christian's strong arms wrapped around her, pulling her against his chest. He alternated rubbing her back soothingly and smoothing over her hair.

Too weak to stand any longer and too emotionally spent to care, she leaned into him, taking the comfort and strength he offered.

He held her tighter and murmured soft assurances, letting her cry it out until her tears ran dry. She sniffled and moved an inch back, wiping at her eyes as she did. She could only imagine how red and puffy her eyes and face had to look at the moment.

She avoided looking him in the eyes. "I'm sorry. I was just thinking how scared I'd been and if it had happened five miles later, how differently things might've been, and then I thought how scared Henry must've been when he realized he was crashing, and—"

Christian pulled her close again and gave her a tight hug. "It's okay. I understand. It's perfectly understandable." He slowly released her.

She let him steady her, then she took a step back. She needed a little distance from him. Being so close, where she could smell the outdoors that clung to him like a favorite cologne, made her not be able to think as clearly as she should. She stared at the ground. "Thanks. I'm fine. Really. I guess I just needed to get it out."

With a single finger, he lifted her chin until she slowly met his stare. "Harper, you've been through a lot in a very short time. It's only natural that your emotions are tangled. Anyone would be all over the place."

She nodded, and he dropped his touch.

"And don't ever apologize or be embarrassed for having honest emotions around me. I care about you, and I'm here for you."

"Thanks." Heat settled in her chest, not yet making it to her face.

A breeze filled the space between them, carrying the scent of autumn promises with it. The vibrant yellow and red leaves rattled on the limbs. In that moment, she couldn't remember a time when she'd ever been so aware of the living and breathing nature of her surroundings. It was a little unexpected and surprising, but also reassuring.

"Well, let's see about getting this tire changed, shall we?"

"Please, and thank you."

"It's really not a problem. Happy to help out a friend." He set about loosening the tire's lug nuts and situating the jack.

Friend. She swallowed. He was right…her emotions were all over the place. Yes, they were friends. Newly forged friendship, but as she thought about it for but a split second, she had enjoyed her day with Christian and his family more than she'd ever imagined. Spending the day as she had had been just what she'd needed. How he'd known that, she couldn't imagine, but she was so thankful.

"Hey, Harper?"

She joined Christian at the rear of the SUV where he'd just placed the blown-out tire. "What is it?"

"Look here." He pointed to a hole in the tire.

"That's what caused the blow out?"

Christian nodded. "And look at the way the slit goes. No nail did that." His face twisted into a scowl.

"Then what did?"

Christian let out a breath and met her stare. "I'm not an expert, but if I had to make an educated guess, I'd say the tire had been punctured."

"Punctured?"

"Yeah. Like with a knife or something."

Her heart started pounding again. "Like on purpose?"

"Harper, can you think of any reason that a knife slices a tire isn't on purpose?'"

She slowly shook her head. The implications filled her head. Was it the same person who came after Henry? Why?

One thing was clear…she needed answers, and she needed them now. She was going to do whatever it took to get them.

11

"The mechanic confirmed what you said. The tire was cut." Harper's voice wobbled just a little. Maybe most people wouldn't have noticed, but Christian did. "I filed a police report, not that it'll do much good. As the officer told me, they'll check the surveillance video from the diner, but if there's nothing there, there isn't much chance on them finding out who did this."

Christian switched to his earbuds so he could work on his laptop while he talked. "I'm sorry, Harper. That's really terrible."

"It is, but the police don't seem too worried about it."

"Even with what happened to Henry?" Yep, the cops were as useless as a raft without a paddle.

"They still have Henry's wreck as an accident."

"Despite the recording?" Christian opened the email from Laurie Fisher. It simply stated: Call me.

"Apparently. I know Father wanted it to stay ruled as an accident and he spoke to the officers who handled Henry's case, so I'm sure it will stay an accident."

Christian pushed back in the chair. "Why on earth wouldn't your father demand they look until the truth was revealed?" Henry had been Elliott's only son…how could he *not* want to know what really happened to him?

"Who knows why Father does what he does? At any rate, the shop is putting on a new tire and they'll deliver my car to me here at Henry's."

"I'd be happy to take you to pick it up."

"Thanks for the offer, but it's already set. Besides, I'm hoping to finish packing up everything from here tonight. The movers Gabe recommended had a job already lined up for Tuesday through the end of next week, but were more than willing to take it on this weekend and Monday when I offered to pay more than their weekend rates. So, they're packing up my stuff at the guesthouse now. Henry's housekeeper, Nell, is heading over there this afternoon to clean the place top to bottom so Father will have nothing to complain about on that end. The moving guys are coming in the morning to move Henry's stuff to the storage building I rented, then they'll move my furniture in and put the boxes in the garage. Monday morning, Nell is going to start cleaning over here and start unpacking for me. It's surreal that this place is mine now."

"Wow, you're moving fast. How did your dad take the news of you moving out?" Christian could imagine Elliott Wolfe's reaction—furious that his only remaining child was moving out from under his control.

"I haven't had a chance to talk to him yet. I've been a little busy."

Christian grinned to himself. "Do I smell avoidance?"

"No. Father is playing golf with some lobbyists at The Greenbriar in White Sulphur Springs today." But she chuckled anyway. "Still, I'd much rather have the bulk of packing and moving done before I have to tell him. I'm not quite sure how he's going to accept the news."

Probably just as they imagined. Time to change the subject. "Have you found anything that might be related to Henry's inquiry into the EPA report?"

"Nothing yet, but I've mainly been working on packing up the kitchen and bathroom. I'll look more closely as I pack up the living room, office, and master bedroom. But hey, I talked with Janet to let her know what I was doing. Two of the four labs she called hadn't gotten any request from Henry."

"It's so odd." Henry went to Peter to ask about the report. First off, why? And secondly, where did he go next to get the information Peter didn't have?

"Maybe it's unimportant, but I have that twin thing that tells me it's what Henry was referring to when he called you."

"I know. There's something there. Whatever it is has to be important enough that Henry correlated the EPA report to something to do with Wolfe Mining. Enough that he went to Peter to ask about an independent study."

"Well, I'll keep looking here. I'll call you if I find anything."

Christian disconnected the call and popped out his earbuds, his mind trying to process everything he knew. One, Henry had been upset about something to do with the EPA report, an independent lab, and Wolfe Mining. Two, Henry died in the wreck and the police don't seem to want to investigate it as more than an accident. Neither did Elliott Wolfe. Three, someone cut Harper's tire.

What did it all mean? Was Henry's wreck associated with what he'd called Henry about? Was Harper's cut tire connected to Henry? Why would anybody cut Harper's tire? Sure, she was an Assistant Prosecuting Attorney, but had her job made someone angry enough to cut her tire? It was possible, but likely? And the timing...so close to Henry's wreck.

He turned back to his computer and saw the email from Laurie. No time like the present. He punched in her number.

She answered on the first ring. "Hey, you." Her voice was as sultry as ever. It was one of her most unique features.

"Hi. I got your email."

"Well, hello to you, too. I'm doing fine. My day off is going swell, even though I've been doing some side work for a friend."

Christian chuckled. "Good afternoon, Laurie. How're things with you?"

She giggled. "Much better. I'll get you trained yet. Seriously though, I finished analyzing that dead Candy Darter."

"And?"

"I found an overabundance of selenium—about ten times what is required by fish—which turned it into a poison to your darter. I also found a bit of telangiectasia of the gills...they were pretty swollen upon closer observation."

"Gill swelling? Is that a thing?"

"It is, and which can be caused by selenium contamination and toxicity. I would dare to say, looking at these levels in your dead darter, the mortality of larval fish will be drastically increased as well, if it isn't already."

"They wouldn't even stand a chance of survival?"

"Not with these levels of selenium. I haven't seen levels this high in such a small fish in...well, I can't remember when. So high that it was toxic to your little guy. If the levels are this elevated in the area you found him, then I would have to guess that the overabundance of the selenium has probably killed more fish, and will be killing off the little larval fishes as well, if it isn't already."

"Wow. That's not good."

"No, it isn't. That's why when the report hit my computer and I reviewed them, I knew I had to let you know as soon as possible, even on a Saturday. What does this mean for the aquatic eco system here?"

"The darters are only found here, so if their larval fish aren't able to fully develop and swim against the currents, they could easily become extinct." He made notes on his ever-ready notepad beside his computer.

"This could be very bad."

"You're telling me. I'm going to get a water sample from different locations on the Gauley and specifically test for the selenium levels. It could be detrimental to more than just the darters. This could affect all the aquatic life in the river." He scribbled more notes.

"Well, let me know if I can help you with anything else. You know I'm more than happy to do what I can."

"I really appreciate it, Laurie."

"Of course." There was a heavy pause over the line. "You owe me dinner, Christian Gallagher."

He smiled as he tossed his pen back onto the desk. "Name the day, and I'm all yours."

"Seriously?"

"Of course. I've been owing you for some time."

"How about next Tuesday night?"

He glanced at his calendar open on his desk. No guiding trips had him scheduled for late that afternoon. "Looks good to me. How about I pick you up at six?"

"Sounds like a plan."

"Good. It's a date. I'll see you Tuesday night, and thanks again." He disconnected the call and jotted down the dinner with Laurie. She'd been so helpful so many times, he felt bad he was just now going to take her to eat. He'd pick someplace nice to take her. Maybe Prime 44 West. It was in White Sulphur Springs, about an hour away, but the steaks melted in your mouth. He made a note to call and make reservations for seven-thirty on Tuesday.

That settled, he grabbed his collection gear and headed out of his cabin. If memory served him correctly, Katie had a group heading to the Upper tomorrow morning. He could get her to grab a couple of water samples from there. He'd see if Gabe was doing a Lower anytime tomorrow and could get a few water samples from the Lower. He'd not only check the selenium levels, but also compare how concentrated each part of the Gauley was.

Something very strange was happening on the Gauley River, and he intended to get to the bottom of it.

∽

"I CAN'T BELIEVE you're moving in here so soon after Henry...well, after he passed. It would creep me out." Janet walked around the living room, void of anything except the furniture and the boxes.

It was a question Harper had asked herself many times over, but had always come to the same conclusion. "I thought I would be, too, but I actually feel really close to Henry here, and it brings me comfort. Peace." She smiled as she stared at the custom-made shades that looked out the front of house. "I remember him asking me to help him pick out those shades to go with the paint we'd selected for the walls. He was so worried he'd turn this house into a bachelor pad and he really wanted it to be a home."

Tears welled in Janet's eyes. "It was a home."

Harper stopped sorting the law books she was putting in boxes. Some of them, she'd keep on the shelves. "Did you come here often?"

Janet dabbed at her eyes. "Often enough. We spent a lot of time watching movies. Henry said it was one of his favorite ways to unwind."

Harper nodded. "He was a movie buff. Did he ever ask you to play movie trivia with him?"

The other woman shook her head. "No."

"Good thing. He won every round I ever played with him, and that's saying something. In case you didn't know, we were extremely competitive."

"Oh, I know. I heard all the tales." Janet plopped down onto the couch Harper had decided to keep and move to the extra bedroom she planned to turn into a study of sorts.

"Really?"

Janet crossed her arms over her chest and stretched out her long legs. "He said you were always better at academics than he could ever ben, but he had the most common sense."

"Did he now?" Harper stopped packing and rested her hip against the table that still held Republican and Democrat in their respective bowls. She had never gotten that impression from her twin.

"He did. He told me that you were the best in your law class and that you could run circles around most of the lawyers he knew, but sometimes, you didn't have the common sense to come in from a snowstorm."

"Well." She didn't know Henry had felt that way. It was a little insulting, and Henry had never been insulting or rude to her. He'd always said to insult her would be like insulting himself since they were twins.

Janet sat upright, eyes wide. "He didn't mean anything by that. We were just talking and joshing around. He kinda said it off the cuff."

Harper forced the smile.

"You know Henry was your biggest fan."

That much was true. He'd always pushed her to be her best and to believe there was nothing she couldn't do. She was going to miss having that. She'd miss it very much. "Yeah, he was."

"I still have a hard time believing he's really gone." Janet's voice sounded thick, heavy with emotions.

"Me, too." She pushed back the emotions and shoved off the table. The movement jolted the table a bit.

"Oh, you've made Democrat upset. He doesn't like the rocking." Janet nodded to the fishbowls.

Harper glanced at the fish. Both seemed the same as before to her, so she didn't see how Janet could know one fish was upset. Unless... "You know, I want you to have something of Henry's that he cared about."

"You don't have to give me anything." But her eyes lit up.

"Henry loved these beta. He picked them out himself. I'd like for you to have them." Harper smiled at the other woman.

"The fish?" A shadow flickered across her eyes, just for a millisecond before she smiled. "Of course. I'd love them. Henry adored them."

"I'll get a box for them and their food. Henry bought the stuff in bulk."

"Okay. Thanks."

Harper boxed everything up, then saw Janet out. She was thankful for the information about the lab, but some of what Janet had told her that Henry had said about her really hurt her feelings. Why hadn't Henry ever mentioned anything to her if he thought she really was lacking in the common-sense department?

She fed Atticus, then as she was filling his water bowl, a knock on the front door nearly had her jump out of her skin. Atticus started barking, his most ferocious-sounding one.

"Atticus, back up. Let me see who it is." She peered through the front door peephole and smiled.

Christian stood there, wearing a grin and holding a pizza box.

She pulled the door open, blocking Atticus access. "What are you doing here?"

"Delivering a pizza? Here to help you pack up stuff?" His sheepish grin was infectious.

"Well then, you best get inside, hadn't you?"

"Only if you call off the beast I heard bellowing."

"Atticus? He's my gentle giant. Come on in." She grabbed the pizza box and moved aside.

Christian got one step inside the house before Atticus was trying to love him to death. "Goodness, you are a pretty boy, aren't you?" Christian bent over and rubbed the Mastiff behind his ears. Atticus was in heaven.

"You'll spoil him." As if she didn't.

"He's beautiful. And huge." Christian laughed as Atticus pushed his head against his hip, nearly knocking him over.

Harper gave Atticus the command to eat, then led Christian to the kitchen. She sat the pizza box down on the island. "I've already packed up Henry's dishes, so we'll have to eat on paper towels."

"Works for me." He plopped down on the tall barstool.

She opened the refrigerator. "I have water and juice and milk. That's it. Henry wasn't into sodas or anything."

"Water sounds good to me."

She passed him a bottle and opened the pizza box.

Christian bent his head and without waiting for permission, said grace out loud. Luckily, he kept it short.

"Thank you for the pizza."

"Figured you'd be hungry and might need a little help." He took a bite of the slice he'd grabbed. Cheese stretched down his chin and he wiped his mouth with another paper towel.

"I am and I will. I was going to call you anyway."

He grinned and waggled his eyebrows. "Missed me, did you?"

She shoved his elbow off the island. "You wish." Truthfully, though, she had kinda missed him. "Janet came by. She found a lab who said they had been hired privately to research into the damage to the environment caused, directly, by Wolfe Mining."

"She did?" Christian's eyes widened as he set down his slice and opened the cap of his water bottle.

Harper nodded. "Yeah. Enviro Labs got a request earlier this year to run an independent analysis of damage done to the environment by Wolfe Mining's practices."

"Did they?"

She shrugged. "They wouldn't tell Janet. They said it was confidential."

"But it was okay for them to confirm they'd been contracted for it?" He took another bite of his pizza.

"Apparently." She took a swig of water. "But I'll call them first thing Monday morning as legal counsel and employee of Wolfe Mining and see what I can find out."

"Things keep getting more and more strange, don't they?"

She nodded. "They do, but I'm determined to keep on until we get to how, if at all, everything is connected."

He saluted her with his bottle. "I'm with you. I promise, I'm in this for the long haul, until we get to the truth."

She believed him, and that alone reassured her.

12

"Can you please have these water samples checked for selenium levels?" Christian stared over the desk at Peter. "Laurie's swamped with the autopsies on those two dead Allegheny woodrats that were brought in by Park Rangers early this morning."

"Why are the important items always so early on a Monday morning?" Peter took a long pull from his coffee cup.

"I'm sorry, Pete. Really, I am. If this wasn't important, I wouldn't ask."

Peter laughed. "Yes, you would, but I get it." He picked up the phone on the corner of his desk and pushed a single button. "Allison, could you please come get some water samples to test for me, please?" He hung up the phone and took another drink from his mug.

"Thanks, man, I appreciate it." Christian set the four vials on the desk. Two were taken from the Upper Gauley and two were from the Lower.

"Why are we testing for selenium levels?"

"Remember that dead Candy Darter I brought in for Laurie to autopsy?"

Peter nodded, taking another drink.

"She found a toxic level of selenium in his system. Enough that it poisoned and killed him. I'm hoping it was a freak accident of some sort, but I have to report things like this to the EPA as well as Fish and Wildlife, and I need to know if it's an isolated incident, or if we have a bigger problem on our hands."

Alert now, Peter sat up straight in his chair and set down his cup. "If it's a freak accident, what could account for it?"

The same question Christian had asked himself many times on the drive over. "I don't know. That's why I need to see if the high levels are in the river. If they aren't, then I'll have to figure out some possible ways the darter could've ingested so much. Laurie also said there was quite a bit of sediment in his stomach, so that might be the correlation." He ran his hand through his hair. "I just don't have enough information right now."

A tap sounded on the open door of the office before a lab-coated lady with bright neon-green, spiky hair stepped inside.

"Thanks, Allison." Peter handed her the four vials. "I need you to check the selenium levels in each of these." He looked over to Christian.

"Also," Christian said, "can you run a comparison of the levels in each of the samples? If a higher level is present, I'd like to see where it's most concentrated."

The woman, probably around Christian's age, nodded. "Of course. Should I check for anything else?"

Christian shook his head. "Not right now. Just the levels and concentration comparison."

She smiled as she pocketed the vials before turning back to Peter. "I'll have the results to you within an hour or so. Will that be okay?"

"Perfect." Peter smiled. "Thank you, Allison."

She left and Christian stood. "Thanks, man. I really appreciate it," he reiterated.

"I'm anxious to see what's going on."

"Me, too." Christian had an obligation to report any unusual data to the Fish and Wildlife Services. Especially when it concerned an endangered species. Also, he'd have to consider reporting to the EPA if there was a high content of selenium in the Gauley. Because of the way water flowed around the Gauley, there could be a chance of high levels of selenium in the vegetables grown in the area. It could also possibly affect drinking water, thus increasing human exposure to the toxic levels of selenium.

The phone on Peter's desk rang. He answered the call. "Peter Swisher."

Christian turned to leave, but Peter snapped and held up a finger to Christian.

"How many of the plants are dead?" Peter asked into the phone.

Dead plants? Christian leaned against the doorjamb.

"Yes, you're right. If you bring in the plant with as much of the roots as possible, we can analyze them." He paused, listening to the person on the other end of the connection. "Yes. You can leave it with anyone in the office. I'll write up an order for the testing." Another pause. "Okay. Thank you."

Peter replaced the phone and looked up at Christian. "A Park Ranger found about fifty to a hundred dead Virginia spiraea over at Carnifex Ferry Battlefield State Park."

"Really?" The Virginia spiraea was a rare plant species indigenous to the area. It was on the Endangered and Threatened Wildlife and Plants list with Fish and Wildlife Services…protected.

"Yeah. She said she'd get a sample and bring it in and another Ranger is securing the site."

Christian shook his head. "Sediment in dead fish's stomach, high levels of selenium, and now dead Virginia spiraea? What's going on?"

"I don't know, but my next call would've been to you."

"I think I'll head over to Carnifex and look at the site. Depending on what I find there, I might be bringing samples back here." This lab was where most all of Christian's tests were run as they were approved by the EPA and FWS, and Peter could direct bill to both agencies.

"Good deal. I'll probably be back soon." The state park wasn't far from downtown Summersville.

Peter nodded. "I'll call you as soon as Allison gets results."

"Thanks."

Christian headed to his cabin. He'd need to grab his work backpack to make sure everything was documented correctly. Federal agencies were precise in how they accepted reporting.

He stopped into the shop of Gauley Guides by Gallagher to see if Gabe, Rory, or Katie had noticed anything odd on their recent rafting trips. If there was a lot of dead foliage, they would've noticed. He opened the door to find Hunter behind the counter. "Where is everybody?"

His brother-in-law's smile came quickly and easily. "Both Gabe and Katie had groups today and Rory's splitting time doing his video thing."

"She put you to work, didn't she?" Christian grinned.

The FBI agent shrugged. "I don't mind. I actually find it relaxing."

Christian could only imagine what his brother-in-law went through daily when he was at work, so the river work was probably a nice reprieve. "I get it. Something about being out in nature is very calming. Always soothes my soul."

Hunter nodded. He picked up a pencil and rolled it between his fingers. "So, how's Harper today?"

"I don't know. Haven't talked to her." He rested against a rack of wetsuits for sale and stared at Hunter. "Why? Has she called here?"

"No. I just figured you might have talked to her, seeing as how crazy you are about her."

Heat burnt the tips of his ears. "We're just friends. She's going through a rough time and I'm trying to help her out."

"Yeah. Sure." Hunter leaned his elbows on the counter and studied Christian. "I'm trained to read people, remember. Not that it's too hard to tell that you like her when you look at her. Your emotions are all across your face."

Christian swallowed. Hard. He rubbed the end of one of the empty hangers on the wetsuit rack. "She just lost her twin and there are a lot of questions that need answered. Henry was my friend."

Hunter tapped the pencil on the old counter. "Tell me you don't like her more than a friend," he dared.

Swallowing again, Christian looked down. "Well, yeah. I mean, she's successful, beautiful, funny, and smart. What's not to like?"

"You missed something."

"What's that?"

"I don't think she's a believer." Hunter's voice had carried a lightness of teasing up until now. He'd turned somber.

"I don't either, and maybe that's what's holding me back from asking her out on a real date. That, and she's got a lot she's going through right now."

"Want some brotherly advice from your favorite brother-in-law?" Hunter grinned and stabbed the pencil into the can by the register.

"My only brother-in-law." Christian smiled back, pushing off the rack to shift his weight to the other leg. "Yeah, sure."

"Don't discount her just because she doesn't seem to share your faith. She could just be going through some issues that God's dealing with her about."

"But Scripture preaches about being spiritually matched."

Hunter nodded. "If I had accepted that I needed to only become emotionally invested in someone who was as strong in faith as I am, I would've never have fallen in love with your sister, and that would have had me missing out on the greatest adventure of my life."

"Katie-cat? Oh, she's an adventure all right." But he grinned at Hunter. His older sister could be a pain in his side sometimes, but she was fierce in her love and loyalty...and now in her faith.

"It's true. I would've missed out on the love of my life. I can't imagine how my life would be now without her, but you know how mad she was at God when we met. If I hadn't given her time and gently coaxed her into talking to God, there's no way I would be this happy in life."

All true. Katie had been furious that their mother left, even though their father had believed until his dying day that something had happened to her and that she hadn't just up and left them. She'd been mad that God allowed them to endure such pain. She'd been mad that God had let their father die years later. Truthfully, Katie had just been angry all around. But now that she was married to Hunter... she was happy. The fun-loving sister he remembered from when they were kids.

"God can change anyone's heart. Just be open to bring up the faith subject gently, yet often. Enough that the Holy Spirit can move in her. Jesus is in the saving business, remember."

Christian nodded. It was something to think about.

The phone rang and Hunter reached for it. Christian gave a mock salute and headed out the door. Now, more than ever, he wanted to see Harper. Something about Hunter's advice had really resonated in him. Maybe he could go ahead and ask her out on a date, see where things went.

If he could work up the nerve to ask her. It might be too soon for her, with just losing Henry and all. She had an awful lot on her plate.

He'd just have to play it by ear.

~

HARPER'S HANDS TREMBLED, shaking the papers she held until the words blurred.

She sunk into her chair at Wolfe Mining and reread, hoping against hope that she'd misread. The enormity of what type of impact of this could have on their company slammed against her.

The logo at the top of the first page mocked her—the U.S. Environmental Protection Agency. No denying the importance of the listed findings.

According to the report, the EPA had recently estimated mountaintop removal valley fills (the process of diverting mountain streams because of mining debris, thus polluting the waterways as well) were responsible for burying over 2,000 miles of Appalachian headwater streams that were vital to the area. Many more of the waterways were poisoned by the practice, so the report stated.

The report concluded with a testing result that water downstream of mountaintop removal mines had higher levels of selenium as well as sulfate, and also increased the electrical conductivity of the water, which was a true measure of heavy metals. Significantly higher levels. Such changes in the water could kill water life, or if not kill them immediately, disrupt their life cycles so drastically that their population would dwindle, or even disappear entirely.

The second report, the one from the lab Janet had found who said they'd been hired by Wolfe Mining, had faxed over their report upon Harper's call this morning. It confirmed they'd been hired to run the same analysis, and had reached the same conclusion. Not only the same conclusion, but worse. That not only were aquatic life at risk due to mountaintop removal mining, but certain clonal root system plants were also at risk.

Harper let the papers fall to the desk, and rubbed her temples. All the possible lawsuits they could be slapped with spun through her head. The results of this report, if accurate and if they were to be released, could effectively cause significant loss to the company, if not shut them down completely.

She tried to imagine Henry finding this report. Kind, caring Henry. Her heart tightened as she glanced at the file the report had been stuck inside. No way would he have buried such a report. It just wasn't in his nature.

She checked the date of the EPA report—over a month ago. The date of the report from the independent lab was a little over three weeks ago. Henry had called Christian's friend's lab last week to see if they'd been hired to run the same test. Why? Did he suspect the EPA and the first report were incorrect? That didn't sound like Henry.

It didn't make sense. If he saw the EPA report over a month ago and became concerned, as Henry would have, he would've ordered an independent study, which he did. When that report came in three weeks ago, what action did he take? What did he do? Janet said he'd never mentioned anything about this to her. So he waited a week or so and then began calling other independent labs to see if they'd been hired to run private studies. Why?

Was Henry afraid someone else knew about the dangers that were specific to the area by Wolfe Mining practices? Just by what she had uncovered, it seemed like Henry might have been covering up for Wolfe Mining.

Harper's chest tightened to where taking a deep breath was difficult, if not almost impossible. Had her twin abandoned his morals and scruples to protect Wolfe Mining?

No, that couldn't be. Harper couldn't accept that. Wouldn't.

She picked up the papers again, putting them back in order. On the last page of the independent lab's report, she noticed something she hadn't before—who ordered the analysis on behalf of Wolfe Mining. She'd just assumed it was Henry, since he was legal counsel and had called Christian's friend at his lab. She was wrong.

The name typed in bold across the very bottom of the page was none other than Elliott Wolfe himself.

Oh, Father, what have you done?

13

"Ranger? I'm Christian Gallagher. I'm a Wetland/Environmental Consultant. Peter Swisher informed me about the dead Virginia spiraea another ranger found."

The older man in uniform turned and extended his hand. "Ranger Hopper, nice to meet you." He squinted despite the wide brim of his uniform hat.

Christian's hand ached from the stiff shaking. He tugged gently, then harder, to withdraw from the man's clasp.

"Yep, Ranger Kettle found herself a passel of dead plants. We don't usually have them around here—not close enough to the water, I guess. That's why we were baffled to find a clump of the plants."

Christian nodded. True enough. The species relied on periodic disturbances, like moderate, occasional high velocity floods, which eliminated competition from trees and other woody vegetation to flourish. While the park was close to the Summersville Dam, it wasn't close enough for the plants to take root in the immediate area.

"As soon as Ranger Kettle found those and we identified which plants they were, well, we knew we needed to get them tested before we moved into action."

"Smart. Can you show me the plants?"

"Yes, sir. They're right over here." He turned and led Christian toward the area sectioned off with bright yellow, nylon rope. "Ranger Kettle took a couple of the plants to the lab already."

"I was there when the call came in." Christian set down his backpack, pulled out his cell, and began snapping photos of the pile of plants and the surrounding area. There was no question they'd been dumped in bulk. "You have no idea how they got here?"

"Not a clue. No one has reported anything fishy, either. Well, not since the last night of *Thunder on the Gauley*. We had a group of those protestors against anything to do with the Civil War show up with their signs and chants that the War Between the States shouldn't be revered, especially not the Confederate side." He shook his head. "I just hate when people try to deny history. It happened and we can't change it. Seems like nobody wants to learn about the history so we can change what was wrong."

Thunder on the Gauley was a lively history event recalling the Battle of Carnifex Ferry that took place on September 10, 1861. Various living history demonstrations depicting Civil War military life were scheduled over the course of two days. The event was scheduled every other year, and most often than not, drew a fairly decent crowd to the area. Some people, however, weren't too keen on the reenactment still taking place.

Christian had learned long ago not to engage in such discussions, but this one might be motivation for damage to the area plants. "What did the group do besides march with their signs? Were they in the park close to here?" He took off another set of photos before pocketing his cell.

"No, they just stood out at the entrance and chanted. We had to ask them to move a couple of times to let cars in or out, but they did as soon as we asked, thank goodness."

Dead end. Time to get back on track. "How did Ranger Kettle discover the plants?" He pulled out some of his sample bags and knife.

"We'd had a couple of reports of people littering off the paths, so we'd been checking different places around the main grounds. She came across these here during one of those checks. Don't know why people toss their trash on the ground when we have trash receptacles all along the paths."

Christian recorded the information for his sample onto the bag and pulled a couple of the plants into the bag. "My family owns a rafting guide business and I'm always amazed at how often many people have such little respect for this land."

Ranger Hopper shook his head and snorted. "People have no respect anymore. It's a crying shame."

Christian took another sample, then shoved them all into his backpack before standing and looking around the area again. "I'm going to guess nobody reported seeing someone dump off anything."

"Nope. Nothing, but we'll certainly be keeping a lookout."

"Are you and Ranger Kettle the only two rangers at the park?"

Ranger Hopper nodded. "Yep, for right now. We get extras to help prepare for *Thunder on the Gauley*, and cleanup after, of course, but on the regular, it's just me and Ranger Kettle."

Christian nodded. "Well, okay." He passed the man his business card. "If you uncover anything else, or find more plants, please call me."

"Will do." The NPS Ranger put the card in his shirt pocket before extending his hand again.

Christian inwardly groaned, but shook the man's hand with a matching firmness. "It was nice to meet you." He jerked his hand free and swung his backpack over his shoulder.

"Pleasure was all mine. I'll let you know if we learn anything."

Christian nodded and headed back to his car. He took note that the park looked basically empty with the exception of a young couple who seemed to be looking more for a place to make out than take in the sights around them. No wonder the ranger had been so outgoing. He was probably bored out of his mind.

He'd just made it to his car and slung his backpack into the passenger's seat when his cell rang. He checked the caller-ID before answering. "Hey, Peter. What's up?"

"Allison just brought me the results from your water samples."

"And?" Christian shut the driver's door and stuck his key in the ignition, but didn't turn over the engine.

"As suspected, considerably high levels of selenium was found in all samples."

"Define high."

"About seventy-five times the normal concentration."

Christian let out a low whistle. "That's definitely what I'd call high."

"Most definitely." Peter paused, then continued. "Allison also said that the samples marked Upper Gauley had the highest concentration, in the seventy-five times the normal concentration, while the samples from the Lower were in the mid-fifties."

"So whatever is causing the higher amounts of selenium is closer to the dam and running down."

"That would seem a logical conclusion. Now, what do you think is causing such a rise in the levels?"

"I really don't know at this point." Christian sighed. Now he'd have to file multiple reports and do whatever follow-up testing they requested.

"You know, I read something about increased selenium levels in rivers recently."

"Oh yeah?"

"Yeah, but I just can't remember exactly where right at the moment. I mean, I just read it in like the last month or so."

"It would really be helpful if you could remember, Peter."

"I'm trying. It will come to me once I stop trying so hard." He chuckled. "It's rough getting old."

Christian laughed. "You're only two years older than I am, man."

"See what you have to look forward to?"

"All right. Email me the results and I'll file my report tomorrow morning. I've got some of the dead plants and saw where they were dumped. It's pretty close to the main site, but I can easily understand how nobody would have seen anyone dropping off anything. The park is basically vacant."

"I'll send them, and when I think of where and what I read about selenium, I'll give you a shout."

Christian disconnected the call and started the Challenger. Something was definitely going on in his field of expertise, and right in his own backyard. Time for him to sit down and do a little research.

He was going to get some answers.

~

THIS WAS GOING to be interesting.

Harper set the papers back on her desk and wiped her hands on the sides of her slacks. She hauled in a deep breath, then released it slowly. Just knowing she had to confront her father had her tied up in knots. She wiped her palms again, then grabbed the documents. She scanned them for the hundredth time, almost memorizing the contents verbatim.

How to interpret the EPA report and the follow up results from Enviro Labs with Elliott's name as the person who ordered it? She needed to know not only how much Henry had known, but also what did her father plan to do with the results.

Last night, when memories of her twin kept her wide awake, she'd come to a plausible theory: that her father had ordered the independent analysis from Enviro Labs, hoping to disprove the EPA report's findings. When it didn't, he tried to bury the information so Wolfe Mining wouldn't be held culpable. Henry probably came across both reports and confronted their father. By all accounts, Wolfe Mining should cease and desist mountaintop removal mining immediately and look into reparations to damages to the community.

It was time to find out answers.

She drew in another breath and rang her father's extension. His secretary answered immediately.

"Mrs. Sommers, is my father available right now?"

"I'm sorry, Ms. Wolfe, but your father isn't in today."

"He's not in?" Her father was always in. When she had ballet recitals, he was at work. When she was in gymnastics, he was at work. When she was in the hospital with appendicitis, he was at work.

"He called a little bit ago and said he'd gotten in late last night, so he'd be working from home today."

"Okay, thank you." She hung up the phone, wanting to kick herself. All that worrying and fretting, and for nothing.

Her cell rang. She pulled it out and checked the caller-ID. "Hey, Nell. What's up?"

"You need to come home. The house has been broken into." The woman's voice sounded cracked.

"Where?"

"Your new house, honey." Bless Nell's heart for not calling it Henry's.

"But I haven't even unpacked yet!" Nor had a chance to install a security system.

"I know. But all the boxes in the garage have been cut open and it's a big mess. I'm going to call the police as soon as I know you're on your way."

Harper shoved the papers into her purse. "I'm leaving now."

A break-in? For what? The furniture and art she'd hung yesterday were more valuable than anything in her boxes. Maybe whoever broke in thought she had jewelry or something.

She grabbed her keys and purse, told her secretary she'd be out for the rest of the day, then headed down to her SUV.

The movers' van had been in and out of the driveway a bit over the last few days, so anybody would have known she was moving in. Criminals, she knew from her experience, would consider breaking into boxes easier than searching for valuables all over the house.

The drive didn't take long, but the Nicholas County Sheriff's Deputy cruiser was already parked outside the house when she pulled into the driveway. The garage door stood open only about two feet from the cement floor, but it was too dark to see anything inside. She entered through the front door and found Nell talking with the two deputies at the kitchen table. Both uniformed men stood as she moved into view.

"Ms. Wolfe." The older man, Lt. Lyons, nodded in her direction. She was happy to see him as he'd been the officer on several of her cases. He was thorough and did his job by the book.

"Lt. Lyons, what have we got?"

"So far, it looks like someone pried the garage door open and slipped inside. They cut open all of the boxes and dumped them. We need you to look and see if they took anything, or if they were looking for something specific."

She nodded, then looked at Nell. "Where's Atticus?"

"I put him in the backyard when the police got here so he didn't knock them over."

"That dog is probably what stopped whoever broke in from coming into the house itself," the younger deputy said. Harper didn't recognize him.

"Then it must not be somebody I know because all my friends know he's nothing but a big baby."

"Maybe you shouldn't broadcast that anymore." The young deputy was probably only trying to be helpful, but it rubbed Harper the wrong way. Especially when he added, "A young woman, living by herself. You really should have an alarm system, too."

"I haven't even technically moved in yet. It's on my list of things to do." She swallowed back the snippiness she felt brewing.

But Mr. Young Know-It-All wouldn't let it go. "I'd move it up on my list, ma'am. Especially considering you probably make a lot of enemies in your profession."

Lt. Lyons had been studying her. He jabbed Rookie Cop. "Ms. Wolfe is well aware of that, Deputy Davis."

"The crime scene unit should be here any minute." Lt. Lyons got the conversation back on track. "Hopefully, they'll be able to pull prints off the garage door."

She nodded. "Any idea what was used to pry it open? I'm guessing we aren't lucky enough that they left it behind?"

"No, ma'am." Deputy Davis hugged the silver, standard issued clipboard to his chest.

"Well, let's go have a look." Harper walked to the garage door and swung the door open. The light came on automatically.

She gasped. Even though she'd been told that the boxes had been dumped, she hadn't been prepared to see all of her belongings littering the garage floor like it sprawled out before her. Thank goodness her clothes had been hung directly into the closet and she'd never emptied the drawers of her dresser for the move over. Her entire wardrobe would've been ruined with this mess.

"Just remember not to touch anything," Deputy Davis reminded her.

"Yes, I know." She descended the four stairs down into the garage and surveyed the damage.

Her lion bookends were smashed. Some of the classic hardbacks she'd collected were open, face down on the floor. No telling what damage had been done to the interiors of many of the books strewn around.

Photo frames broken, with glass shards haphazardly all over the garage floor. Some of the photos had to be damaged, and it made Harper want to cry. Especially when she saw her old photo albums, the ones her mom had made for her since birth. They were all over the floor, some open. The one she looked at first had a dirty footprint on top of her mom's writing. She resisted the intense urge to snatch it up and try to wipe off the dirt. Instead, she fell back on her position as Assistant Prosecuting Attorney and pointed to it. "Make sure the crime investigators take note of that. I can guarantee that footprint is from the culprit."

Deputy Davis scrawled on his clipboard as Harper moved on.

She passed the ripped box that had her coin collection spilling out. As best as she could tell, none were missing. Some of the most valuable ones were still mounted and visible. She nodded toward them. "Doesn't look like robbery was the motive. They would've taken the coin collection for an easy fence."

Deputy Davis nodded as he wrote.

The most damage seemed to be from the box with her home office papers. They were mostly all facing up, as if they'd been searched through. "Have the investigators check these papers for prints. It looks like this is what the break-in was really about. The rest is just for show." Or meanness.

"What are those papers?" Lt. Lyons asked.

"Old case notes, law citations I use frequently...things like that."

"From any of your open cases?" Deputy Davis chimed in.

She shook her head. "I'm on a leave of absence from the Prosecuting Attorney's Office for the next several weeks. I don't have any files from any criminal cases here."

"Do many people know you're on leave?" Lt. Lyons asked.

Harper thought about it, then shook her head. "Not too many."

The familiar rumble of a muscle car vibrated in the driveway. She bent over to look through the couple-of-feet opening.

Christian.

She straightened and turned back to the officers. "Also, the person would have to be pretty small to fit through that space. The investigators should not only check the garage door for fingerprints, but also the ground directly below." Squeezing through might have made them put a full hand on the ground.

Nell opened the garage door, Christian and Hunter on her heels.

"What happened?" Christian asked before she could greet him.

"A garage break-in. How did you know?"

Hunter shrugged. "I get notices of any crimes against government employees in the area where I am."

Ah, the perks of being a senior FBI Special Agent. She quickly introduced Christian and Hunter to the two officers.

"What was taken?" Christian peered around the room.

"Nothing that I can see without touching, but to me, it looks like whoever did this was mainly interested in my papers."

"What kind of papers?" Hunter interjected.

"Old case notes, citations I use frequently, case research I wanted to keep...just things like that."

Another vehicle sounded in the driveway.

"That's probably the crime scene investigators," Officer Reynolds offered.

"We'll get out of y'alls way." Harper took Christian by the arm and started into the house, following Nell who rushed to the front door.

"If it's all the same to you, I think I'll stay out here and watch." Hunter kinda posed it as a question, but it really was more of a statement of fact.

She nodded and passed Investigators Hamm and Reynolds on the way back to the kitchen.

"I just put on a pot of coffee. Y'all go sit in the living room and I'll bring you a cup when it's ready." Nell smiled at the two of them. "Nice to see you again, Christian." She winked at him.

"You, too, ma'am." He got the drift of what Nell was telling him. He gently took Harper's elbow and led her to the overstuffed leather couch. It was very different from Henry's itchy fabric one. "Now, what's going on?"

14

"So, you know as much as I do." Harper stirred the cup of coffee Nell had just brought to her. "I have no idea why anyone would break into my place. I've never felt threatened before."

"That's because you lived on your father's estate, which is almost as secure as Fort Knox." Christian took a sip of his coffee, which did nothing for his already tense nerves.

He'd about had a heart attack when Hunter had called him and told him the Sheriff's Office was responding to a break-in at Henry's—er, Harper's house. As they'd sped over, a million different scenarios, none of them good, had raced through his head. And when he'd mentioned her cut tire to Hunter? Well, the FBI Agent had pressed even harder on the accelerator.

It would seem that someone was out to get Harper. Why? He hadn't a clue, but he was worried. Yet, he didn't want to worry her. Especially not since she'd just moved out on her own for the first time. Even Hunter agreed she seemed to be targeted.

Atticus barked outside as he spied Harper through the window.

"Where was the beast baby when the garage was broken into?"

"In the house. The deputies figure that's why whoever did this didn't come into the house." She wrapped her hands around the hot mug. "He was probably barking his head off. Most people don't know his bark is all bluff."

Christian looked at the huge Mastiff staring at them. "I don't know, Harper. If he thought you were in danger, he might attack."

"Maybe. Anyway, a lot of the stuff is ruined beyond repair."

"I'm sorry." He reached over and rubbed her shoulder.

Shrugged. "It's mainly just personal stuff, nothing of much value."

"Sentimental value, though, which is more important." He knew how much Gabe clung to stuff that had belonged to their mother. Katie had things that had been their dad's that she would be devastated if any of it was ruined.

Harper nodded, blinking rapidly.

Christian hated to see her upset. Hated that she was going through this at all, but needed to figure out what was happening so he could stop it once and for all. "Any idea who might have thought there was something in any of your home office papers?"

She shrugged and shook her head. "No one comes to mind."

"Maybe someone who thought you had something incriminating on them?" In her line of work, that would be an easy assumption for a criminal to make.

"No, but, not to change the subject, I did finally get in touch with Enviro Labs. They did, in fact, do an analysis and confirmed the findings described in the EPA report."

"They did? When?"

"That's what I've been working on. The article in the EPA came out almost a month ago. The confirming report from Enviro Labs was dated about three weeks ago."

Christian shook his head. "Then Henry calls me last week, basically to ask me what to do. At least, that's what I got out of the voice message." He twisted on the couch to face Harper. "Why do you think there's the week between him getting the report and him calling me?"

"I'm not sure. I've been playing around with the theory that he took the Enviro Labs report to my father, and that's why there's the week delay in contacting you." Harper chewed her bottom lip.

"Because why? Henry would know what needed to be done.

Despite us being at odds on many subjects, I can't imagine him not doing what's right after he got a confirming report."

"Me, either. But there's another theory, Christian."

"What?" His stomach had already tightened.

"Henry didn't order the analysis from Enviro Labs."

"Who did?"

Harper licked her lips. "My father."

He tried to break that down into what that meant.

"It's possible—probably likely that when the report came in from Enviro Labs, he didn't tell Henry. Father wouldn't have even told Henry he'd ordered anything from Enviro Labs, so when the report came in and it wasn't favorable to Wolfe Mining, he buried it. That would explain the week's delay. Henry probably found it, asked Father about it, then when Father wouldn't act on the facts, Henry called you."

"That's the most logical explanation, at least from Henry's angle. Not Elliott's though. If he wouldn't have had any intention on acting on what the results were, why did he order the analysis in the first place?"

"I haven't figured that one out yet, unless it's just that Father was so certain the discoveries in the EPA article were wrong and this Enviro Labs report would substantiate what he's been claiming for years: that mountaintop removal mining wasn't harmful."

"So when he got the Enviro Labs report, he—what? Decided just to bury it and not say anything?"

She nodded, her heart sinking. "My father would never admit liability, nor would he spend upwards of hundreds of thousands of dollars to fix any damage he didn't feel responsible for."

Wow. He'd known Elliott Wolfe was a manipulator and power monger, but if what Harper said was true, it took it to a whole new level. "Has he ever given any indication that he'd done something like this before?"

Harper hesitated a long moment, then nodded. "I remember a big hoopla in a neighboring community. Cowen, I think. It had been mine and Henry's last year of law school. It was an especially rainy season that year, and Wolfe Mining had just begun mountaintop removal mining for coal. For whatever reason, there was a huge mudslide and many of the residents of Cowen lost their homes. They banded together to form a class action suit against Wolfe Mining."

"I remember that. Donnie Castro was one of the attorneys who was involved in that. For the residences, of course. He's the former member of the Coal River Mountain Watch, who are very much opposed to mountaintop removal mining. He's now running for US Congress in the third congressional district. Running against none other than the man your father supports, Vince Parsons." This was getting more and more convoluted.

Harper nodded. "I remember now. Father had been livid to have been blamed. He hired a full team of lawyers to make the class action suit go away. He probably paid them more in fees than he would've had to pay in damages, but he wouldn't admit any responsibility. Months passed as the ongoing case went through a multitude of pretrial motions and responses, all ending in the class action suit falling apart."

Christian finished off his coffee. "Donnie had been devastated. So many of the named plaintiffs took it really hard. One committed suicide. One became a drunk and died while driving under the influence, and I think another went bankrupt and lives on the streets. It's a sad story. It was hard on most everybody involved."

"Not everybody. Father celebrated like I'd never seen. It was then that he really started pushing Henry hard. Promised him the Porsche and just about anything else for Henry to commit to being the company's main litigator. Maybe he was just making sure he'd never have to pay such exorbitant legal fees again. Regardless, he had Henry from that moment forward."

Christian set down his empty mug on the coffee table in front of them, then took Harper's hand in his. "I'm so sorry. I had no idea it was so hard for you."

As if he'd said the magic words to open a dam, she bent over in tears.

"Whoa." He slid next to her and pulled her against him. She felt so frail and fragile in his arms. He wrapped his arms around her. She felt so cold. He drew her closer, giving her as much of his body warmth as he could.

Christian held her, letting her cry it out, and sent up silent prayers.

Please, God, help her. I don't know how to, but You know exactly what she needs. Wrap her in Your comfort and love. Let her feel Your love and presence.

∼

"I'M SORRY. I'm really not a crybaby." Yet Harper felt like she'd been doing that a lot around Christian. He must think her a weak, emotional mess.

"It's okay. You've been going through a lot. Seems like it's one thing after another." He released her from his hold.

Harper missed his touch, but she dabbed her eyes. She must look a mess. Definitely testing the claim of her waterproof eyeliner and mascara. "All my life, at least after Mom died, it was always 'Henry this' and 'Henry that,' to the point where it was nauseating." She let out a breath. "But, that's in the past. Henry was my twin and I loved him dearly, despite Father's attempts to turn us against one another."

Lt. Lyons and Deputy Clark came out of the garage. "Ms. Wolfe, we've finished taking your housekeeper's statement. The investigators are almost finished as well, so we'll be getting out of your hair now."

Standing, Harper smoothed down her slacks and hoped she didn't look like a racoon. "Thank you both."

"You know the drill...if you think of anything, or anything else happens, just give us a call." Lt. Lyons smiled. "You have our number."

She nodded and led them to the front door. "I do."

"We'll keep you updated on your case as we progress." Lt. Lyons stopped at the door. "I would highly recommend you do get a security system installed as soon as possible, Ms. Wolfe. Especially considering who you are." He gave a curt nod, then followed Deputy Davis out of the house.

She shut the door and stood there for a moment.

"He's not wrong, you know." Christian spoke softly just behind her. She hadn't heard him approach. "You should get a system. I can install one for you, if you like."

She'd really intended to get one. It just wasn't on the top of her to-do list. It wasn't like she didn't have a gazillion other things going on. But they were just concerned, not talking down to her. "Thanks. I'd appreciate it. Where do I get one?"

"You know what? Why don't I pick one up for you and bring it over and install it? I could do it tonight."

"Okay, if you don't mind." That'd be one less thing she had to worry about. "Just bring me the receipt so I can pay you back."

Christian nodded. He opened his mouth to say something, but the two investigators and Hunter emerged from the garage.

"We got several prints off the garage door," Investigator Hamm told her. "And a couple off the floor."

"We gathered as much evidence as we could." Investigator Reynolds held one of her scrapbooks, as well as her mom's old leather journal, each in clear evidence bags. "These two items are likely to have other sources of evidence, so we need to take them in."

She cleared her throat to move the lump that'd settled in as big as *Pillow Rock*. "I'd like those items back as soon as possible, please."

"Of course. As soon as we finish pulling evidence, we'll bring them to you at your office," Investigator Hamm said.

"Right now, I'm on a leave of absence. You can just call me and I'll come pick them up."

"We should be done in a couple of days. We'll call you." Investigator Reynolds turned and shook Hunter's hand. "It was a pleasure meeting you, Special Agent Malone. Thank you for all your assistance. I'll keep you updated." He nodded at Christian and Harper, then led the other investigator out the front door.

Nell took the opportunity to come in from out of the kitchen. "The officers said it was okay to move things now. I thought I'd start getting rid of the stuff that's definitely broken like the glass and such, if that's okay with you, Harper."

Harper met her in the living room. "Oh, Nell, you don't have to do that. I can do it."

"Honey, I work for you now and this is what I do." She glanced around the room. "Did you put those fish out in the garage? I just realized I haven't seen them."

"I gave them to Janet. She needed something of Henry's."

Nell chuckled. "And, of course, you gave her those fish."

Harper couldn't stop herself from giggling in response. "I had nothing else to do with them, and I couldn't keep them here. Atticus would have knocked the bowls down a thousand times over. It's better this way."

"I agree." Nell put her hands on her motherly hips. "I'm going to go ahead and get started." She smiled at Christian and Hunter. "I'll see you later." She grabbed a broom, dustpan, and trashcan on her way into the garage.

"I should go help, but I need to do something first." Harper had made up her mind. She needed to confront her father about the report. She had to know if her twin had been involved in a cover up, or if their father was the only one responsible. What she learned would make a difference in what she did with the information.

Christian threw her a puzzled look.

"I'm going to give my father the key to the guesthouse and confront him."

"Confront him?" Hunter crossed his arms over his chest.

Harper filled him in on the details, but in the back of her mind, she appreciated that Christian hadn't violated her trust and told his own brother-in-law details about what her brother and/or father had done.

"Has it occurred to you that it's possible this break-in and your tire slashing could be related to this?" Hunter leaned his back against the white, round pillar separating the living room from the dining room.

"How? It seems the only people with a vested interest in any of this being made public would be my father or Henry, and I'm leaning toward my father acting alone." But how far would her father go to protect his company? No, that was ridiculous. "I can't imagine my father cutting my tire or breaking into this house. He doesn't even know Henry left it to me and that I've been moving in. He's been playing golf this whole weekend."

"Maybe a stock holder?" Christian stood next to her, his stance so casual that he looked like he'd stepped out of a fashion magazine. "Someone who would stand to lose money if something happened to cause Wolfe Mining to take a loss?"

"Wolfe Mining is a private company. There isn't a group of stockholders involved." Only she knew about the twenty-five stocks Henry had left her.

Could it have been possible Henry *did* know about the report and agreed to cover it up because he had a vested interest in the success of the company? He did own this house without a mortgage. Had he made the money to pay for the house from payouts from the stocks? Was that why he might have been willing to look the other way until his conscience got the better of him and he called Christian?

Surely not. Harper couldn't take knowing that about her twin now that he was gone. Where was the redemption?

"Your father could have hired someone." Hunter's voice was low, pulling her from her frantic thoughts.

He could have, but would he? "No. That's beneath him. He wouldn't harm me." Not physically. He'd already done an emotional number on her and had for years. Always making her feel inferior to Henry, just because she was female. Never noticing her accomplishments. "No, he's not responsible. This isn't the connection."

"Maybe not." Hunter straightened and shoved his hand into the front pocket of his jeans. "But make no mistake about it, Harper...you *are* a target. I'd bet my badge on none of this being coincidental."

She believed him.

And it scared her.

15

"Christian, we have a problem."

Christian set down the drill he'd used to install the security cameras outside of Harper's garage and pushed the phone closer to his ear. "What's up, Donnie?"

"The bill is about to be dead in the water. No pun intended."

"What?" They'd been working so hard on getting the Appalachian Community Health Emergency (ACHE) Act reintroduced into Congress. "I thought Congressman Ziglar was all set to take it to the floor. What happened?"

The bill was critical to stop all new mountaintop removal mining permits until the feds could study the health effects of that method of coal mining in the affected communities. It would call for a comprehensive analysis of the health dangers. While the bill focused on health issues, stopping the permits could only help the environment.

"Lobbyists, that's what. Ziglar had enough people to move it through the House to get to the Senate, then the coal mining lobbyists descended upon some of those representatives who'd been willing to back the bill. I'm not sure what they were promised, but Ziglar says over half of them have pulled their support."

"Let me guess...one of those lobbyists was Sammy Johnson."

Christian pushed to his feet and walked to the back door. He pulled the second door sensor from his pocket and grabbed the screwdriver.

"How'd you know?"

He wedged the phone between his shoulder and chin, leaving his hands free to install the sensor. "After Henry's funeral, back at Wolfe's place, I saw Sammy with Elliott Wolfe. I wondered what those two were up to when they were deep in conversation. Now I have a pretty good idea." Christian finished attaching the base plate to the top of the door frame and walked back into the living room.

"Wolfe's got deep enough pockets to kill the bill for sure." Donnie sounded more than upset. He sounded downright despondent. "I've been using the bill as the groundwork in my platform for my campaign. If the bill is dead, then what little chance I had in the election just died. I can't fight Parsons and all of Wolfe's resources without a leg to stand on against the coal mining in the area."

"Is Ziglar still willing to sponsor the bill?" Christian set the screwdriver down and sat on the couch.

"There's not enough support for it, even if he is."

"Just keep the faith, Donnie. Let me see what I can do. There are some things going on that might shake Wolfe's foundation, which would trickle down to Sammy and the like. All might not be lost."

"It's hard to have the faith when we're getting smacked down from every angle."

"Just hold tight. Let's see what happens over the next couple of weeks."

"What do you know that I don't, Christian?"

"Just let things play out."

"Okay. I'll let you know if anything changes, one way or the other."

"Thanks." Christian pocketed his cell phone and headed into the garage where Nell was diligently working. "Need some help?"

She glanced over to him. "I thought you were installing the security system for Harper?"

"Already done. Just need her to download the app on her phone and I'll help her get it set up."

"She's not back yet?"

He shook his head. "Not yet."

Nell shrugged. "Then I guess you can help. Take those two bags out to the trashcan to start, then you can bring those law books into the house and put them on the shelf in the study by the others."

"Yes, ma'am." He took out the trash bags, then stopped and filled Atticus's water bowl before rejoining Nell in the garage. He grabbed an armful of the heavy books and headed to the shelves.

Nell followed, carrying a couple of the volumes. "Don't you hurt that girl." Nell never looked at him, just began rearranging the books he'd put on the shelf.

"I'm not. I'm doing my best to protect her."

Nell turned to face him and put a fist on her hip and wagged a finger at him. "You know what I'm talking about, Christian Gallagher. Don't you play with Harper's heart. She's been through enough and I've heard the talk about you being a womanizer."

A what? "I'm not a womanizer. Never have been." He ran a hand over his hair. "I admit I've dated several women, but I've never played with anyone. I've been upfront and honest with every woman I've ever been out with."

"Harper's extremely vulnerable. Losing her momma about did her in. Now, losing Henry...she's lost and doesn't need anybody messing with her head, let alone her heart."

Christian had endured a lot of 'talks' from fathers of the girls he'd dated, but none were more intimidating than Nell right now. He let out a long breath. "I'm not going to intentionally hurt her. I like her...I mean, really like her. She's smart and funny and beautiful and strong. She's pretty much everything I've ever wanted in a woman."

"Pretty much? Boy, that girl is perfect."

Christian smiled. "Really close."

Nell narrowed her eyes. "But?"

"But she doesn't share my faith. Henry was a man of God, so I just assumed Harper was a believer as well, but she isn't." That fact broke his heart a thousand times over, more than just for the obvious reason.

Nell surprised him by chuckling. "Oh, I take it back, Christian, you will be good for her."

"But she's not a believer."

"Honey, she's a believer. She's just mad and doesn't know how to reconcile herself to that anger at God. He'll call her back to Him, don't you worry. You just do like I do and keep praying for her."

"I have been praying for her. For comfort and peace and to feel His presence."

Nell smiled wide. "That's what we do. We just keep loving her. Showing her God's love through our actions and words. We pray for her. Soon enough, the Holy Spirit will get ahold of her. Just watch."

"And if He doesn't?"

"Now who has so little faith?"

"Touché." He grinned, liking the housekeeper even more.

"You know, you should do something special for her for her birthday."

"When is her birthday?" He was a little shocked he hadn't remembered that Henry's birthday was near the end of raft season.

"Thursday."

"*This* Thursday?"

Nell nodded. "She'll be turning twenty-five. A monumental birthday, wouldn't you say? I'd hate for it to be overshadowed by everything she's been dealing with lately."

That would be sad, for sure. "What does she normally do for her birthday?"

"She's always taken her birthday off. She says she likes sleeping in on her day. sHer and Henry used to make sure they had lunch alone, then most times, Elliott would take them out for dinner."

"But with Henry gone this year…and so recently…" It could be a major upset for her.

Nell smiled. "Think about it."

"I will." Something low-key. Maybe a private lunch—a catered lunch here. Roses, definitely. Or maybe a small lunch at his place with Katie, Hunter, and Gabe. He'd have to give it some thought. "Thanks, Nell."

She looped her arm through his and led him back to the garage. "You're welcome."

"May I ask you something about Henry?"

"What?"

"If Henry found out his father knew something the company was doing was hurting people, do you think he'd keep quiet?"

Nell stopped in front of the remaining law books and picked up two. "That's a hard one. Henry loved his father, and he and Harper both were forever looking for his approval, even if neither would admit it." She switched the books to Christian. "On the other hand, Henry was an honest and good man. I can't see him letting people go on getting hurt if he could help it."

Christian bent and grabbed four more books and held them tight with the other two. "It is a conundrum for sure." He headed to the shelf and deposited the books.

Nell moved beside him and slid the last two volumes onto the shelves. "I would say that Henry, slick thinker that he was, would figure out a way to help people and stay in Elliott's good graces."

A sickening thought hit Christian. "If he couldn't, and he chose to betray Elliott, how would Elliott have reacted?" He turned to face Nell.

Her face said it all. "Oh, that wouldn't have been good. Not at all. Elliott could deal with a lot but betrayal wasn't one of them."

If Henry had confronted Elliott about the report and Wolfe Mining's covering it up, it wouldn't have gone well for Henry.

Now, Harper was at her father's ...confronting him about the same report!

∽

HARPER KNOCKED on her father's study, telling herself under her breath that she would not be intimidated. She rubbed her thumb over the key to the guesthouse she held tight.

"Come in." As usual, he sounded annoyed at being disrupted.

She pushed open the door.

"Harper, what are you doing here? Why aren't you at work?"

"I could ask you the same thing, Father." She stepped into the room and approached his desk.

"Don't get snippy with me. It doesn't become you."

Probably not, but not much did become her in his eyes. "I came to ask you something."

"That you couldn't ask over the phone?" He sat back in his chair. "If it's that important, then by all means, ask away." Sarcasm dripped from his words.

Harper licked her lips and swallowed. "Why did you order an independent study to follow up the article in the latest EPA report?"

He frowned. "What are you talking about?"

"Following the article in the EPA report about the dangers of mountaintop removal mining, you ordered Enviro Labs to run a study to see if the details in the article were accurate. Why did you hire them to conduct the study if you had no intentions of changing Wolfe Mining practices?" There, she'd said it.

His brows furrowed. "You've been hanging around that treehugger too much. He's polluting your mind. I ordered no such study from any lab."

Now he was lying right to her face. It stung. She blinked, refusing to back down. "Father, I saw the order. Your name was the one listed for having requested the study at Enviro Labs."

"I did No. Such. Thing. You've been misinformed."

"I saw it with my own eyes." She kicked herself for not bringing the papers with her. They'd been in her purse. Why had she taken them out and left them at home?

He shook his head. "Then the document is incorrect. I don't know what this is all about."

She let out a breath. Was it possible everything was wrong? "Do you know about the article in the EPA report?"

"Of course, I know about that. This is my business, Harper. I keep up with anything that has to do with mining in the area."

"So you knew about that, but you didn't order an independent study from Enviro Labs to prove or disprove the article's claims?"

His face turned bright red. "Harper, I've answered that already. No, I did not. And I'm getting more than a little tired of your constant accusation that I did." His tone was even harsher than his stare. "For the record, my advisors told me that the article was based on outdated information and couldn't be proven at this time."

Even now, he would rather lie to her face than to admit he knew how Wolfe Mining's practice hurt the people in the community and the environment itself.

She couldn't take it anymore. Harper crossed the few steps between them. She tossed the key onto the desk, her stomach tangling into a taut knot.

"What's that?" He didn't even bother to pick it up.

Her entire abdomen tensed. "The key to the guesthouse. I've moved out."

"You what? When? To where?"

"Over the weekend. Henry left me all of his belongings in his will, including the house. Don't worry, it's all cleaned. Nell finished that yesterday afternoon." She could feel the waves of nausea starting to roll.

"Henry left you everything? You've already moved?"

She nodded, not trusting herself to speak. Harper resisted the desire to put her hand over her stomach. Was he upset because she'd left, or that she'd left without his permission?

He took the key and stared at it for a minute before slipping into his top center drawer. "Very well then."

So she didn't even rank missing period, apparently. She licked her lips again. "Also, you need to find an attorney to replace me within the next two weeks. I'll be finishing up my leave of absence then and will be going back to the Prosecuting Attorney's Office."

He shot to his feet. "What? You said your leave was through the end of the month."

Harper took two shaky steps backward. "I changed my mind." How could she work for him now that she knew the truth?

His face grew even redder and his hands trembled slightly. "You begged me to let you fill in, and now you just walk out on me?"

"Beg you? Father, I volunteered so I could help you, but now I see that was a mistake." She wanted to vomit. "And I'm not walking out on you. I'm just telling you to find a replacement. I won't be coerced into staying."

He fisted and unfisted his hands several times. "Coerced, are you? Then how's this, how about you just clean out whatever personal belongings you have in the office tomorrow? I don't need you to stay for two weeks."

"Fine, if that's what you want." Bile burned the back of her throat.

"That's most definitely what I want."

"Okay then." She turned on her heel to leave.

"Oh, and Harper?"

She spun and faced him. "Yes?"

"Don't bother coming around here anymore either."

The catch in her breath stole all air from her lungs.

Harper left before he could see the sag in her shoulders and the moisture burning her eyes. Her father might be dismissive and hard to love, but he was all she had left.

Now she was really all alone.

16

"I can't believe he just looked me in the eye and lied to me." Harper paced around Atticus's sleeping form on the living room floor. "He didn't even care about me moving out."

Christian set down her cell, having finished setting up the security system in the app on her phone. "Is it remotely possible he wasn't lying?" The last thing he wanted to do was to take up for Elliott Wolfe, but Harper was hurting.

She snorted. "The proof is in black and white, Christian. His name is on the order to Enviro Labs. He gave the authorization to have their study conducted. I would find it extremely rare for him not to have seen the final report."

Christian couldn't argue with that. Having grown up with his sister, he fell back on his experience when Katie would have emotional outbursts: he sat there quietly, nodding when necessary.

Harper plopped down on the end of the couch. Atticus rose and put his big head in her lap. She pet him as she continued. "I knew Father was ruthless at times and emotionally distant ever since Mom died, but this takes his mercilessness to a whole new level."

Again, Christian sat in silent support.

She shot to her feet again. Atticus grunted in protest, but settled back on the rug.

"He actually acted like he didn't know what I was talking about. Like I would believe him. I saw the copy of the report with his name there as clear as a cloudless day."

She was on the edge, and he needed to pull her back. Give her a focus instead of emotions.

"Harper, I don't know the inner-workings of Wolfe Mining, but is it likely your father would've ordered the study himself, or have someone else do it?" Elliott seemed above doing the mundane like requesting a study. "Why Enviro Labs? Is that one Wolfe Mining has used in the past for testing purposes? Could such a request have been made by someone else and the lab just listed everything from the company under your father's name?"

She opened her mouth, then shut it. She sank to the couch. "I don't know."

Nell came into the living room. "Okay, honey, everything is cleaned up and put away. Call me if you can't find where I put something."

Harper stood and stepped into Nell's hug. "Thank you. I didn't want to have to face the mess in the garage. Everything looks amazing."

Nell patted her back before releasing her. She looked at Christian and winked. "That's my job, and I had a little help." Her gaze shot between Christian and Harper, and she hesitated. "Are you sure I can't put something on for dinner for you?"

"No, I'm fine."

"Okay. Well, you be sure and get plenty of rest tonight. You'll be drained after the day you had." Nell spoke to Harper, but stared at Christian.

He gave a slight nod. Message received—don't stay too long.

Apparently satisfied she'd set the boundaries, Nell said a final goodbye.

"Let me show you how to work your new security system." Christian stood and handed Harper her cell phone. He gave her a thorough walk-through of all the system's features, and how to control them all with voice or a tap in the app.

Harper returned to the couch. "I was thinking while we were going around to all the doors and windows. If anybody at work would order a study on Father's behalf, it would be his secretary/assistant, Mrs. Sommers."

She was going to keep on this track until she ran it off the rails. "Can you ask her about procedure?"

She worried her bottom lip between her teeth. "I doubt it. The woman has never really liked me, ever since I was a teenager. I've never known why. Anyway, she holds Father's business close to her chest. I guess that's what makes Father hold her in such high regard."

He was running out of ideas.

"I don't think the company uses Enviro Labs commonly, though. If they did, Janet would have known to call them first. They were her fourth call."

Made sense. "Unless Henry didn't know that because he was more into the legal side of things?"

She shook her head as she rubbed Atticus's big ears. "I would think he'd know all the places the company did regular interactions with because of business contracts."

"What about payment? If Elliott ordered the analysis, he would have had to pay them, right?"

"Yeah, that won't confirm he knew about the report. Everything is set up through purchase orders. As soon as a work order or anything is requested, a purchase order is generated. When the bill comes in, the PO number is matched and paid, attributed to the ordering department. There's no distinguishing between departments in the PO. Everybody uses the same batch of PO numbers, and a management signature isn't required for amounts less than five thousand."

Five thousand? That was a lot of trust in the employees. "How many people have access to these purchase order numbers?"

"Probably just about everybody in the company."

Another dead end. Seemed like that's what they kept circling around. More and more questions, less answers.

His cell rang. He dug it from his pocket and glanced at the caller-ID. "I need to get this," he told Harper before answering the call. "Hey, Pete. We've got to stop meeting like this."

"Tell me about it. We go weeks without talking, then we're in each other's faces and on the phone almost non-stop."

Christian laughed and relaxed against the couch. "What's up?"

"A couple of things. First, I just finished the prelim testing on those dead Virginia spiraea from Carnifex Park. You aren't going to believe what I found."

"What?"

"The roots show the plants died from selenium toxicity."

That was rare. "How elevated were the selenium levels in the roots?" At high doses, selenium acts pro-oxidant, causing oxidative stress in plants. That could kill them.

"Best I can determine, about forty micrometers selenate."

"Are you sure? That's about double the high-end readings."

"I know, and yes, I'm sure. I performed the testing myself. Twice, just to be sure the first time I ran it the sample wasn't contaminated."

"Man." That would definitely explain why the plants had died. "We still don't know where they came from, but this can't be a coincidence. First the Candy Darter and now the Virginia spiraea...both dead from selenium toxicity? No way this is a happenstance. I'll get some soil samples from around the Gauley for you to test. If the selenium levels in the soil are high, we have more problems coming our way."

"I know. This is getting freaky." Peter's words were light, but his tone told of the somberness of the situation. "There's something else. After I got the results, it bothered me that I couldn't remember where I recently read about the high selenium levels, so I did some checking. I finally found where I'd read it."

Peter paused for a beat before continuing. "It was in the EPA article. The same one that had Henry stirred up."

Now things had just passed eerie into evil.

"Thanks, Pete. I'll get the soil samples to you tomorrow morning." Christian disconnected the call and looked at Harper. "I'm guessing you don't happen to have the EPA report and the one from Enviro Labs?"

She got to her feet. "Actually, I do. Hang on." She left the living room and went into her bedroom, then returned just a minute later. As she sat back down on the couch beside him, Harper handed him several papers. "Here. The EPA article is on top."

He scanned until the word 'selenium' jumped out at him. He read slowly.

VARIOUS TESTING RESULTS have shown that water downstream of mountaintop removal mines have increased levels of selenium as well as sulfate, and also increased electrical conductivity of the water. Such changes in the water can kill aquatic life, or disrupt their life cycles so drastically that their population would dwindle, or even disappear entirely. This high level of selenium and sulfate has the potential to kill natural plant life, further disrupting aquatic life and possibly human life due to the selenium poisoning in vegetation.

CHRISTIAN DROPPED the papers onto the coffee table and lifted his gaze to meet Harper's, rage simmering in the pit of his stomach. "Your father clearly knew about this report and authorized an independent testing that confirmed these findings, yet did nothing. He's..." He couldn't finish his statement without insulting Harper. She might be angry and hurt by her father, but he was still her father.

Tears welled in her eyes. "He's immoral and terrible and responsible for so many awful things, I know." She held his gaze despite the tears sliding down her face. "I'm so sorry, Christian. I had no idea. I promise you I'll do whatever it takes to hold him accountable."

His anger vanished as she stared at the pure goodness radiating from her. "It's not your fault." He scooted closer to her and put his arm around her shoulder.

"It's my father. His company. He's made so much money, but at what cost? And to whom?" She got the tears under control, but he could see the struggle.

"You aren't your father, Harper. I believe you never would have allowed this to continue had you known."

She shook her head. "When I think of how many lives have probably been destroyed by Father's greed and power lust...it makes me sick."

In that instant, whether it was the innocence in her eyes or the way he'd been drawn to her, all that mattered was her. A tendril of hair fell over her forehead, almost grazing her long eyelashes. Without forethought, he gently smoothed it behind her ear. He caught a whiff of her shampoo—like bottled sunshine. It was intoxicating.

She gave a little gasp, and it nearly unraveled him. Slowly, and holding her gaze, he lowered his mouth to hers and ever-so-softly grazed his lips across hers. He let his fingers caress her jawline, not surprised by the softness of her skin.

He gave her another tender kiss, then remembered himself. He sat back. "I'm sorry. I shouldn't have done that. You have so much to deal with right now. I didn't mean to complicate things." He moved a little further from her.

~

"No, it's okay." Harper had no idea how she managed to keep her voice steady when her entire world had just been tilted on its axis.

Christian's touch and kiss left her breathless and her heart doing somersaults.

And he apologized?

He took her hand. "I'm really sorry. I know you don't need this added complication in your life right now. I just...just wasn't thinking, I guess."

"I said it's okay." She didn't mean to sound snappy, really, but apologizing for kissing her hurt her feelings. Especially since that kiss had rocked her to her core. Sure, she should appreciate that he was considerate of what she was going through, but still... "Now, more than ever, I can't believe Henry was involved in anything nefarious that has to do with this. It wasn't in him. You know that."

Christian nodded. "I do. I figure that he'd just found the reports and that's why he called me. Maybe he even busted your father on it."

Harper shook her head, still reeling from Christian's touch. "I don't think so. Father's reaction when I confronted him was honest surprise. I'm pretty sure this was the first time he'd been called out about what he'd done."

"Then maybe he called me to know how to progress in addressing the subject with your father?"

She shrugged. "Maybe, but the message made me think he'd already made the decision to take action. He might've called you to see which agency to contact first." If he was going to apologize for kissing her, he needed to stop looking at her like he was because the intensity of his stare made her want to fling herself into his arms.

The way he held her...it made her forget everything but him with his sincerity, goodness, and honesty. His embrace made her feel safe. Like nothing in the world could hurt her when he held her. Christian was smart and funny and easygoing, fun to be around and always adventurous. Just what she needed.

Spending time with him these past few weeks or so had made her realize how empty her life was. She was wrapped up in work and enjoyed what she did, but that was really all she had going on in her life. She and Henry hung out, of course, but now that he was gone...

"How would you like to proceed?" he asked. Caution lurked in his eyes.

She could appreciate him letting her take the lead. "Of course, I want my father held accountable, along with Wolfe Mining, but I need all the details first. We still don't know why Henry called your friend's lab. If he had the report from Enviro Labs, why call your friend? It doesn't make sense."

"I don't know. It baffles me, too."

"I'd like to know before we move forward. Mainly because Henry never did anything without a reason. With something as important as this, there was a reason he called the other lab. I want to know what that reason was."

He slowly nodded. "I get that, but I don't see how we can get an answer to that. We've tried and haven't been able to get any traction on that. That might be something we never know."

She couldn't accept that. "What if we've gotten everything wrong?"

Christian's eyes widened and he pointed at the papers on the coffee table. "You're saying that's wrong?"

"No. Not that. I believe those reports are very accurate, which puts my father and the company responsible for so many wrongs."

He crossed his arms over his chest. "What are you saying is wrong?"

Therein laid her problem. "I don't know."

A pregnant silence filled the room. They'd been so easy with each other, but now...now, since the kiss, everything seemed too awkward. If only he hadn't apologized. Did that mean he wasn't attracted to her? He wasn't interested? She didn't know if she could take such rejection. At least not now, when she'd allowed that little glimmer of hope to fan in her.

Christian broke the silence. "What if Henry hadn't seen the Enviro Labs report, but found, perhaps, a purchase order vaguely written for the analysis, but it didn't list the company? He would have called around to find out the details, starting with a call to Peter since he knew him. He made the rounds like you did, and finally got the report from Enviro Labs. That's logical, yes?"

A weight lifted off of her. "That would mean the date of the report had nothing to do with when Henry learned about it. Maybe the PO was charged to a case and Henry found it and did the calls, just like you said. When he got the report from Enviro, he understood, like us, the enormity of what Wolfe Mining was doing."

Christian smiled and nodded. "He said on the voice message that he'd found something at the office *today* that was concerning, implying he'd just found the report from Enviro."

She knew Henry hadn't been able to cover up anything so wrong, no matter what! She grabbed Christian's hand. "He asked to meet you so you could advise him what steps to take next. He was going to do the right thing immediately, without even confronting Father, which is why Father looked surprised when I called him out about the report."

Now it all made sense. Relief washed over her like a class five rapid and without thought or hesitation, she leaned over and hugged Christian.

He tensed for a moment, then wrapped his arms around her and held her, really held her.

So many emotions swirled in her chest and head. She could almost feel him tremble against her, but that had to be her imagination.

She pulled back, staring him in the eye. Harper didn't care that her feelings for him were probably marching across her face for him to see. She needed him to know she cared about him. Liked him. Wanted him to kiss her again.

He groaned, then kissed her. Harder than before, but hard with intensity.

She wrapped her arms around his neck and tried to melt into him. His hands were on either side of her face, his thumbs rubbing her jaw.

Suddenly, he pulled back, keeping his hands on either side of her face, and rested his forehead against hers so their eye contact was locked. "You're killing me here, Harper."

Before she could reply, he moved further back and bent her head to plant a kiss where his forehead had been on hers. He cleared his throat and took her hands in his. "Look, I'm not going to apologize again because I'm not sorry. I am about this happening right now, and I think we need to take it slow, but you need to know that I want us to have a chance, a real chance. I don't want you to get into anything right now because you're in an emotional hurricane, but know that I'm here when our time is right. Okay?"

She found it hard to speak. "Christian, I really like you. Yes, there's a lot going on in my life right now—"

"You're having major life changes: you lost your twin, you took a leave of absence from your job and took on your brother's work, you've moved, and you just found out your father isn't the man you thought him to be. That's more than just a lot going on, Harper. Let's not rush into anything. Please. I don't want us to take any missteps. This is too important."

Just that he acknowledged they were important was enough for her. For now. "Okay." She forced a smile.

"Okay." He grinned and stood, tugging her to her feet with him. "It's getting dark and I need to go get some soil samples. I'll get them to Peter tomorrow and he'll start analyzing them. Once we have all the facts, then we can move on to reporting what we've found. Sound like a plan?"

She nodded.

"Good. I'll call you tomorrow, okay?"

She nodded again, feeling that if she spoke, she'd spew her emotions all over the place.

He gave her a quick hug and led her to the front door. "Lock up behind me and be sure and set your alarm."

Harper finally found her voice. "Yes, sir."

Christian bent down and pecked her cheek. "Talk to you tomorrow." He opened the door and was gone.

She had a sneaky suspicion that he'd taken part of her heart with him.

17

"You kissed her?" Gabe leaned against the counter at Gauley Guides by Gallagher and stared at him.

Christian fought the urge to squirm under his scrutiny. It was times like this that the oldest Gallagher looked so much like their father it was unnerving. "I didn't plan on it, Gabe. It just happened."

His brother scowled at him as he restocked the postcard rack. "No, things beyond your control just happen, not you kissing some woman. Especially not Harper Wolfe. She's everything you stand against."

"She's not like that. Not at all. She's providing me with all the documents to file my report with the EPA and FWS. I wouldn't have been able to get that report from Enviro Labs that shows Elliott Wolfe culpable without her." Christian straightened the 'sale' sign over the rack of last season's stock of wetsuits.

"Do you have that report yet?" Gabe finished filling the rack and slid the box with the remaining postcards under the counter.

"Not yet. She's going to give it to me in time to file my report, along with the reports on the dead Candy Darter, the plants, and anything I get from the soil samples tests."

"I wouldn't hold my breath until it was in my hands." Gabe straightened and glanced at the clock. His next tour group would arrive in about an hour.

"She's not like that, man. You haven't even seen her in years, much less gotten to know her. How can you make a judgment?"

"Fair enough, but what I know is I didn't see her turning down any of the money Wolfe Mining made by such questionable practices when she went to law school, or while she lived on Daddy's estate, or when Daddy bought her a new luxury SUV."

Christian set his jaw. "She didn't know about the ultimate dangers mountaintop removal mining caused." His brother was usually the calming sibling, the thoughtful one. The one who considered all the facts before making a decision. Why was he so against Harper?

Gabe snorted. "You really believe that? C'mon, Christian, you know how this community opposes the company, even some of the old-time miners. She'd have to have buried her head in the sand to not know."

That much was true. Like with the lady outside the diner—now that he thought about it, Harper had said she was used to such encounters. At the time, Christian had been so taken aback by the woman's mean streak and confrontational manner that he hadn't considered how calmly Harper had handled the situation.

No, he wouldn't believe that. Couldn't. He'd seen the pain in her eyes when she'd found out. Acknowledged the determination she had to see her father be held accountable. "She's not like that, Gabe. Even Katie admitted she'd had a preconceived idea about her that was wrong."

Gabe raised a brow. "She has Katie's stamp of approval?"

Katie had always been protective of both of her brothers, ever since middle school, and even more after their dad had died. It was rare for her to like anyone they were involved with.

"I think so. I know I have Hunter's, and that's half the battle."

Gabe stood silent, clearly thinking through the whole situation. Now that was the brother Christian was used to. "Well, I suppose I should meet her and make up my own mind. Why don't we have dinner all together this weekend?"

Christian grinned. "Actually, I was thinking about Thursday. It's her birthday. I'd like to make her dinner and let it be low-key with just us family." He dug his hip into the counter. "If she'll come. I mean, I *kissed* her. Despite knowing better, I did it anyway." He paused. "I mean, I apologized for it, but I don't—"

The bell over the store's door chimed and Katie and Hunter, both wearing wetsuits, breezed in. Her Blue Heeler, Shadow, pranced in on her heels. "You apologized for what?" Katie tugged at his loose hair—she always had to pick on him in some way about his hair being shoulder-length. "I'm sure you have a lot to apologize for. What was it this time?"

Heat crept up the back of his neck.

Gabe chuckled. "Tell her."

"Yes, tell me." Katie took a seat on one of the stools behind the counter. Hunter stood off to the side, his eyes on his wife.

Christian's face blazed. "I kissed Harper."

Katie's mouth opened. "And you *apologized* for it?" She facepalmed her forehead and shook her head.

He met her gaze. "Well, yeah. She's got so much going on right now that I shouldn't have done that. I told her I was sorry, but she still seemed upset with me."

"Why, of course, she was upset with you, doofus. You don't kiss a woman and then apologize for it. Sheesh."

Hunter chuckled, then immediately choked it back when Christian stared at him.

"But she's got so much going on that I didn't mean to put anything else emotional on her." What had he done so wrong?

Katie snorted. "That might be so, and is considerate, yes, but that's not how a woman would take it."

What was his sister talking about? "How else could she take it?"

"That you were sorry for kissing her." Katie gave him the blankest stare.

"I am. I mean, I'm not, but my timing is way off."

Katie pointed at him. "Then that's what you should have apologized for—your lousy timing, not for kissing her."

Christian furrowed his brow. "That's the same thing."

His sister groaned. "You have so much to learn about women."

"What?"

Hunter cleared his throat. "What my wife is trying to explain is that when you apologized to Harper for kissing her, she would immediately assume that you were sorry for kissing her...the act itself, not the timing."

Gabe nodded. "It probably hurt her feelings that she thought you regretted kissing her, having nothing to do with your timing."

"But I explained that I wanted to take things slow and not rush into anything."

Katie tilted her head. "Then you're probably forgiven, but she no doubt felt the sting when you initially apologized. You'll need to prove to her that you're interested in her, and that telling her you just wanted to take it slow wasn't an excuse."

That made sense. "I can do that."

"Good. I like her. I think she might be too good for you, but that's beside the point." Katie leaned over the counter and tugged his hair again.

"You give your approval?" Gabe asked his sister.

She nodded. "I do. I was ready to not like her, expecting her to be snobby and uptight, but I owed her an apology before our trip was over. She proved me wrong, and that's rare." She jerked her chin in Christian's direction. "The question really is if you like her a lot."

Christian's throat tightened like a rapid's undercurrent pulling a swimmer into a death cave. "I do. A whole lot."

His sister held his gaze. "Then you need to let her know by showing her. So what if your timing is off? It doesn't matter." She glanced over to her husband and smiled. "Love comes when you aren't looking and you least expect it."

Hunter smiled back at Katie. "Yet it's the greatest thing in the world, to love someone and be loved by them."

"Okay, y'all are making me sick now." Gabe laughed.

Everyone else joined in.

"Okay. Thursday is her birthday, her twenty-fifth. Her housekeeper told me she usually has lunch with Henry and dinner with her father. Since neither will happen this year, I wanted to surprise her with a home-cooked meal at my place Thursday. I was thinking of grilling steaks."

"Count me in. You've always been good on the grill." Katie inattentively bent to scratch behind Shadow's ears. "What time?"

"Yeah, I don't have to go back to work until Monday, so I'm in." Hunter nodded.

"About five? I know I have that one group, but I should be back before two, which gives me plenty of time to cook."

"Good deal," Gabe said. Everyone else nodded.

"Great. See y'all then. I'm off to take these soil samples to Peter, then I'll run by the store and pick up steaks to grill. Where's the best place to order a birthday cake?"

"That little bakery over off Main Street." Katie didn't miss a beat in answering. "Una B's. Her cakes are amazing." She smacked her lips.

Christian grinned. "That sells it. I'll call Nell and find out what flavor is her favorite, then I'll order one from Una B's." He turned and headed to the door, then paused and looked over his shoulder. "Thank you. All of you. I love you guys." Embarrassment singed his face as he rushed out to his car.

Just thinking about Harper made him all mushy inside. Was this how Hunter felt about Katie? If so, no wonder he'd changed his field office and his work schedule to be able to spend more time with her.

Christian grinned to himself as he started the car. Maybe, just maybe, Harper was *his* happily ever after.

∽

"I'm so glad you called, Janet. Dinner out with a girlfriend was just what I needed. How're you doing?" Harper gave her a smile as she lifted her glass of water and took a sip.

"I'm doing as best I can. Same as you, I imagine." She set down her spoon in her almost-empty bowl of French Onion soup. "Thank you for inviting me to this place. I've never been here before."

"Shame on Henry for never bringing you. Prime 44 West is named after Jerry West, NBA legend and West Virginia native."

Janet shrugged. "I don't pay much attention to sports."

Harper raised a brow. "Then how on earth did you put up with Henry and his addiction to all sports?" She shook her head at the memories. No, this wasn't the time for memories that were still too painful to remember. It was too soon. "Anyway, Father's been a member at the club here for as long as I can remember."

"Well, the soup was marvelous. Have you settled into Henry's house now?"

Harper finished the last bite of her caprese salad, trying not to show her annoyance. It was only natural that Janet would think of the house as Henry's. No matter how long Harper lived there, to Henry's girlfriend, it would always be Henry's house. "I am. You heard I had a break-in, didn't you?"

Janet nodded. "That's just awful. Did they take anything?"

"Not that I've noticed. They left my coin collection, so I'm thinking they were looking for something specific."

"Any idea what?" Janet lifted her glass of tea and took a big swallow.

Harper shook her head. "No. The police got some prints and are running them now. Maybe once we know who broke in, we can figure out what they were after."

"I guess." Janet swirled her glass making the ice clank. "What did you ever find out about the Enviro Lab report?"

"Well. Let me tell you what's going on with that." Harper started to give Janet the details, but the waiter came to the table, refilling Janet's tea and removing their soup and salad dishes. Once he left, Harper finished giving Janet the facts. "As soon as Christian gets the soil sample results, if the selenium level is elevated, we'll have plenty of proof for him to report his findings to the EPA and Fish and

Wildlife. Enough to hold my father accountable for what he's ignored."

Janet set down her glass with a thud. "You would do that—turn in your father?"

"I would." Harper felt the familiar turmoil churn in her gut. "He's my father, but I can't accept him turning a blind eye to all the damage and hurt he's caused."

Janet just stared at her.

"I have to do what's right." She shared the theory she and Christian had come up with that involved Henry.

"That makes sense." Janet took another long drink of tea. "I guess I didn't expect you to be willing to hold your father accountable."

"I am. Henry would've, too. We figure that's why Henry called Christian, to ask him to help in reporting Father."

"I guess I wouldn't have expected Henry to betray your father, working for Wolfe Mining and all."

Harper shot her a quizzical stare. Did this woman even really know Henry? She immediately swallowed back her snap judgment. It wasn't too long ago that she herself had questioned if Henry would've done what was right.

Before the conversation continued, the waiter appeared tableside with their entrees. "Bay of Fundy Salmon with enhancement of a lobster tail for you, ma'am." He set the delectable-looking plate in front of Harper.

He placed a beautifully presented plate at Janet's place. "And the filet mignon, medium, with Béarnaise sauce for you, ma'am."

He set down two bowls between them. "Creamed spinach and Broccoli Gratin with Gruyere Sauce and Panko."

The waiter took a step back and refilled Harper's water glass. "Is there anything else I can get you at this time?"

Harper smiled. "No, thank you. This looks wonderful."

He smiled. "Then, please enjoy. I'll check back on you in a few minutes." He left as quickly as he had appeared.

"I guess that recording of the accident was just that: an accident, then." Janet cut her steak and shoved a piece in her mouth.

That had been one of the things that kept her tossing and turning last night. Well, mainly it was remembering Christian and how it felt to be in his arms...how his touch on her face felt...the headiness of his kiss. Yet, she had thought about Henry's wreck, too. "I still don't think so. Maybe it was a coincidence, but I really don't believe in them either."

Janet swallowed. "So what are you thinking?" she asked as she plopped a spoonful of the broccoli gratin onto her plate.

"I really don't know. I don't have an answer there, but I know someone was in his lane and didn't move, didn't stop when he went off the side of the road. The investigators say that the car had to..." She licked her lips, struggling to breathe normally. "...had to explode soon after his car left the road. Whoever ran him off the road had to have heard and seen that. Still, they didn't stop or even make an anonymous call to 911."

Janet chewed slowly.

Harper took a bite of the salmon and closed her eyes in appreciation of the softly smoked flavor tickling her tastebuds.

"I wonder if your father found out Henry was going to get Christian to help report him," Janet mused as she spooned the cream spinach onto her plate.

"I don't know." Harper took another bite of the moist fish.

Janet's fork clanked against her plate as she stared at Harper across the table. "What if your father did find out and he was the person in Henry's lane?"

The fish spoiled in Harper's mouth. She forced herself to swallow. "No, Father couldn't have done that."

"I meant, had it done. Had someone cause Henry's wreck. Isn't that possible? Think about it."

Harper reached for her water. Her knee-jerk reaction was to dismiss Janet's theory, but she just couldn't do that without considering the idea.

Her father *had* gotten the media to hold off reporting Henry's death. He *had* been influential with law enforcement to close the case quickly. He *had* been more than a little annoyed when Harper had given a copy of Henry's voice message to the police. He *did* stand to lose a lot, both financially and in reputation.

But could he have ordered his son to basically be murdered? His only son, his golden child? Harper couldn't buy that.

Yet...she could see him having someone do something to distract Henry from acting. Maybe the person wasn't supposed to cause Henry's death, but it all went terribly wrong?

Harper found she couldn't eat anymore. She felt like she'd downed a bottle of wine by herself, and she didn't drink.

"It is possible, isn't it?" Janet had never made any bones that she didn't think highly of their father. Maybe she was able to see him in a clearer light because she wasn't close to him.

"I think it is." Harper thought she might be sick. She put her napkin on the table and stood. "I need to run to the restroom. I'll be right back." She rushed toward the ladies' room, weaving amid the natural and dark wood of the restaurant.

She made another turn, then stopped dead in her tracks. Her heart slipped past her stomach into her toes.

Christian sat at a table with a woman. A very beautiful blonde woman who leaned into Christian's space. They were both smiling and engaging in what looked like intimate conversation. The woman's hand casually rested on top of his forearm.

They chuckled together.

If Harper hadn't felt like she was going to be sick before, she definitely did now.

Christian looked up. For a fleeting second, he wore a blank look as he stared at Harper. Then, as if he'd been shaken, his eyes widened and he paled.

As if in slow motion, he stood.

Harper spun and ran into the bathroom. She didn't know whether to cry or throw up as the sting of double betrayal whelped in her heart.

18

"Excuse me." Christian barely got the words out to Laurie before he rushed after Harper. He'd seen the look on her face...the hurt...the betrayal. It had turned his heart inside out.

If he'd ever questioned or doubted his feelings for Harper, he didn't any longer. The thought that he hurt her made him want to raft the Upper Gauley River without a paddle.

He made a turn. She ran into the ladies' restroom. He was three steps following just as the door swung shut behind her.

Christian knew how it must have looked to Harper. He and Laurie had been quietly laughing about the antics of her new kitten. While it was innocent, it had to have looked like he and Laurie were on a date.

He leaned against the wall outside of the ladies' room. He had to see Harper. Had to explain that there was nothing between him and Laurie. They were friends and he owed her a nice dinner for all that she'd done for him. How was he to know Harper would be here?

Anxiety pushed him to pace the small space. He groaned. He'd just apologized for kissing her, then told her he wanted to take it slow. Now she sees him out with another woman on what looks like a date.

It was an extremely nice and intimate restaurant, so her assumption would be correct, except, it wasn't.

Christian pushed down the desire to run into the ladies' room and explain, make Harper understand that she was the only woman he was interested in. Probably the only woman he would ever be interested in.

Wait...what?

He self-checked himself. Was he really thinking that she was it for him? The one and only? The one he...loved?

"Hello, Christian. What are you doing here?" Janet stood in front of him, pulling him from the realization that he might be in love with Harper Wolfe.

"I, uh, owed a friend a nice dinner."

Janet glanced at the ladies' room door. "And you're waiting out here for her? Is she sick or something?"

"No. She's at our table." Aw, man. Now he would seem like a creeper. Or a stalker. Maybe both.

Again, Janet glanced at the door to the ladies' restroom. Then awareness must have hit. "Oh. You're waiting on Harper to come out."

He nodded. "I think she got the wrong impression when she saw me and Laurie."

"The wrong impression?"

The air whooshed out of him like a punctured raft. "Laurie and I were laughing over something she told me about her new kitten when Harper saw us." He shifted his weight from one foot to the other. "It probably looked like we were on a date, which we most definitely are not."

"Ahhh. You like-like Harper." Janet grinned.

He nodded, not trusting himself to speak.

"When she saw you, did she say anything?" Janet asked.

"She didn't have to. Her face said it all." Acid seared the back of his tongue.

"Oh. Does Harper like-like you?"

"She did." He spoke before he thought.

Janet raised her eyebrows.

"I seem to mess up with her every time I turn around. All unintentionally, but it doesn't matter."

Laurie walked up on them. "Leaving me for another woman here, Christian?"

"I'm sorry. I didn't mean to abandon you." He hesitated, then gestured to Janet. "This is Janet Meyers, she was Henry Gallagher's girlfriend. Janet, this is my friend, Laurie Fisher. She works at A+ Alliance Labs, and does a lot of testing for me."

"Oh. I'm so sorry for your loss." Laurie always seemed to say the right thing.

Why couldn't he learn from her?

"Thank you. It's nice to meet you." Janet turned to Christian. "I can understand why you're worried."

His heart tightened.

"Why are you worried?" Laurie asked.

He hesitated. He and Harper hadn't made their relationship public yet. Heck, he didn't even know if they had a relationship. It was all so new and they hadn't really talked about them, except that they needed to take it slow.

And now she saw him out with Laurie, no matter the reason.

"Christian?" Laurie's big, brown eyes were locked onto his. "What's going on? Why are we standing outside the restrooms?"

Janet lightly grabbed his bicep. "I'm going to go into the ladies' room. Why don't you talk to Laurie back at your seats? I'll see what I can do." She smiled at Laurie. "It was very nice to meet you. Excuse me." She brushed past them and into the ladies' room.

Christian didn't want to explain to Laurie, but he owed her that. He had just left her at the table. He led her back there, pulling out her chair. He took a breath, gathering his thoughts, or rather, his emotions. "Over the past few weeks or so, I've been seeing a lot of Harper Gallagher. She and I have gotten close." That was putting it mildly.

"We're at the start of something, I think, so it's all very new and uncertain." He noticed Laurie's eyes growing wider and a tinge of pink dotting her cheeks. "She just walked by and saw you and I here."

He swallowed. And again. "By appearances, it probably looked like we were a couple on a date. She had no way of knowing we're just friends and I wanted to take you out for a nice dinner for all that you do for me."

Laurie blinked several times. "Are we just friends, Christian?" Her voice was even huskier than normal.

His pulse throbbed in his temples. "Of course, we're friends, Laurie. You know that."

"But is that all we are? All we can be?" Laurie ran her fingertip around the lip of her wine glass. "I'd hoped that this could be the start of something more." She laid a hand on his. "Truthfully, I've been attracted to you for some time now. I've just been waiting for the right time to see if there could be something between us. When you called this a date, I thought perhaps now was the right time. Finally."

Christian was at a loss for words. He'd never even suspected Laurie could be attracted to him. He'd always thought of her as a friend. Honestly, he really didn't think about her until he went to the lab or called her about tests. Wow, how shallow was he? He felt even lower than he already did.

"Look, it's okay if you don't feel anything. I mean, I wanted to give us a try, but if you aren't interested, I don't beg any man." Hurt echoed in her words and tone.

"Laurie, I didn't know."

She lifted her half-full wine glass and downed it. "Of course, you didn't. How could you? I'm just the woman who does your bidding in the lab."

Ouch. That stung.

She rolled her eyes. "I'm sorry. That was rude."

"No, it's okay. You're right. I've mistreated you. I'm really sorry, Laurie."

She shook her head. "It's okay, Christian." She gave him a weak smile. "You can't blame a girl for trying though."

"I'm truly sorry, Laurie. I feel like a heel."

She smiled and shook her head. "It's okay. I'll get over it. There are plenty of other fish in the sea, right?"

He nodded and bullied up a smile, doing his best to alleviate the awkwardness of the situation. "You're an amazing woman, Laurie."

"Yeah, yeah, I know. I'm smart and pretty, right? I've heard it before."

He couldn't blame her for being flippant, but he didn't know what to say to make things right between them. Or between he and Harper, who hadn't come out of the bathroom. He knew because he'd been watching out of the corner of his eye.

She smiled wider. "Look, it's okay. I'm okay. Better to find out now that you aren't interested. Really. It's okay." She either buried her hurt or she'd processed the rejection and opted to just move past it.

Laurie Fisher was a class act.

His smile came naturally. "Thanks, Laurie."

"Anything for you, Christian. I mean that." She tapped her wine glass at the waiter as he walked past. "I really do mean it."

"I know you do. Thanks."

Now if he could only make it right with Harper. Funny, he had that awful sensation that it was going to be much, much harder to make things right with her.

∽

"Are you okay?" Janet caught Harper's gaze in the mirror over the sink. "I told you, they're just friends."

"I'm fine." Harper studied her reflection. Her face looked puffy, announcing to all the world that she'd been crying. Stupid, fair skin. It always went blotchy when she cried.

"She works in the lab for his friend. She runs testing on his samples and stuff."

Harper balled the paper towel into a wad. "She's just a friend that he brings her *here* for dinner? An hour away and to a place known for its private atmosphere? And you saw the prices. It's not cheap." She'd thought it all through when she'd been bawling in the stall.

"Come on. He's so upset that you're upset."

Harper turned from the sink and shoved the wadded-up paper towel into the trash. "I'm fine."

"So you keep saying." Janet leaned against the other end of the sink. "Look, as best as I can tell, he's out there beating himself up for how it looked to you. That doesn't say, to me anyway, that he's not sincere in how you two feel about each other."

It made sense, but Harper's aching heart wouldn't accept what Janet said. "I don't even know how he feels about me. I mean, he kissed me yesterday, but then apologized for it, for Pete's sake."

"He what?"

"Apologized for kissing me. He explained that he hadn't wanted to put any more of an emotional load on me at the moment, that he just wanted to take things slow." He'd said they were too important. She'd clung to those words.

Then to see him cozying up to another woman...it just hurt, even if they were only friends.

"Men are clueless, Harper, you should know that. Especially when it comes to women they like."

Maybe so, but it didn't make it any less painful.

"I met her. They didn't seem like a couple to me. She works in the lab he uses for testing. I imagine they're only friends because of her working there."

That didn't make Harper's situation any better. Now she was embarrassed. Embarrassed that Christian had seen her jealous upset. Embarrassed that the 'other' woman knew Harper was jealous of her. Embarrassed that she was hiding out in a ladies' room at one of the swankiest restaurants in a hundred-mile radius.

Mostly embarrassed that she felt so strongly for Christian that she allowed herself to be jealous.

Harper hung her head and groaned.

"Oh, come on now." Janet patted her back. "Henry made plenty of missteps when we were first dating. He didn't mean to, of course. He just didn't know better."

Straightening, Harper asked, "He did?" Her twin always seemed to be so smooth with the girls. Always seemed to know the right thing to say and do.

"He did. He sent me flowers, a nice gesture, but not knowing I can't stand them. He made an off-the-cuff remark about me must have been a daddy's girl, not knowing that my dad died in a car accident when he hit a tree head-on. He assumed my cousin was a guy I was secretly dating when he saw the name and picture pop up when my cousin called." Janet smiled and shook her head. "All were misunderstandings, but definitely blunders."

Harper smiled. "Well, we are twins so I guess it's natural we both would have issues in the relationships department."

"See, there you go." Janet stepped back. "Now, I'm going back to the table. I had the waiter box up the rest of our food to go. I hope you don't mind."

"Thank you." It still didn't help alleviate her suspicions about her father and Henry's accident, but she could worry about that later. She had a much more pressing problem at the moment.

"Um, Janet..."

Janet paused at the bathroom door. "Yeah?"

"How do I get out of the bathroom gracefully?"

Bursting out laughing, Janet shrugged. "You got me, but I do know you can't just stay in here forever. They will eventually kick you out. Best of luck." She opened the door and rushed out before Harper could stop her.

Harper was able to laugh despite her situation.

She drew in a deep breath. She had to go out there and face him. Face her. Face her own jumping to conclusions and letting jealousy get the best of her.

Harper shook her hands, taking several cleansing breaths. Might as well get it over with. She opened the door and stepped out of the ladies' room.

At least he wasn't lurking right outside the bathroom door like Janet said he had been. Harper squared her shoulders and straightened her posture, then sucked in more air. With all the grace she'd learned from her mother, she walked around the corner and right up to Christian's table. "Hey, Christian."

He scrambled to his feet. "Harper." There was so much emotion in his voice when he just spoke her name that she wanted to crumble.

"Hi, I don't believe we've met. I'm Laurie Fisher, Christian's friend from A+ Alliance Labs, so we kinda work together."

"Hello. I'm Harper Gallagher." She felt smaller than the wine spot on the tablecloth. This woman oozed friendliness.

"Christian tells me you're the woman he's dating. It's a pleasure to meet you."

Okay, now she wanted the floor just to open up and swallow her whole. Anything to save face. She'd lost her ability to speak.

He stood. "May I speak to you for just a moment?"

She finally found her voice. "I don't want to interrupt y'alls meal any more than I already have." Could she feel more like a louse? Her mind screamed *retreat, retreat*!

He took her by her elbow. "It'll only be a moment. Will you please excuse me, Laurie?"

"Of course. I'll just have another glass of wine."

Christian led her out the front door. "Look, I'm sorry for how this looks. I didn't even think about mentioning it yesterday. I'm sorry."

"No need to apologize." She flashed a sheepish smile. "My legs are tired from jumping to conclusions. Not even right ones, either."

"Look, I need to talk to you anyway. Could I come by later tonight?" His eyes held such hope.

Even so, today had been emotionally draining for her. She needed to unpack all the emotions she was having about the possibility of her father being involved in any way in Henry's wreck. She needed to deal with her own feelings for Christian, and how that dictated how she acted from now on. "How about you call me later? I'm planning on a long bubble bath and snuggling with Atticus in my jammies."

He hesitated, then nodded. "Whatever you want."

Oh, she wanted a lot. She wanted her father to be a decent human being. She wanted to be wrong about him maybe being involved in

Henry's death. She wanted to step into Christian's arms and lose herself in his strength.

But she could do none of that right now. Instead, she smiled. "You know my number."

He leaned down and pulled her into his arms, kissing her softly, soundly, and speedily, then releasing her just as quickly. "I'll call you tonight. I promise." He found her hand and enclosed it in his as he led her back inside.

Christian stopped at her table. "Nice to see you again, Janet. You ladies drive safely on the way home." He locked eyes with Harper, sending her heartbeat into overdrive. "I'll call you tonight." He bent down and pecked her cheek before disappearing toward his table where Laurie waited.

They had to be friends, because no woman would be that patient if they were involved.

"I'm guessing y'all made up?" Janet chuckled. "Now I don't feel guilty about leaving you the check."

Harper laughed as she pulled out her credit card and slipped it into the little leather folio. He'd held her hand and kissed her in public...firming up that they were...dating?

She kept smiling. It would always be an adventure with him, that was for sure.

And she was looking forward to all of it.

19

"The soil samples have the same high elevation of selenium." Peter's leg jiggled as he tossed the results across the desk to Christian. "Now what are you going to do?"

"Basically, I'm going to file a complaint against Wolfe Mining with the EPA and FWS. Harper has the report from Enviro Labs to prove Elliott knew the damage his company was doing to the environment, yet did nothing."

Peter nodded.

"I do need to run some facts by you and make sure we're on the same page, because I'll have to list you and the lab as collaborating since you ran the tests." Christian opened his notebook.

"Hit me with your best shot."

Christian grinned as he took out his pen and tapped against the notebook. "I'm just going to read you what I have. Feel free to interrupt and stop me if something needs clarification or correction, okay?"

"You got it." Peter leaned back in his chair, interlacing his fingers behind his head and closing his eyes.

"Proven health concerns aside, mountaintop removal mining is detrimental to the environment in areas around this practice. To begin with, waters downstream of mountaintop removal sites have increased levels of selenium as well as sulfate, and also increased electrical conductivity of the water. These elevated levels in the rivers, lakes, and run-off creeks can kill aquatic life, or unsettle their life cycles so radically that their populace would diminish, or even disappear completely. This increased level of selenium and sulfate has the prospective to destroy natural plant life, further disturbing water life and possibly human life due to the selenium poisoning in vegetation. This information is included in the following report from Enviro Labs and their analysis of the Gauley River."

Peter opened his eyes and nodded. "Good opening."

"Thanks. Here's what I have next: Mountaintop removal mining is regulated by the Surface Mining Control and Reclamation Act and the Clean Water Act, under supervision of the EPA and FWS, which are under the direction of the US Department of the Interior. Recently, the U.S. Environmental Protection Agency estimated that "valley fills" from mountaintop removal mining practices are responsible for submerging two thousand plus miles of vital Appalachian headwater streams."

"Watersheds from these headwater streams are critical as their runoffs move to a watershed, which ultimately drains down to other bodies of water, like the Gauley River in this instance. It is crucial to contemplate these downstream effects when developing and applying water quality protection and restoration actions." Christian looked up from his notebook. "How's that sound so far?"

"Sounds good so far. You've covered the basics of why the report from Enviro Labs is so important in regard to mountaintop removal mining. It connects the action to the results, which I'm assuming you're about to get to..." Peter waved his arm. "Therefore, please continue."

Christian grinned and went back to reading. "Just this month, tests from A+ Alliance Labs confirm high levels of selenium in the soil surrounding the Gauley River, which led to a vast amount of dead Virginia spiraea, a rare plant species indigenous to the area, which is currently on the Endangered and Threatened Wildlife and

Plants list with Fish and Wildlife Services. Further testing completed by A+ Alliance Labs revealed high levels of selenium in the Gauley River. Samples taken from both the Upper Gauley region and the Lower Gauley both presented with levels ten times what is required for fish's intake requirement. The levels recorded were higher in the Upper Gauley region, indicating the watershed effect from the mountaintop removal mining is the root cause of this increased level in the Gauley River."

"Finally, a dead Candy Darter was autopsied and analyzed by A+ Alliance Labs, and extremely high levels of selenium were found in his bloodstream, which turned it into a poison to kill the Candy Darter. Also noted was telangiectasia of the gills, which can also be caused by selenium contamination and toxicity."

"It should be noted that Candy Darters are freshwater fish native to the Gauley, Greenbrier, and New River watersheds, and are found nowhere else in the world. The Candy Darters are vital for maintaining a healthy, balanced water interdependent food chain in that they help to convert and transfer energy in aquatic ecosystems. They also contribute to the reproduction of freshwater mussels, who filter out impurities in the rivers to help keep waterways clean."

"Freshwater mussels are exceedingly sensitive to water pollution, so doing everything to help their reproduction, like the candy darters provide, are critical to the lifelong care of the Gauley River. Since 2018, the candy darters have been listed on the endangered species list." Christian paused and stared at Peter. "I'll just conclude with something like evidence included proves…blah, blah, blah."

Peter straightened. "I think you've covered everything. You just need to link Wolfe Mining to the mountaintop removal process and that should be enough."

Christian nodded. "When I talked to Harper last night, she said she'd get documents that show Wolfe Mining has been the sole company that has been utilizing mountaintop removal practices on Gauley Mountain and surrounding elevations." They'd avoided talking about the misunderstanding and where they stood, but she had agreed to dinner at his house on Thursday. Those plans were coming along easily.

"Yeah." Peter stared at him, hesitating.

"What?"

"It's really none of my business, but it kinda is since you use our lab exclusively."

"What?"

Peter's cheeks filled as he blew out a rush of air. "Laurie came in today in a bit of a mood. When I asked her what was bugging her, she clammed up. About twenty minutes later, Allison comes in almost in tears because Laurie snapped at her. I called Laurie into my office. She apologized to me, and later Allison. When I pushed her on what had her in such a mood, she implied that you took her to dinner, but blew her off."

Christian groaned. He couldn't win for losing. "It's not an intentional blow off. I took her to dinner as a friend, and a kind of thank you for all the times she's rushed a test for me, or worked me in on a weekend. I had no idea she had any feelings for me other than friendship. Trust me, I never meant to lead her on or give her any false ideas about how I felt."

"Didn't it ever make you wonder *why* she always rushed your tests or worked you in on a weekend? Did it ever occur to you that she wasn't doing a friend a favor, but was showing you that she cared about you by taking care of things you needed?"

"No, it didn't." Christian ran his fingers through the tangle of his hair. "Honestly, it never occurred to me. I feel so lousy, I really do, but I can't make myself interested in her or anyone else because of Harper."

Peter grunted, kind of. "You're really that crazy about Harper Gallagher?"

Why did everyone seem so surprised by that? "Yeah, man, I am."

"I'm not sure how to respond." Peter wore a wide-eyed expression. "You two just don't seem to fit in my mind."

"Seems to be going around." Christian set his notebook in the chair beside him. "Look, we might be an unlikely pair, but we both feel this strongly toward each other." At least, that's what he sensed from Harper, and the reaction she'd had last night.

Peter was quiet for a moment. "Okay, then. I wish you the best of luck. But please, for the love of everything that is sacred in this world, don't be alone with Laurie anymore. It gives her mixed signals, even when you don't mean for it to."

Was being a couple with Harper always going to be this difficult? "Okay. I have to say, though, Laurie showed her classy side last night. Even if she was upset with me."

Peter smiled. "Yeah, she's like that. It's one of her many admirable qualities."

Wait a minute...he recognized that cracking of the voice because he'd heard it in his own when talking about Harper. "You like Laurie, don't you?"

Blushing, Peter shook his head. "It doesn't matter. I'm her boss, so that puts her out of the dating pool for me."

"You know...I might have a contact at Enviro Labs and can see if they're hiring."

"Um, no." But the blush still stayed.

Christian chuckled. "Okay, just thought I'd offer." He and Harper might seem like an mismatched couple, but at least there wasn't a legitimate rule that would keep them from exploring their feelings for one another.

That would be the worst.

～

HARPER SET the last framed photo into the box on the desk. She hadn't been there long enough to really decorate the office and make it hers. Made packing up her personal effects much easier.

Her father hadn't appeared, which was probably a good thing, but also made Harper realize even more that he wasn't the man he once was. When her mother was alive, he'd been different. Oh, he was still a tyrant of sorts, but her mother had always been able to keep him in check.

What she wouldn't give to be able to ask her mom for advice right now. Everything in her life had gone through an upheaval, some good...some bad. She desperately wished she could know what her mom thought about everything.

And Henry. Oh, the ache was still so fresh. She'd always been able to talk to her twin about any and everything. He was always the perfect sounding board—from mean girls in junior high to boys she had crushes on, to changing hair and makeup styles. It didn't matter that he was a guy...he was her twin, and always there for her.

Now she was alone with her father, which was basically the same as being all alone. Alone was a lonely place to be.

Behold, I am with you always, to the end of the age.

Harper gave a little gasp. She hadn't thought of Scripture in years. Why now? And why so perfectly meaningful at this time?

It wasn't surprising she knew Scripture. After all, her mother had made sure she and Henry grew up in a Bible-believing church from the time they could walk. Even after she died, Henry had kept attending church there. Not Harper, though. She just couldn't. Not when God hadn't intervened and saved her mother.

Shall we receive good from God, and shall we not receive evil?

She froze. The Bible said over and over that as a Christ-follower, it wasn't a matter of if trials and tribulations would come, but when. As that verse in Job implied, how could she accept only the good and not some bad?

But her mother and her twin? Wasn't that too much? Especially when it was on the threshold of losing a relationship with her father?

Yet...

She had found Christian in the midst of the recent losses. A relationship that could bring her joy that would last a lifetime. Had God sent Christian to her? For her?

Christian had experienced a lot of losses in his life, too, yet he was still faithful. Had he worked through his anger and hurt and disillusion with God? Maybe she should talk to him about it. He certainly seemed open to talk about his faith and beliefs. His sister and brother-in-law, too.

"Harper?"

She turned and faced her secretary. "Yes?"

"Mrs. Sommers just informed one of the other secretaries who told me that your father has arrived and he's asking if you're still here. When that call comes, what would you like me to say?"

Harper smiled sadly. "He won't be asking to see me. He just wants to make sure I'm gone, which, I'm almost finished here. I'll be leaving in just a few minutes."

The young secretary nodded and slipped out of the office, shutting the door behind her.

If her father was here, she needed to hurry. Harper quickly printed out the project reports for all the mountaintop removal mines in the Gauley River region. There were a lot more than she'd imagined. Christian might want to get a sample or two from these other sites to back up his complaint.

She shoved the printouts into her purse and removed the building's key from her keyring. Holding it tightly to pass off to her secretary, Harper lifted the box to her hip and reached for the office door.

It swung open and her father stood there, looking much worse for the wear.

Harper took a step back and took a moment to regain her composure. "I'm leaving now. I was going to leave the key with my secretary, but here." She shoved the key out to him.

He shut the door behind him and brushed past her. "We need to talk." He took a seat in the executive chair behind the desk.

Talk? Funny, coming from him. She set the box back on the desk, but kept her purse over her shoulder as she leaned against the side of her desk. "Okay." If they were going to talk, she was going to ask hard questions. Ones that had kept bouncing around in her mind, even after she talked to Christian last night and he told her that he just couldn't believe Elliott would be in any way involved in Henry's accident.

Considering how her father had been of recent, Harper wasn't so sure.

"I do think it best that you leave, but I wanted to reiterate to you that I knew nothing about a report to confirm that article in the EPA. I've had several of my advisors, some of the smartest scientists, physicians, and analysists out there, assure me that Wolfe Mining is not responsible for any of the claims about mountaintop removal mining causing health or environmental issues."

"Then they're just as foolish as you are, Father." Harper struggled to keep her anger in check. "There is so much proof of the health issues alone that I can't believe that even you can turn a blind eye to the data."

Her father's jaw clenched and the muscles in his cheeks pulsated. "If we're so responsible, how come we haven't been sued."

"Many have tried! I've seen the suit reports. You've managed to get every case dismissed or the plaintiffs withdraw, probably because they were paid off."

"Can you prove that, Harper?"

"No. You manage to hide your tracks very well, Father. Maybe too well. You've gotten too cocky, too confident. But your day is coming. A reckoning is coming."

More cheek pulsations. "Maybe trying to talk to you was a bad idea after all. You can't listen to reason."

"Reason? Are you kidding me? What lengths will you go to in order to protect yourself and this company? Is making the money that you do worth it? Worth causing people to get sick or die? Worth causing such changes to the environment that it might never recover?"

"See, there you go, just trying to blame me for everything wrong in the world. When did you become so self-righteous, Harper?"

"Father, I've never been self-righteous, but I do believe in doing the right thing. Even now, knowing the data because I gave you a copy of the Enviro Labs report, you haven't done anything to right the wrongs this company has made. You're still going on, business as usual. Where do you draw the line? Where does the greed end and the morality begin? Do you even have any morals left?"

"That's about enough."

No, she had one more thing to get off her chest. "Would you go so far as to be involved in your son's death?"

His face lost all color. "What are you talking about?"

"What if Henry found that report, just like I did, and was going to act on it? What if you found out he was? What lengths would you have gone to in order to keep Henry from taking action?"

"What are you accusing me of, Harper?" Her father's voice had gone flat, emotionless.

She was too far gone to stop herself. "Would you have had someone do something to distract Henry? Maybe supposed to just cause an accident that would take Henry out of play for a little while...just time enough for you to cover everything up like you usually do? Maybe something went wrong with that plan and Henry's wreck was worse than ever expected."

She'd never seen her father so pale, not even after her mother or Henry had died. She'd pushed too far. Fear snaked up her spine, slithering around her neck and practically choking her. He was going to explode.

He did explode, but not with the rage she expected. He burst into tears, sobbing like she'd never imagined him capable of. His entire body shook as waves of sobs rolled over him.

Harper didn't know how to react. The great Elliott Wolfe, man who raised her to not display emotion in public, was having a breakdown of sorts. Did she dare speak? Apologize? Just leave? She wasn't sure, but as she stood there, silently watching him release grief, she realized that she wasn't going to leave. She wasn't going to apologize, but she wasn't going to walk out on him. Even though that was probably what he would have done if the tables were turned.

Moments later, he regained his self-control. He looked her in the eye. "Harper, I swear to you on your mother's grave that I had nothing to do with Henry's accident. I'm more than hurt that you would even consider for a moment that I could be involved, but I suppose I can understand why you might think that. Still, I had nothing to do with anything in that regard."

She considered him, meeting his stare dead-on, something she wasn't accustomed to doing. All she saw back was sincerity. She could almost taste her relief. "Okay. I believe you had nothing to do with Henry's wreck."

He nodded.

"But," she continued, "someone was responsible for causing the wreck and left him alone to die. I won't rest until I find out, too, and I have a strong feeling, it has something to do with the Enviro Labs report and this company."

"I don't know how." Her father's full composure had settled firmly back in place.

"I'm working on figuring that out."

He stood. "Let me know what you find out, if you will."

She nodded, not committing to anything.

He nodded back and headed to the door. He hesitated. "Good luck, Harper. I hope you find whatever it takes to bring you peace about Henry. In regards to my company, we are not responsible and no amount of your saying we are will make it so." He left before she could respond.

Well, they'd just see about that.

20

"You're just going to let him off the hook?" Janet asked.

Harper switched the phone to her other ear. This wasn't how she wanted to start her birthday. "I'm not letting him off the hook for what Wolfe Mining has done. I'm helping Christian finalize his report to file a formal complaint directly against the company."

She set her cup of coffee down on the counter. "Having said that, I don't think my father had anything to do with Henry's wreck, but I do believe someone was responsible and I will keep looking to find out who that was."

"You're being gullible. Who else would want to hurt Henry? Nobody. Only your dad, just to keep him quiet."

"You really believe that?"

"I think Henry started to distrust your father weeks ago."

Harper took the last sip of coffee and rinsed out the cup. "Really? You never mentioned that before."

"I didn't think it might be important until now."

Shutting the dishwasher door, Harper then wiped the counter. "Henry never mentioned any of that to me." Just how well did she know—or rather, not know, her own twin?

"It wasn't some big announcement or anything. Just little things. Like he'd tell me to tell your father he had lunch plans already when your father would call. Or he wouldn't be available to take his calls. Just little things like that, which is why I never thought much about mentioning it to you before now."

Logical. "Henry asked you to lie to my father for him?" That didn't sound like Henry at all.

"More like little fibs."

They were one and the same to Harper, and they certainly had been to Henry.

The door monitoring system chimed inside the house, setting Atticus off on a barking episode.

Harper glanced at the monitor on the counter that showed the image of the motion activated camera. A man in a suit and holding a briefcase stood at the door. Lawyer. "Janet, I've got to go. Someone's at my front door. I'll talk to you later."

Atticus continued barking until she moved beside him and stroked his head.

She continued to pet the dog as she spoke through the electronic doorbell's speaker, using her cell. "Hello, may I help you?"

"I'm here to see Harper Wolfe."

"And you are?"

"Terrence King. I'm an attorney with Quarles, Saks, and King." He held a business card up to the camera.

She knew the firm. They didn't handle anything criminal. Their main line of business was estates, wills, and business law.

"I'm here on behalf of Nicolette Wolfe's estate."

Everything in her went cold. "Just a moment."

She grabbed Atticus by the collar and put him in the fenced backyard. She didn't even know her mother had an estate. This was the first she was hearing about it, and it unnerved her. She opened the front door. "Please, come in." She waved him inside, then led him to the living room. "Would you like a cup of coffee or a bottled water?"

"No, thank you." He took a seat on the couch.

Harper sat at the other end. "How may I help you?"

"First," he smiled, "Happy birthday."

"Thank you, I think." She felt displaced, like she was awake in the middle of a dream.

"I need to explain something to you. Years ago, back when your parents started Wolfe Mining, your mother and father were equal partners in the business. I know, because I helped set it up."

"I had no idea." Why hadn't her father ever mentioned it? Or her mother before she died, for that matter.

"After your mother was diagnosed with cancer, she began making arrangements for the time to come when she would no longer be around. As such, I was instructed to give you this on your twenty-fifth birthday, and answer any questions you might have after you read it." He handed her a red envelope. He lifted his phone and became very engaged in an app on it.

Harper would've stood up and moved to read whatever was inside the red envelope in private, but she didn't trust her legs to support her. Instead, she slit the envelope open and pulled out the pages folded inside. Recognizing her mother's handwriting, she absorbed the gasp.

"Please, excuse me. Make yourself at home." She carried the letter into the kitchen and read.

MY DEAREST HARPER,

We always wish we had more time on this earth to be with the ones we love, but each of our days are numbered. I am confident in where I will spend eternity, and know that you are strong in faith and will join me in Heaven when your time on earth is through.

Your father and I set up Wolfe Mining just after we got married. I know growing up with your father was difficult at times, but I pray you two have reached a comfortable relationship now that I've passed and you are an adult. Please understand why your father is like he is.

Your father comes from a family of coal miners, be he resented their long hours and low income. To get away from what he thought he hated most, he enlisted in the Army when he was just eighteen.

Eight years later, he was honorably discharged. He returned home, only to constantly argue with his father. He left Harlan County, Kentucky after a dispute with his father—he saw ways to work less but make a larger profit, while his father believed in hard work. His father died soon after Elliott and I married and started Wolfe Mining.

After we had you and Henry, your father began doing more and more to turn a bigger profit so his son would never have to do manual labor in a coal mine. It was a constant fear of his, Harper, that he would somehow lose money and Henry would have to work as he'd seen his father have to work. No amount of me telling him otherwise would convince him.

Because we used the money from the inheritance from my father to start the company, I wanted to divide the shares of the company fifty-fifty, but your father wanted to make sure I never felt like he was taking control of the company. He insisted that I keep one share more than him, so I own fifty-one percent of Wolfe Mining, and your father retains forty-nine percent.

When I began making plans for my final arrangements, I realized I still held the stock certificates. I know your father has looked over you in favor of Henry too many times, and I hope my gesture isn't too little, too late. I know your father has made it very clear that Henry will be the legal counsel for Wolfe Mining, but I want you to know that you are just as valuable.

As such, I've given the twenty-five shares to go to Henry to your father to bestow upon him at the time he selects, as long as it is transferred to Henry by his twenty-fifth birthday. I'm giving you twenty-six shares today, on your twenty-fifth birthday. My estate attorney, Terrence, will have the certificates for you. Together, you and Henry have controlling interest in Wolfe Mining. Your father has no idea that I've given these to you, and if I depart this world as quickly as the doctors think I will, he will most certainly have forgotten all about my extra twenty-six shares by today.

I hope that things are doing well by this date, and this will just be an added bonus to the three of you forging onward into the great things of the future. If not, this is your security.

Always remember, dear girl, that I love you to the moon and back and I've always been so proud of you. I'll be waiting to be rejoined with you in Heaven.

Until then, Love, Mom

HARPER HADN'T EVEN REALIZED she'd been crying until she folded the letter and slipped it back into the envelope and tears dripped to the kitchen counter. She grabbed a napkin and dabbed at her face.

Oh, Mom, I miss you so much.

She took a deep breath and headed back into the living room, her mind still reeling.

Mr. King smiled as she entered. He handed her a manilla envelope. "These are the twenty-six stock certificates of Wolfe Mining." He stood. "I'm also very sorry for your loss. I didn't know your brother, but your mother spoke almost entirely about both of you during the times I was assisting her with estate planning. I can only imagine the loss you must feel."

"Thank you." She walked him to the door. "So, that's it?"

"Unless you have any questions."

She shook her head.

He extended his hand. "Then that's it. Happy birthday, again. I know your mother would be very proud of you." He shook her hand, then turned and left.

Harper shut the door and leaned against it. Her legs almost buckled under her weight. Only one thing kept her on her feet: She now held controlling interest in Wolfe Mining.

∼

CHRISTIAN TOOK in every detail of his cabin. He'd spent the better part of the morning cleaning and decorating, and picking up the cake from Una B's. Four huge bouquets of balloons were weighted down to the four corners of the living room/kitchen combo area. A Happy Birthday banner hung from the exposed wooden rafter of the living room. A bouquet of twenty-five, long-stemmed, red and white roses were perfectly arranged on the kitchen table covered in one of his mother's old lacy tablecloths and alongside the white birthday cake with sprinkles. Lots and lots of sprinkles, just like Nell had told him Harper liked.

The presents he, Katie, Hunter, and Gabe had gotten her were brightly wrapped and sat on the coffee table, awaiting Harper. Nell had even sent over her gift for Harper. The steaks were ready for the grill, the potatoes were already wrapped in foil and on the low-heat grill, and the corn on the cob was husked and ready to go into the big pot of water. He'd cut everything for the salad and made the homemade dressings.

"It all looks awesome, Christian." Katie came beside him and slung her arm over his shoulders.

"I hope so." Was it too much? If she was used to just being taken out with her father and Henry, maybe this would seem too over the top. "I'm not sure about the roses, though."

"They're perfect. Really. Stop worrying. She's going to love everything." Katie squeezed him in a quick hug, then moved to sit on Hunter's lap. "Besides, this is the cleanest I've seen your cabin in years."

Gabe chuckled softly. "She has a point."

"Hey, I'm working two jobs, you slackers, so I have less time to clean than you do."

"You wish. It takes you having two jobs just to keep up the hours we have in just the family business." Katie took a sip of the sweet tea he'd brewed that morning.

Christian spread his arms. "And I'm fighting to bring down a big, bad mining company that's destroying our environment."

"I find it admirable that Harper's helping you bring down her father and his company," Gabe said.

An unexplained sense of pride puffed out his chest. "That's how she is—she wants to right wrongs and see people held accountable for their actions."

Tires crunched on gravel.

Christian jumped to his feet. Suddenly, he was unsure of everything. Maybe she didn't like surprises. Maybe she'd always just gone out to eat for her birthday because she didn't like parties. He second guessed all his planning.

A car door slammed.

"Unless you want us to all jump out and holler 'surprise' when you open the door, I'd suggest you head out to meet her," Hunter said softly.

"Right." He shot to the door, hesitated, then opened the door and stepped onto his front porch just as Harper was climbing the stairs.

"Hi." She wore jeans, a deep blue, slouchy type shirt, and worn-in looking sneakers.

"Hey." He went in for a hug as she approached. The smell of her heady perfume wrecked him. He gave her a quick kiss. "Happy birthday."

Harper pulled back, but kept her hands on his forearms, and gave him a long stare. "How'd you know it was my birthday?"

Christian couldn't read if she was surprised or upset. "Nell, but don't be mad at her."

She shook her head. "Why would I be mad at her? I always love my birthday. It's a bit sad today because Henry's not here. It's the first year I haven't shared a birthday with him and it feels really weird."

"Good. I mean, I'm glad you like your birthday."

"You're acting weird. I couldn't wait to see you because I have something to tell you." She stood at the door. "Are you going to invite me in?"

He hoped whatever it was she needed to tell him could wait. "Yeah." He opened the door and motioned her to enter before him.

"Happy birthday!" Katie hopped up to give her a hug.

Hunter stood as well. "Happy birthday, Harper."

Gabe smiled. "Happy birthday."

"Wow, this is such a great surprise." She gave Christian a hug as he shut the door and moved beside her. "You planned all this for me?"

"Girl, he's been driving me nuts with his planning. Do you want a glass of tea?" Katie was already halfway into the kitchen. "Christian won't tell you this, but he makes the best sweet tea in the family. I think he sneaks in mint or something, but he won't tell me his secret."

Harper turned to him. "Christian, this is the nicest thing anyone's ever done for my birthday. Thank you." She reached up on her tiptoes to plant a kiss on the side of his jaw.

"Come on, sit down." He pulled her onto his sofa with him.

Katie passed her a glass. "Now, you must open your presents. Dad always said it was bad luck to have your cake before you open presents."

"There's cake, too?"

"Oh, there's cake all right." Katie grinned as she sat back on the loveseat with her husband.

Gabe sat in Christian's recliner. "Katie always used that saying of Dad's as an excuse to open her presents first thing in the morning."

"Hey, I usually had a cupcake for breakfast, so I didn't want to have bad luck." She wagged her finger at her older brother. "Besides, Gabriel Gallagher, I seem to recall you doing the same thing a time or two yourself."

"Guilty as charged." Gabe chuckled as he passed a box to Harper. "Here, save me from further insult from my little sister and open mine first."

"You didn't have to get me anything." She looked around the room. "None of you did."

"Don't be silly." Christian took her glass and set it on the end table. "Our dad always made big deals out of birthdays and we carry on the tradition. Finding the perfect gift is almost a challenge to us. We get very sneaky and competitive about gift-giving."

Harper smiled and slowly removed the wrapping paper.

Katie groaned. "Please just rip it. I can't stand the waiting."

"It's her present, let her unwrap it how she pleases." Hunter kissed the tip of Katie's nose. "My wife is such an impatient woman."

Harper grinned, but tore away the paper faster. She opened the box inside and pulled out a resin picture frame with an English

Mastiff on the side. "It looks just like Hopper. Thank you, Gabe. I love it."

"You're very welcome."

Christian knew she'd have it up in her house very soon. He fist-bumped his brother.

Katie narrowed her eyes at her brother. "Did Christian help you?"

"I didn't have a clue, but man, it's dead-on perfect." Christian couldn't be more pleased with Gabe's gift.

"Then who helped you?" Katie pushed.

Gabe leaned back and took a swig of his tea. "I never reveal my sources."

"Cheater." Katie hissed before passing another present to Harper. "Here, open mine next." She inched to the edge of her seat.

The box was long and narrow. Christian had no idea what his sister had bought. Harper ripped the paper off. "Oh, that's freeing. I like it."

"See?" Katie laughed.

Harper opened the box inside and pulled out a paddle. She burst out laughing. "Does this mean I get to go rafting again?"

Katie nodded. "It does."

Harper clapped her hands. "Oh, I love it. Thank you!"

Grinning, she high-fived her husband, then looked at Gabe. "I'd say we're even."

Gabe huffed.

"Here, open mine next." Hunter passed her a heavy gift bag. "I don't wrap."

Harper grinned and tossed the tissue paper aside. She pulled out a small, bronze scales of justice. "This is beautiful, Hunter. Thank you. I love this."

"It fit you." Hunter smiled.

"Very nice." Christian knew that, too, would be up very soon.

"Nell sent this one." Katie passed it to her.

Harper ripped it open. "Oh, y'all check this out. It's perfect."

"What is it?" Christian asked.

"It's a gift certificate for a month's meal prep service." Harper blushed a little. "I don't have a lot of time to plan meals, go to the grocery store, then make something elaborate for dinner. I can't wait to use it."

Christian stared at her animated face and his heart leapt. This would be a moment he remembered forever...the moment he knew she was the only woman for him.

"Okay, Christian, you're up," Katie said.

He nervously passed the last present to her. "Obviously, this is from me."

She smiled shyly and tore off the paper. She opened the box and gave a little gasp. "Oh, Christian. I love it."

"What is it?" Katie asked.

Harper pulled out the tan attaché bag he'd had engraved with her initials, running her hands over the kid leather. "It's so soft and supple."

Hunter nodded in approval. "Every attorney I've ever seen has one of those."

"I've never seen you with one before, so I took a chance." Christian stared at Harper.

Tears welled in her eyes. "This is so amazing...I can't even." She sniffed and gave a quick shake of her head. "I had ordered one almost just like this for Henry for his birthday today, except in black leather. To get this...thank you, Christian. I absolutely love it." She leaned over and kissed his cheek. "It's perfect," she whispered under her breath.

"Then it's a perfect match for you," he whispered back. Because she was truly perfect. At least for him.

21

"I can't thank you enough for tonight. Truly one of the best birthdays I've ever had." Harper sat on Christian's front porch, snuggled beside him on the swing, sipping her tea. She felt right at home and didn't want to do anything to disturb the peacefulness she'd missed for such a long time. "And your family...they really are something special."

Christian smiled and kissed the top of her head. "They like you. They had fun in all the planning."

His siblings and Hunter had left half an hour or so ago, after helping pack all of her presents and the rest of her birthday cake in her SUV. Now she was alone with Christian, and cherishing the intimacy of sitting on the swing with him in the twilight.

"You Gallaghers do go all out. It's such fun, and I love every single present." She closed her eyes into his warmth. "Especially my attaché. I never had one and always wanted one."

"We always go all-out for birthdays because our dad did, but I wanted to make this special for you since I figured it'd be a hard one."

"It was a hard—er, interesting day. Yes, hard because I've been missing Henry. Interesting because of the visitor I had."

"Is that what you were going to tell me earlier?"

She sat up, a little worried how he would take her being the controlling stockholder of Wolfe Mining. But she'd been thinking all afternoon and, on the drive over, had some ideas. If Christian would be onboard with it. "Yes." Slowly, she told him all about the visit from Terrence King, her mother's letter, and the stocks.

He sat very still when she finished. Very silent. She could feel his body stiffen just before he sat up straight. "You now own Wolfe Mining?"

"Fifty-one percent of it. The controlling interest."

He bent and ran his fingers through his thick, shoulder-length hair.

"What?" She could feel his angst.

"Harper, as a lawyer you should realize, after I file my report and lodge a formal complaint, every suit that comes against Wolfe Mining will also come against you."

"That's what I was thinking about on the drive over. You can just not file your report."

"What?" The incredulous look on his face said it all.

"Hear me out. You don't file your report or lodge a formal complaint. As the major stockholder, Father can't fight me on changes I make in the company. Changes like immediately ceasing all mountaintop removal mining, but keeping those miners employed by having them work at cleaning up the environment. Investing in the community. Making reparations for the damage Wolfe Mining has done."

"How will you get the money to fund these changes if you cease the mining?" His expression of disbelief hadn't changed.

"I said I'd stop the mountaintop removal mining. I'd continue with the other avenues of coal mining to keep funds coming in to make payroll for our employees, but we don't need the extra income derived from the mountaintop removal practice." He didn't look convinced. "Down the road, we could invest in cleaner energy like windmill farms. Just about two hours away, in Thomas, there is already a windmill farm. We could buy one or build one."

Disdain shadowed his expression, even in the dim light of the porch light. "How long down the road will that be? Years? And do you have any idea the price of the upkeep of a windmill farm and the cost of doing business versus the profit? That farm over in Thomas? It produces less than three percent of the electricity used in the state."

"I don't know, Christian. What do you suggest? I'm open to ideas."

He sat up and stared at her. "I don't think I have a choice. I have to file my report. It's part of my job as a Wetland/Environmental Consultant. It would be unethical for me to withhold my report."

"Then could you hold off…delay filing it? Give me time to start turning around Wolfe Mining? Maybe that would appease the community—seeing the positive changes." She knew she was asking a lot, but there was a lot on the line for her. "It's not like I asked for the stocks. My mother left me some and Henry left me his. I want to turn the company around, do the right thing. Give me that chance."

"I don't know, Harper. I want you to change Wolfe Mining policies, you know I do, but I can't withhold or delay information. I'd lose all credibility. My reputation would be in tatters."

She could understand. As it was, once she took over the helm of Wolfe Mining, and when the report became public, her dreams of being Prosecuting Attorney were dead in the water. No one would ever believe she hadn't been involved with the company or didn't know she'd get shares of it all along.

Looking at Christian's face, she realized that she had damaged their fragile beginning of a real relationship, and possibly changed the feeling of what had been a wonderful evening. She put a hand on his forearm. "I'm sorry for even asking. I'm just trying to figure things out. I want to do the right thing for the community, but it was really unfair of me to ask you to not file your report or even to hold off filing it."

Her heart pounded so hard that surely, he could hear it. His expression hadn't changed. Her chest ached. She'd blown it big time and only had herself to blame. "Look, I'm going to go ahead and go home. It's getting late and I have things I have to do tomorrow." She stood.

He pushed to his feet as well. "You don't have to leave."

"It's best if I do." He'd said she didn't have to leave, not that he wanted her to stay. Emotions rolled in her chest, and she grappled to deny tears the release they demanded. "Thank you again for my party, the dinner...everything. You'll never know how much this meant to me." She turned and headed toward the steps.

He grabbed her wrist and tugged her against his chest. He looked down into her face with an unreadable expression. His breathing was labored against hers. When Harper placed her hands against his chest, she could feel his heart pounding, almost racing hers.

His hands were on either side of her face, holding her ever-so-gently in his grasp. His eyes locked with hers.

Oh, goodness, she could stay lost in his eyes.

He bent, his forehead nearly touching hers. Their breath intermingling.

Slowly...deliberately...softly, he kissed her.

She leaned into him, her heartbeat matching his.

Christian deepened the kiss until she could almost taste forever.

Then, he straightened. His eyes were glassy as he looked at her. His arms moved around her, and he pulled her into his embrace, hugging her. A good thing, since she didn't think she could stand. She finally knew what it meant when women said a man made them go weak in the knees. Harper definitely could relate at the moment. She could stay in his arms indefinitely and be perfectly content.

He stepped back, holding her steady until she wasn't so unsteady.

"Christian, I'm really sorry for asking. I just wasn't thinking." Her voice sounded shaky even to her own ears.

"Shh." He planted a quick kiss on her lips. "Let's just do some thinking tonight and try to come up with some ideas on where to go from here tomorrow." He kissed the top of her head and hugged her again. "I'm going to pray for wisdom. I hope you do, too."

She didn't have the nerve to tell him that she'd been so far from God for so long that He probably wouldn't listen to her prayers. Then again, she couldn't just ignore what her mother wrote in her letter. "I'm just so sorry. I feel like a jerk for asking."

He didn't reply, but walked her to her vehicle, kissed her again, then watched her drive off.

How could she have been so stupid to ask him not to file his report?

Harper drove slower than usual because she didn't want to disturb the box holding the rest of her birthday cake on the passenger's seat.

She'd already run through a dozen ways to make this right, but as Christian had pointed out, there wasn't a way that didn't hold her responsible in some way.

As she pulled into her neighborhood, she realized she only had one option that would save herself, her reputation, and her relationship with Christian: to dissolve the company.

That would stop all mining immediately. She could let the employees go with a nice severance package, then the rest of the company's assets would be split 51/49 between Harper and her father. She could take her fifty-one percent and invest it in environmental endeavors to repair the damage done by Wolfe Mining.

The more she thought about it, the more she liked the idea. Christian could recommend places to donate in order to make private reparations to the community. Why she hadn't considered that to begin with, she didn't know.

She pulled into the driveway to see Janet's car parked. Janet got out of the car as Harper did. "Janet, is something wrong? Are you okay?" It was barely ten, but still a little late for an uninvited visit.

"I needed to talk to you."

"Okay." Then it must be important. "Let me carry this in and I'll make us a cup of decaf." She opened the back door and reached for the bags of presents.

"Let me help you," Janet offered.

"Thanks. If you could just grab the cake box in the front seat, that'd be great."

"Sure."

Harper deactivated the alarm, unlocked the door, then rushed inside. She set the bag down on the kitchen table. "Just put the box on the kitchen island, please. I'll let Atticus out right quick." She bent down to give him a head scratch. "You need to go out, don't you, sweet boy?" She led him to the back door and set him free into the backyard.

Back in the kitchen, Harper stared a pot of coffee. "Would you like a piece of cake with your coffee?" She opened the cake box.

Janet glanced over at the cake. "It's your birthday?"

"Yeah." Harper smiled, then froze and just stared at the other woman. Janet didn't know today was Henry's birthday? Something didn't ring right about that. *You're madly in love with someone and you don't know his birthday?*

Janet recovered quickly. "I'm sorry, I sometimes forget you and Henry are twins. I've been sad all day about Henry."

Harper nodded, but she still felt like something was *off*. "So, what did you need to talk about?"

"I heard you were let go from Wolfe Mining. I wanted to make sure you were okay."

The coffee maker hissed, signaling the end of the cycle. Harper grabbed two mugs and began to pour. "Where did you hear that?"

"A friend of mine who's a temp."

Harper passed a mug to Janet. "Actually, I gave my father notice and he opted to let me go immediately." She turned and pulled out two dessert plates and forks. She couldn't find her cake server, so just grabbed a butcher knife to cut the cake.

"My friend said there was some yelling involved."

Slicing the cake, Harper passed a piece to Janet, cut one for herself, then closed the box back and set the knife on top. "I guess there was. He didn't appreciate me calling him out for the horrible things he's done to the community—people and environment all in the name of making a profit." She shrugged. "I didn't like that he kept denying he ordered the report from Enviro Labs." The cake didn't taste as delightful as it had earlier.

"But Christian's still going to file his report and complaint, right?" Janet took a bite of the cake and chased it with a sip of coffee.

Harper nodded. "Of course." She set the fork on the plate and pushed the cake aside. As delectable as it was, she didn't feel like eating anymore. "Even though I asked him not to."

"You what?" Janet set down her mug with a loud clank. "Why on earth would you do that?"

"Because as of today, I own controlling interest in Wolfe Mining."

Janet's eyes widened. "What? How?"

With just the basics, Harper filled her in on the stocks. "But, I was wrong to ask Christian to hold his report. It won't matter anyway."

"Why?"

"Because I made a decision on the drive home. I'm going to dissolve the company." Excitement built in her chest again, just like it had when she'd considered her options just before she'd reached home.

Janet passed pale and went straight to ashen. "You can't do that."

"I can. I'll have all mining halted first thing, then set up the severance package plans tomorrow morning, then call a company-wide meeting tomorrow afternoon to inform the employees. I'll make sure that even the miners are pulled in and told. The dissolution can be done once some reports are completed and business affairs are in order. The actual resolution of dissolution can be done online and is only a twenty-five-dollar fee. In two-to-four business days, it's all done." It was freeing to say it all out loud, and as she did, Harper realized it could actually work!

"But your father won't pay for what he's done."

"Probably not, but losing his beloved company will have to suffice as his comeuppance. After all severance packages are paid, and final bills and taxes are paid, the remaining assets will be distributed between me and my father. I'll use my fifty-one percent to invest back into the community. While I can't undo the bad my father did, I can work to make reparations in the community."

"No." Janet jumped to her feet. Her voice raised several decibels. "You can't dissolve Wolfe Mining. Your father has to pay." Janet's eyes were wide and her face was no longer pasty. It was sunburnt red.

"I've explained that there's nothing more to do." Harper set her cup in the sink, not sure why all the hairs on the back of her neck were standing at attention like little army soldiers. "Look, Janet, I hate to run you off, but it's been a really long day and I have a busy day ahead of me, so I really need to take a bath and turn in." She turned to lead Janet to the door.

Crash!

Harper turned around and nearly stepped on the broken glass of the coffee mug. She jumped back to the other side of the island from Janet, then froze. Janet wielded the knife Harper had used to cut the cake.

"What are you doing?" Harper forced her voice to be calm and not warble even as she sidestepped to keep the island between her and Janet. "Put the knife down."

"No, I won't let you ruin everything. I worked too hard to set this all up to let you destroy my plan." Janet waved the knife through the air like some crazy woman.

"What plan?" Harper steeled herself to not show her fear, but she was terrified.

"Your father has to pay for what he did to me. My family. He has to pay." Janet's eyes creeped Harper out with the way they darted around the room, not settling on anything but Harper every few seconds.

"You're upset because he fired you?" This was a little excessive of a response. And a little late.

Janet narrowed her crazy eyes. "For a lawyer, you sure are stupid. No, this has nothing to do with him firing me. I would've quit anyway because I'd already set my plan in action."

There it was again, mention of a plan. "I don't understand." Harper stuck her hand in her back pocket, hoping she looked unassuming as she gripped her cell phone in the pocket.

Janet erupted in humorless laughter. "Of course you don't. Because you don't want to see. But I see. I know. I can't let you dissolve the company or your father will never pay, and I've worked too hard for too long to see that he does."

Harper casually moved her hand holding the cell phone in front of her, below the island. "What did my father do to you?" If she could just keep Janet distracted and ranting, she might be able to dial for help without Janet realizing it. While she couldn't chance looking down long enough to dial 911, she could just hit redial. And hope her last call wasn't to Janet.

"He destroyed my family. You already know his greed kept him removing mountaintops, even though it was dangerous. You know about a lot of it, but you never considered that it also changes where the water flows as well as removes trees and plants that slow the water during a rain season?" Janet didn't look as crazy at the moment, but she still brandished the knife at Harper. "It can cause a landslide which just washes away a home. A lifetime of belongings, gone in minutes. That's what your father did to my family."

This sounded really familiar...Harper took only enough time looking at her phone to tap the redial icon. She could only hope the last person she called would be able to help. She clicked the phone to silent, and held it carefully hidden from Janet by the kitchen island.

"Ah, I see by your expression that you're starting to understand. The Cowen community suffered such loss that night. Enough that we all banded together to bring a suit against Wolfe Mining. They needed to replace what we'd lost. It's not like anyone just wanted to get rich off the suit...we all just wanted to be able to rebuild our homes and lives." A myriad of emotions shadowed Janet's expression.

Oh, no. The class action suit.

"My father was one of the main people named in the suit. Funny, but just before we were set to go to trial, the judge refused to certify the case. We had no flood insurance, so we lost everything. My father didn't know what to do after the case fell apart. We had no money and were basically living on the street." Janet's eyes weren't crazy at all anymore—they were filled with nothing but sadness and grief.

Harper glanced down and saw that the call had connected. Now if whoever was on the other end could get what was happening, maybe they'd call 911 and send help her way.

"He took up drinking and one day, just ran his truck into a tree." Janet wiped her tears on the sleeve of her shirt. "Your father did that. Because of your father, I lost my home, everything I owned, and my father." The crazed look was back. "I have a plan. He has to pay. I can't let you undo everything I've set up."

"What have you done, Janet?" Fear pooled in the pit of Harper's stomach. While she felt for Janet's losses, she also believed in the legal system. People couldn't just take the law into their own hands.

22

Christian clicked his phone into the dash mount of the Challenger. He knew he should call the police, but he didn't want to miss hearing what was happening with Harper. He peeled out of his driveway, throwing gravel everywhere.

He skidded to a stop outside of Katie's cabin. He double checked to make sure Harper's call was muted before he honked his horn. In seconds, both Katie and Hunter spilled out.

"What's going on?" Katie asked.

"Listen. It's Harper. She has me on a call."

"My plan was flawless until Henry messed it up. And just when I got it back on track, you come along and mess it up. What is it with you two?"

"That's Janet, Henry's girlfriend," Christian informed his sister and brother-in-law.

"What did you do, Janet?" Harper's voice was steady, but there were levels of fear in her delivery.

"Do you really think your father would order a report from Enviro that could in any way implicate him and his precious company of any wrongdoing?"

"You ordered the report?"

"Of course I did. And I made sure I used his name, then I also cross-referenced the purchase order to make sure it appeared as if he alone had ordered and authorized payment for the report."

"You set it up so it would look like he'd known about the selenium and did nothing, making him blameworthy and liable."

"Not quite as dumb as a rock, are you?"

"All this time, you were using Henry?"

"I went out of my way to meet Henry and worm my way in as his assistant. I never managed to seduce him, though, despite my best efforts. Still, at least we were casually dating so I had access to just about everything. All was going according to plan until he found the report and told me he was going to confront his father about it."

"Janet, could you please put down the knife? I want to hear what you have to say, I do, but every time you wave that knife, it makes it hard for me to concentrate."

Every muscle in Christian's body tightened. Hunter looked at Katie. "Christian and I are going to go to Harper's. You call 911 and tell them that there is a woman with a knife threatening Harper. Let them know an FBI agent is on the scene." He looked at Christian. "I'll be right back." He ran into his and Katie's cabin.

"Tough. I'm about tired of this conversation anyway." Janet didn't even sound like herself. "Don't move." Her voice raised.

"I'm not."

Christian quickly gave his sister Harper's address. Hunter rushed back to the car, his gun on his hip and his badge hanging around his neck. He gave Katie her cell and a quick kiss before he climbed in the passenger's seat of the Challenger.

"I'll be praying," Katie said as she turned and raced toward her cabin.

Christian slammed the car in reverse.

"You said you loved Henry. You were devastated at his funeral. You can't fake tears like that."

"I was crying because I could've been the one killed in that wreck. If he hadn't swerved when he did, we could've had a head-on collision."

"You killed Henry."

Christian raced down the road toward Harper's. He could only imagine how Harper felt right now. She was about to lose it. He would. He sent up many small prayers. *Help her. Protect her. God, please.*

"You caused Henry's accident?" Harper's tone was flat, emotionless. It terrified Christian, pushing his foot down harder on the accelerator.

"I'd had a GPS tracker on his phone for weeks. When he told me he was going to talk to his father and get everything straightened out, I smelled a cover up and, once again, Elliott Wolfe wouldn't be held accountable. I couldn't let that happen."

"You planned to kill him?" Harper's tone was still just as flat as before, but it had flickers of emotion hitting some of the syllables.

Christian sent up more silent prayers.

"Actually, I didn't. I liked Henry, I did. I wasn't goo-goo in love with him, but he was fun and took me to nice places and we had a good time. I only planned to make him wreck and put him in the hospital, hopefully unconscious for a few days until I could figure out how to get around him. If that didn't work, I had a gun to make sure he couldn't talk to your father. But, fate worked it out so I didn't have to intervene."

"Fate had nothing to do with it, Janet. You planned it, you executed it, and you killed my brother." The emotion was definitely back in her voice now. Christian clenched and unclenched his hands. He'd never felt so helpless before.

"Nuh-uh-uh. Don't you move." Janet's voice had a sing-song cadence.

"Don't point that knife in my face!" The anger trembled in Harper's voice.

"It's going to be okay. We're almost there and the police should be right behind us," Hunter said as Christian swerved around a car going the speed limit.

"You still wouldn't have gotten your revenge on our father. Eventually, Henry would have talked with him. What was your plan for that?"

"That's the beauty of how things worked out—I saw your father's carefully placed façade fall at Henry's funeral and that's when it hit me...I would just take everything from Elliott. First his son, then his daughter, and finally, his company."

"You were planning to kill me, too?" Fear mixed back into Harper's voice.

"Were?" Janet laughed, but it sounded too loud and too fake over the phone. "Why do you think I kept cozying up to you at the funeral, after, up until today?"

"To get close enough to me to kill me."

"Right, but it wasn't as quick as I'd originally planned. When you started finding the trail I'd laid out that would lead to Elliott, you were angry and ready to turn your father in. I hadn't planned on that. Then it struck me that I could make Elliott suffer even more than killing you. You betraying him would hurt much worse."

"That's why you kept encouraging me to help Christian get information to report my father."

Christian recognized the controlled anger humming in Harper's voice. *Lord, please keep her safe and in control. I claim Deuteronomy 31:6 over Harper right now, in Your name, that You will not leave her or forsake her. That You will go with her.*

"Everything was going according to plan. I figured once you turned on him and exposed what he had done, a lawsuit would be easy to file and he would finally have to pay. I had a lawyer ready to go as soon as Christian's report became a matter of public record." There was a pause. "I'm glad I stopped by to check and make sure things were still in motion. I had to be sure. While the office was bugged so I could hear everything Henry and you were doing, I lost the bug here once you put Henry's old furniture in storage."

"You bugged the office and Henry's house?"

"Are you dense? That's what I just said."

Christian gripped the steering wheel tighter as he turned into Harper's subdivision.

"So, now what?"

"Now, well, the grief over losing your twin was too much for you to bear. Especially on y'alls birthday."

Heart pounding, Christian ran a stop sign and squealed tires around the corner.

"You'll stab yourself, in the heart, as you ate a piece of cake for your precious twin."

"Nobody will believe I'd commit suicide, Janet."

"Oh, but they will. Because I'll be the one to call it in. I came over to wish you a happy birthday. We talked about how miserable this life is without Henry. I tried to stop you, I did, but you moved too fast. I wasn't—"

Oof!

A clatter as the phone dropped. Sounds of crashing blasted through the speaker.

Scuffling. Grunting. Heavy breathing.

Metal against tile. More crashing of glass.

Christian whipped into the driveway and jammed the car in PARK. He didn't even take the time to turn off the engine or close the door. He only had one thought: get to Harper.

Sirens wailed in the distance.

His legs pumped as he ran to the front door, outrunning Hunter. The door was locked. Christian punched the code in the keypad deadbolt and the lock disengaged. He and Hunter dashed inside.

They raced to the kitchen and found both women on the floor. Wet blood was on both of their shirts. Harper kneeled over Janet's still body.

"Harper!" Christian slid to her.

She had blood on her hands and tears streaming down her face as she had her fingers pressed against Janet's wrist. "I can't find a pulse! Help me find a pulse!"

Sirens howled in the driveway.

Hunter holstered his gun and felt Janet's neck. He shook his head at Christian. "Don't move. This is a crime scene."

"I stabbed her. I didn't mean to kill her. I promise." Harper rocked back and forth as Christian held her. They sat together on the stretcher in the emergency room.

"I know you didn't. We heard everything."

"I just lunged for her to knock the knife out of her hand. It went flying to the floor, then we were scrambling for it." Tears blurred Harper's vision. Everything seemed to have happened at once. One minute she scrambled over the kitchen island to knock the knife out of Janet's hand, the next they were punching each other and fighting for the knife. "It just went into her. I'm not even sure how that happened."

Christian kissed her head and held her tighter. "It's okay. You're okay."

"But Janet's dead because of me." She'd taken a life. Harper couldn't even remember how she'd stabbed her.

The doctor returned, with a nurse on his heels, carrying the electronic tablet. "X-rays are back. Nothing is broken, but your wrist is sprained. We'll get it set and wrapped up for you." He pulled the little light back out and tested her eyes.

He looked at Christian. "She's in shock, and I can't rule out a concussion. She'll need someone to be with her, at least for the next twelve hours. During this time, wake her up every two or three hours and ask her a simple question, such as her name. Be sure and then look for any other changes in the way she looks or acts. If anything seems off, bring her to the hospital immediately."

Christian nodded.

"I'm going to write a prescription for an anti-nausea medication, just in case she feels woozy. It's natural. Also, she might have a headache. She can take Acetaminophen or Ibuprofen every four hours for that." The nurse tapped on the tablet.

This was ridiculous. "Hey, I'm right here."

The doctor smiled at her as if she was an impudent child. "Yes, but because of the shock, you probably won't remember your at-home care instructions."

Or maybe he just didn't trust a killer. That's what she was now. Tears burnt the scratches on her face, but she didn't care. How could she be an officer of the court when she was a killer?

Christian tightened his hold on her.

She drew from his strength and warmth. Why was she so cold? Her teeth chattered.

The nurse slipped out of the room as the doctor grabbed a roll of Coban. "How do you like bright yellow?" He held up the almost neon-colored self-adhesive wrap.

Harper shrugged. She didn't care. Did killers have a color preference? She shivered.

The nurse returned and placed a warm blanket over her legs. Heat radiated through her immediately. "Thank you." The nurse also had the nicest smile.

Hunter stepped inside. "The Prosecuting Attorney himself is on his way to talk with you. You'll be able to give your statement to me, with him present. Since Christian heard everything via the phone, he'll give a statement to your boss, too, and that should be it. Until the PA gets here, just rest."

Harper nodded, and Hunter left. On some level, she recognized she'd acted in self-defense, but right now...she couldn't process anything.

The doctor hummed as he wrapped her left wrist. She still didn't remember how she had hurt it during the struggle. It wasn't really hurting now, but the x-ray tech had told her it was probably because she was still on an adrenaline high following the rush.

She must have started coming down off that adrenaline high as weight pulled at her muscles. Harper closed her eyes and leaned against Christian. She couldn't think anymore. Didn't want to. She just wanted to let Christian hold her and keep the guilt at bay.

He has delivered us from the domain of darkness.

Harper stilled as the words whispered in her head. Her pulse slowed.

He has transferred us to the kingdom of his beloved Son, in whom we have redemption, the forgiveness of sins.

Opening her eyes, Harper glanced at Christian to see if he had whispered the words to her. He talked with the doctor about rafting. The doctor had slowed his motions of wrapping her wrist, and told Christian he hadn't been on the Gauley River in years and he missed it. Neither man spoke to her, certainly not in whispers.

In Him we have redemption through His blood, the forgiveness of our trespasses, according to the riches of His grace, which He lavished upon us, in all wisdom and insight making known to us the mystery of his will, according to His purpose, which He set forth in Christ as a plan for the fullness of time, to unite all things in Him, things in heaven and things on earth.

Her heartbeat stuttered. *God?*

The Lord is near to all who call on Him, to all who call on Him in truth.

The doctor finished wrapping her wrist and set her hand gently in her lap. He spoke in quiet tones to Christian, something about her falling asleep. He stood and slipped out of the room. She ignored him as her pulse raced. *God, is that You?*

Behold, I am with you and will keep you wherever you go.

The image of her mother passed through Harper's mind, making her smile to herself. Her mom was safe in God's love. She was in heaven. How could Harper stay mad at God for calling her home?

I am with you always, to the end of the age.

Harper thought about Henry, with their mom, in heaven. She ached for feeling all alone.

I will not leave you as orphans; I will come to you.

Suddenly, Harper knew in her heart, she wasn't alone. She'd never been alone. God had always been with her, and He still was. And He wasn't upset that she'd been angry with Him.

Neither death nor life, nor angels nor rulers, nor things present nor things to come, nor powers, nor height nor depth, nor anything else in all creation, will be able to separate you from the love of God in Christ Jesus.

Tears spilled down her face again, but this time they were tears of overwhelming, all-consuming, joy.

"It's okay," Christian crooned as he held her tighter.

She sat up and looked at him, smiling. "Will you do something for me?"

He wiped away her tears. "Anything."

Harper's entire being trembled with agape love like she'd only begun to understand. "Will you pray with me? Now? Here?"

23

"She's come back into the flock? That's amazing, Christian. I'm so happy." Katie snuggled against Hunter on Harper's couch.

"Yeah, it's pretty amazing. I can't even tell you how elated I am." Christian leaned back in the chair and yawned.

"She did great in her statement. The Prosecuting Attorney declared it self-defense, so that's the end of that." Hunter draped his arm around his wife.

"Is she really planning on dissolving Wolfe Mining?" Katie asked.

Christian nodded. "She's pretty adamant. She refuses to sell it to a hedgie, fearful that it will still function business as usual. That's the last thing she wants."

Katie tucked the blanket around her tighter. "A *hedgie*? What in blue blazes is that?"

"The way it was explained to me is it's a hedge fund or a venture capital firm." Christian chuckled.

The timer on Christian's cell went off, and Katie automatically pushed to her feet. "What question should I ask her this time?"

They'd already asked her name, name of her dog, and her mother's name. Now that they were nearing the eight o'clock mark, Christian struggled with finding a new easy question that wouldn't upset her. "Ask her who the most amazing man in the world is." He grinned at his sister, who stuck her tongue out at him.

"That would be you, Christian." Harper came into the room wearing the sweats Katie had helped her into after she'd showered. She wore a light blanket like a shawl. Atticus followed her out of the bedroom and moved to the couch. He rested his head on Katie's lap until she pet his massive head.

Christian leapt to his feet. "You're supposed to be resting."

"I'm tired of trying to sleep. I've slept enough." She sat on the arm of the chair where Christian had sat. "I've already filed the forms online to dissolve Wolfe Mining and put in an order to stop all mining for the day. Funny how the operations manager seemed surprised." She gave a little laugh.

Christian eased her into the chair and took the arm himself. "Do you feel nauseated? Have a headache? Is your wrist hurting."

"No, no, and a little." She grinned and looked over at Katie, who had settled back on the couch with Hunter. "Is he always a mother hen like this?"

Katie shook her head. "Not really. He's more of just a regular nuisance."

Christian dramatically put his hand over his heart. "No respect."

They all laughed, then the room fell silent.

"Would you like a cup of coffee?" Katie finally asked.

"I would, actually. I'll put on a pot for us." Harper took three steps in the direction of the kitchen, then froze. "I'll need to clean up the... the mess in there."

Christian shot to his feet. "It's already done."

"You didn't have to do that. Any of you." She took the hand of support that Christian gave her.

"We didn't." Katie smiled. "We started to, but then Nell showed up and took charge."

Harper smiled. "She does that." She frowned. "How did she know what happened?"

"She apparently has a cousin that works at the hospital who called her when you came in. She called me to find out if you were okay, and I told her you were being discharged and then I'd bring you home." Christian smiled. "I remembered the mess in the kitchen, so while I had her on the phone, I asked where you kept the bleach. She showed up about fifteen minutes after Katie tucked you in."

"She's amazing." Harper let go of Christian's hand. "I'll go make that coffee."

"Let me help you," Christian offered.

She laid a hand on his. "No. I need to do this myself. Would you let Atticus out for me, please?"

He nodded and did her bidding, then returned to the chair, glancing over his shoulder toward the kitchen several times.

"She looks good," Katie offered. "Steady on her feet, thinking clearly, and her coloring is back to normal."

"Yeah. I just worry about the emotional stuff." Christian looked over his shoulder again. "She's handling everything for Wolfe Mining professionally and efficiently."

"It's hard to deal with taking a life, even when it's self-defense," Hunter volunteered. "If she needs to talk to someone, I can set her up with the counselor the bureau uses. It's mandatory if we're involved in a death that we talk to the counselor to deal with all the conflicting emotions." He shrugged. "It helps."

"Thanks. I'll let her know after her physical wounds heal." Christian glanced over his shoulder again. How long could putting on a pot of coffee take? He stood and moved toward the kitchen. Katie grabbed his arm. "Let her be. She wanted to be alone, so let her be alone. She'll holler if she needs us."

His sister was right, but that didn't make being sidelined any easier. He wanted so desperately to take all the pain she had—physical and mental, away from her and carry it for her, but he knew he couldn't. She would have to walk through this on her own. He could only be there to love and support her.

He drew himself up suddenly.

Love?

The word didn't send spiders of fear throughout him. He didn't even wince. He thought about Harper, how she made him feel and how he wanted to be a better man because of her.

Yeah, love.

He loved Harper!

The electronic doorbell chimed. Christian jumped to his feet to answer the door, but Harper emerged from the kitchen. "I've got it. It's my father."

The room went silent as she opened the door. "Father. Come in."

He stepped just far enough over the threshold for Harper to shut the door before he spoke. "I've been hearing some things. We need to talk."

"Would you like a cup of coffee?"

"I would." He glanced over and saw Christian, Hunter, and Katie in the living room. Ignoring their head nods, he followed Harper into the kitchen. "What's that tree hugger doing here, Harper?" He didn't try to quieten his voice.

"Christian is here because I want him here." Harper sounded as calm and smooth as ever.

"Why would you want that?"

"Because I love him, that's why. I don't have any artificial sweetener in the house. Would you like real sugar?"

Christian went still. Every nerve in his body was on full alert. Had he misheard her. He looked over at Hunter and Katie, both smiling at him. Nope, he hadn't misheard.

His heart nearly exploded. Christian wanted to rush into the kitchen and pull Harper into his arms and kiss her until he couldn't breathe anymore. But he couldn't. Not yet.

She loved him!

⁓

THE LOOK on her father's face was priceless. Harper turned her back to him to stir her coffee, but mainly to hide her smile. If he was shocked by that, he was going to love what she was about to tell him.

She turned back and handed him the black coffee she'd poured.

"I'm fine. I guess I needn't bother asking you how you found out about last night. It doesn't matter anyway."

"You really can't love that tree-hugger, Harper. He's no good for you."

She didn't even dignify his statements with a response. "I have something to tell you, Father."

"Nothing could be worse than what I've been hearing. The operations manager called and told me—"

"I received a letter from Mom yesterday."

His face went slack. "What?"

"The lawyer for her estate paid me a visit. He had a letter for me from Mom that explained how Wolfe Mining was set up."

Her father's face turned white. He understood. Had he just forgotten about the other stocks her mother had?

"He also gave me stocks Mom had for me. Twenty-six shares."

"Well, it was your mother's right to leave them to whomever she chose." A little color seeped back into his face.

Harper ran her thumb back and forth over the top of the cup's handle. "Yes, just like it was Henry's." She straightened while he paled again. "I'm the sole beneficiary of Henry's estate as well, including his shares."

All the blood drained from his face. His jaw locked.

"Yes, that's right. I own fifty-one percent of Wolfe Mining. Controlling interest in the company."

He didn't miss but a beat or two. "We've already established we can't work together, so I'll buy your shares. All of them."

Harper slowly shook her head. He would never take responsibility for everything he'd done. His one-track mind would hurt so many. "I don't think so Father. I have a different plan in mind." Slowly, she informed him she would be dissolving the company immediately, and all her plans that would follow.

"You can't do that. It's my company!"

"But I can because it's *my* company. I won't let you continue to hurt the people in the communities where Wolfe Mountain has implemented mountaintop removal mining. I won't let you continue to poison the waters and plants, damaging the environment. You have to be stopped. Henry is dead because of you, and I was nearly killed because of you."

"What?"

Harper told him about what Wolfe Mining had done to Janet and her family, and how she'd plotted her revenge. She let herself cry when she explained what Janet had done to Henry, and stiffened her shoulders when she told him about Janet attacking her right in that very kitchen.

"It's not my fault that woman was unstable. I told Henry not to get involved with her in the first place."

"And that, Father, is a prime example of you not being willing, or maybe not even able, to take responsibility for anything you've set in motion, which is why my only option is to dissolve Wolfe Mining."

Her father shot to his feet. Rage shook his entire body. "I won't allow you to do this. I've put my own blood, sweat, and tears into my company, and I'm not about to let you destroy what I've worked so hard to build."

"You can't really stop me."

The look in his eyes made her, for the first time in her life, actually afraid of her father. It was like she was looking at a man possessed. Maybe she was.

"Excuse me. I came to get a cup of coffee." Christian stepped into the room, angling himself between Harper and her father.

"It's because of this tree-hugger, isn't it? He's filled your head with such nonsense."

"I think it's time you left, Father. I'll send you a notice about the time of the employee meeting this afternoon."

He went silent, just stood there shaking.

"Sir, Harper asked you to leave now. I think it best that you do." Christian used his body to block Harper from her father.

"Donnie warned me you would be a problem. I had to hire extra lobbyist just to undo all the damage you had lined up."

"Sir, you need to leave."

"This isn't your house, it's my son's. The one I paid for."

"Correction, Father, it's my house."

"I bought it as a welcome-to-the-company gift for Henry. I paid for it."

His admission didn't even phase Harper. She didn't care that he would never accept her for the woman she'd become. It didn't matter to her anymore. "Yet, I hold the title to it."

His jaw clenched again.

"Sir, please don't make me throw you out. Harper doesn't need this right now."

"I wish you'd try to throw me out of a house I bought and paid for."

Hunter walked into the room and flashed his badge. "You can either walk out that door right now on your own, or I will physically escort you out. Either way, you are leaving. Now."

"You won't get away with this," he hollered at Harper, but made his way to the front door.

She turned and collapsed against Christian, who held her against him. He stroked her hair and kissed the top of her head. When she felt strong enough, she looked up and stared into his eyes. "Will you do me another favor?"

"Anything."

"Will you kiss me?"

He smiled and lowered his head. When he was barely an inch from her mouth, he paused. "Tell me." His voice was husky.

She didn't have to ask...she knew what he meant. "I love you."

He smiled wider. "I love you, too."

Then his mouth was on hers, and her heart beat in perfect sync to his.

DEAR READER

Thank you so much for joining me in the adventure on the Gauley River. I loved returning to the Gallagher family.

The research for this story was immense. Yes, the facts about the Candy Darters, the plants, and the State Park are true. Yes, mountaintop removal mining is very real. I took certain liberties in my telling for the sake of the story. I encourage you to look up mountaintop removal mining for more information.

If you are interested in discussion questions for this novel, they will be coming soon. Please visit my website at www.robincaroll.com and click on FOR READERS. You'll find many extras there, just for you, my reader friend.

I would love to hear from you. Please visit me on social media and on my website, sign up for my monthly newsletter to learn first about new releases, contests, events, etc.: www.robincaroll.com. I love talking books with readers, and you can always reach me via snail mail at PO Box 242091, Little Rock, AR 72223. I'd be honored to hear from you.

Blessings! And keep reading,
Robin

ACKNOWLEDGMENTS

I'm so thankful to my husband, Casey, and our friend, Wade, for providing my gazillion strange questions about the Gauley River so I could come up with this story.

I'm very thankful to my beta readers: Lisa and Heather. I don't know what I'd do without y'all.

This book was brainstormed many years ago at a hotel in St. Louis. Special thanks to Colleen Coble, Pam Hillman, Rachel Hauck, and Cara Putman. Thanks to Carrie Stuart Parks, Lynette Eason, and Voni Harris for stepping up when I needed immediate story help.

My extended family members are my biggest fans and greatest cheerleaders. Thank you for being in my corner: Mom, Bubba and Lisa, Brandon, Rachel, and Wade.

I couldn't do what I do without my girls—Zoey Coraline, Remington Case, and Isabella Co-Ceaux. I love each of you so much! And my precious grandsons, Benton and Zayden. You are all joys in my life.

My most heartfelt thanks to my best friend, brainstorming partner, idea-maker, love of my life, husband...Case. You make my days brighter and fill my heart with love every day. Thank you for loving me as I am. I adore you.

Finally, all glory to my Lord and Savior, Jesus Christ. *I can do all things through Him who gives me strength.*

SIGN UP FOR ROBIN'S NEWSLETTER

HOW TO HELP THE AUTHOR

A special note from the Gallaghers:

"Word-of-mouth is the most powerful marketing tool—even stronger than the class 5s of the Gauley River. If you enjoyed reading about Christian and Harper's adventure in *Snares of Death*, we'd appreciate you rating this book and leaving a review. Even just a sentence or two is greatly appreciated."

Thank you—We appreciate you!

GET CHECKED INTO THE DARKWATER INN SERIES

Isn't It Time You Got Lost in the Bayou?

BAYOU SERIES **BAYOU JUSTICE** ROBIN CAROLL	**BAYOU SERIES** **BAYOU CORRUPTION** ROBIN CAROLL	**BAYOU SERIES** **BAYOU JUDGMENT** ROBIN CAROLL
BAYOU SERIES **BAYOU PARADOX** ROBIN CAROLL	**BAYOU SERIES** **BAYOU BETRAYAL** ROBIN CAROLL	**BAYOU SERIES** **BAYOU BLACKMAIL** ROBIN CAROLL

Time For Restitution with the Justice Seekers Series

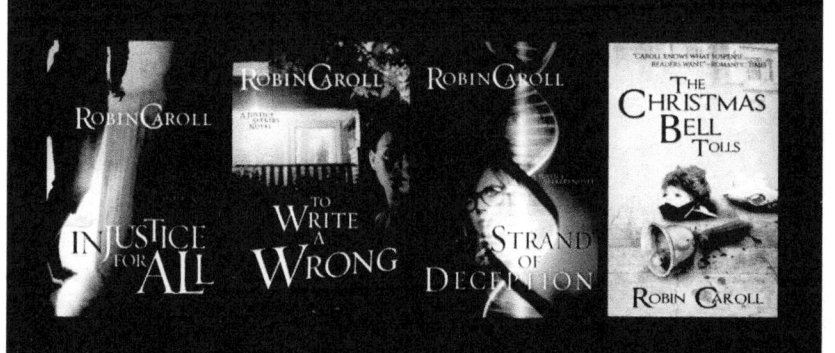

Time To Conquer The Evil Series

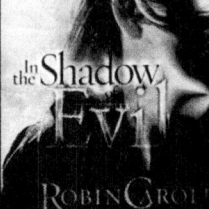

- Deliver Us From Evil — Robin Caroll
- Fear No Evil — Robin Caroll
- In the Shadow of Evil — Robin Caroll

ENJOY READING ABOUT NEW ORLEANS? TRY OUT THIS SAMPLE OF STRATAGEM

"According to your estimation, she has eight minutes to figure out she can't open the door unless her employee uses the key he got in the last room." Pam leaned back in the chair and tilted her head toward the live feed. Her brightly dyed hair shimmered with the movement.

The woman on the screen stumbled around in the room. Her breathing came out labored—harsh in contrast to her platinum-blond hair that caught the dim light. She ran to the only visible exit and turned the knob. Her body slumped against the locked door.

"They'll get it." Grayson was rarely off by more than a few minutes at most. His job was to study the financial, medical, background, and psychological reports on each of the game participants to find their weaknesses and strengths, then use it all against them. To break them to the point where they couldn't escape the game—win—unless they worked as a team. That was the whole purpose of the games, and why they signed waivers.

"I think you read her wrong." Pam tapped the monitor and took a sip of her white mocha. "I bet they won't escape according to your time frame."

Grayson grinned at his collaborator. "Wouldn't be the first time I misjudged." He stared at the blond woman, now on her feet again, running her hands over the walls. "But I don't think that's the case with this one."

"Twenty bucks says you're wrong." Pam dug a bill out of the back pocket of her jeans and slapped it on the long desk they shared.

He shook his head. "Why must you bet on every single game we run?"

"Adds to the excitement." Grinning, she shrugged. "Are you going to put your money where your calculations are, hotshot?"

"Of course." He laid a twenty on top of Pam's and stared at the woman on the monitor.

"Six minutes."

The blond woman's hands fisted at her side. Grayson could almost feel her frustration as he gave the computer command that opened the sliding hidden passageway. The woman's employee all but fell into the room. The blond rushed to him.

Grayson smiled as the woman helped the man stand. Just as he'd predicted, her nurturing instincts kicked in. He pressed another button, and a recording of a child crying out for her mother filled the room. One of the woman's greatest fears was being unable to protect her child.

The woman pounded on the door. Her employee eased in front of her and rammed his shoulder against the door. His protective instinct came right on time, as Grayson had estimated.

"Four minutes." Pam leaned forward, closer to the monitor.

It might be close.

The woman sobbed, shoulders shaking as she hung her head.

"She's freaking." Pam rubbed her hands together and pushed the button to increase the volume on the child's wails.

The woman slumped against the wall beside the door—defeated.

"That's almost cheating." Grayson leaned forward, his nose nearly pressing against the monitor.

This was the most intense part of the game, the flipping of personalities. The employee saving the employer served a twofold purpose: the employee built confidence in himself as a vital part of the company team, and the employer learned that the company can accomplish nothing without the input and dedication of its workers.

The woman shook herself and turned to beat on the door, almost in hysterics. She twisted the knob, rattling the lock.

"One minute." Pam rubbed her hands together.

Come on, man. Figure it out. Grayson locked his jaw, concentrating on the monitor.

"Thirty seconds."

The more frantically she turned the knob, the louder the lock rattled. The man hesitated in his ramming.

That's right. The key. It's in your pocket.

"Twenty."

Slowly, the man pulled the key from his jacket pocket and thrust it at his boss.

"No!" Pam glanced at the timer. "Ten seconds."

The woman turned the knob, and she and the man both slipped through the door.

Grayson stared at the timer. "With four seconds to spare." He grabbed both twenties.

Pam shook her head but grinned. "You make me sick, you know that, right?"

He waggled his eyebrows. "When are you going to learn not to bet against me?" Grayson stood as the monitor flipped to the "recovery room" where the man and woman were taking bottles of water from Grayson's congenial business partner, Colton York.

Pam stood as well. "One of these days, Grayson Thibodeaux, you're going to lose."

Some days, it felt like he'd already lost all that he'd held dearest, but he shook his head at his assistant anyway. "I think I'm gonna call it a day."

"Sure, take the money and run." Pam laughed as she shut down the monitors.

"See you tomorrow." Grayson headed down the hall to his office, ready to grab his laptop and head home.

"As usual, my timing is perfect."

Every hair on the back of Grayson's neck stood at attention. No mistaking that voice. He turned. "Hello, Anna Belle."

"Don't 'hello' me." She marched around the receptionist, who threw Grayson an apologetic look. "Did you think I wouldn't find out?"

He sighed. No use trying to shut up his ex-wife or even get her to speak with him privately. Nothing would work until she had her say. He knew. All too well. "Find out what, Anna Belle?"

"About your dad's duck hunting gig in Plaquemines Parish. You failed to mention that in our divorce, and it's worth over one point five million dollars. I was entitled to half that amount in the settlement."

"My father didn't own that. It's a hunting lease. I was accepted as a legacy." He caught a flash of Pam's lavender-pink hair from the corner of his eye. Humiliation would come later.

"Which is still worth a very healthy amount of money and was passed down to you. You didn't declare it, Grayson."

"But I can't sell the land because I don't own it. That's why it wasn't addressed in the divorce settlement, Anna Belle. It's not something I own."

"I'm entitled to half what the lease is worth." She popped her hands on her hips and tightened her lips into a firm line.

At one time, that move would have made him reverse his stance.

That was then; this was now. "I don't care what you think you're entitled to, Anna Belle. I suggest you call your lawyer if you have a problem with the divorce settlement because I really don't—"

Her slap brought a stinging to his eyes. He grabbed her wrist. Held it. "How dare you, Anna Belle? To come to my job and assault me?" Grayson ground his teeth so hard it was a wonder he didn't crack a couple.

Pam was beside him in a flash, her hand on his forearm. "Don't bother, Grayson. She isn't worth it."

He let go of his grip on Anna Belle with a jerk.

"You should leave. Now." Pam's voice shook with the hatred she felt for Anna Belle.

"This isn't over, Grayson." Anna Belle spun away from him, her long, blond hair flung over her shoulder as she marched toward the front door, her spike heels tapping angrily against the cool tiles.

"Everything okay out here?" Colton stood in the hallway, his embarrassed-for-someone-else look planted firmly on his face.

"We're fine. Just leaving for the day." Pam took Grayson's arm and turned him toward the back door.

The mortification had already wormed its way into Grayson's chest. No telling how many people just saw the exchange. Pam, Colton, Jackie the receptionist, and possibly clients. He didn't need his assistant or his business partner to take up for him with his ex-wife. Every time he saw Anna Belle, the pang of her betrayal nearly strangled him. He didn't want to hate her, prayed daily that his heart would be softened to forgive her, but she still stopped him cold.

He cleared his throat. "I need my laptop."

"Not tonight, boss. Take the night off. Read a book, watch a game, do whatever you need to do to unwind. You've earned it." Pam had that look in her eye, the one that said it was easier just to do what she wanted because she could be almost as relentless as Anna Belle.

Almost, but in a much better way.

He gave a curt nod and dug his keys from his jeans pocket. "I'll see you in the morning."

She rested her hands on her hips, shifting her weight from one leg to the other.

Grayson had one thought when he headed to his truck: he desperately needed a vacation. Soon.

CHAPTER ONE

Home sweet home.

Long weekends were great for a getaway to think and refocus, but Grayson Thibodeaux itched to get back home. He turned onto his street and let out a sigh—he'd sleep in his own bed tonight. Tomorrow would start a new week, and he could put the last couple of months behind him, especially the past two weeks.

Maybe then he could put the last several years in his rearview mirror.

The drive had been slower than usual, but with Mardi Gras coming next week, New Orleans burst at the city limits with tourists and carnival people. Bright, sparkly greens, purples, and golds lined the French Quarter and beyond. The floats housed in the many warehouses would receive final touches before the upcoming parades.

Tension gripped Grayson as he spied a car parked in the driveway of his home. He didn't get random visitors, and very few people knew he'd even left town, much less when he'd return. He didn't recognize the vehicle.

He eased his truck behind the car, effectively blocking them it in. Grayson stepped silently onto the concrete and stared at his front porch. No one there.

Zydeco music blasted from the house next door: an early Mardi Gras celebration in full swing. Smoke from a grill drifted from the couple's backyard, sending a mouth-watering aroma wafting through the garden district neighborhood.

Grayson gently pushed the truck door closed, then headed down the cobblestone path that ran alongside the old house. Even in the waning light, his steps found the stones with no stumbles. He'd grown up in this house, had helped his father place the very cobblestones he now walked on into the sod.

The light by the kitchen door illuminated a man and woman standing on his back porch, their backs to him. The woman had her hands cupped around her face as she pressed against the kitchen window.

Grayson's muscles flexed. "May I help you?"

The man and woman spun at the same time, both setting their hands on the butts of their respective side arms.

Recognition came instantly. "Brandon?" Grayson asked.

"Hey." Brandon Gibbons, Grayson's old college buddy and currently a detective with the New Orleans Police Department, removed his hand from his sidearm. Grayson had worked with Brandon when he was a consultant for the department.

"You remember my partner, Danielle?" Brandon nodded at the woman beside him.

Black-as-night hair, brown eyes, and a chip on her shoulder bigger than a boulder—yeah, he remembered Danielle Witz all right. "I do. Hello, Danielle."

Her eyes narrowed. "Thibodeaux." Apparently she still hated his guts. It'd been months ago—how could she still carry a grudge for his not calling her sister after their blind date?

"What're you doing back here?" Grayson asked. It wasn't like Brandon to creep around backyards.

Danielle leaned against the porch's support beam. "Where have you been?"

In a split second, Grayson took in their body language and the microexpressions most people didn't even realize they showed. Brandon's lips were thinned, and he wouldn't meet Grayson's stare. Danielle, on the other hand, narrowed her eyes and held eye contact, dropping her chin as she glared.

"Why?" Grayson stood a little straighter.

"Maybe we should go inside?" Brandon asked, looking quickly at Grayson, then darted his gaze to his partner.

Grayson crossed his arms over his chest as little pinpricks of apprehension pimpled his arms. "Why don't you tell me why you're here, peeking in my back windows?"

Brandon met his stare. "I think you'd rather us go inside to talk, Grayson."

This wouldn't be good, but now curiosity nibbled at the edges of his mind. He sighed. "Sure. Come on."

Grayson led the two detectives around to the front door. He unlocked it, then stepped inside and punched in the disarming code on the keypad to his alarm system.

Brandon and Danielle followed him into the cool house. Grayson took a seat in his recliner, leaving the two to sit on his couch. But Danielle didn't sit; she stood behind the couch, facing Grayson. She wore her animosity like a shield.

"So, again, why are you here?" Grayson rested his elbows on his knees and let his hands hang loosely.

"Why—"

"Grayson, I'm sorry," Brandon interrupted his partner.

"For?" His gut twisted.

"It's Anna Belle."

Grayson gripped his hands together and squeezed. "She's hurt? Was she in an accident?" Images of the way his ex-wife drove filled his mind. She often forgot to wear a seat belt. "Is she okay?"

"She's dead." Danielle's words were too flat for the information. She had to be wrong. This was a mistake. Had to be.

"D–dead?" No, Anna Belle was too—well, she was just too alive to be dead.

"I'm sorry, bud. I hate to be the one to tell you, but it's true." Brandon leaned forward on the couch. Empathy did little to soften the severity of his expression.

Anna Belle—dead. She couldn't be—he couldn't— "What happened?" She was vibrant and always driven. She couldn't be dead. Not Anna Belle.

"She died from anaphylactic shock."

Grayson snapped his attention to Danielle. "That can't be." He shook his head. Sure, Anna Belle would take risks, but not with her allergy. She'd always been extremely careful about that and never went anywhere without her EpiPen.

"It's true. The autopsy confirmed it. I'm sorry." Brandon's words registered with Grayson, but he still couldn't fathom the finality.

Numbness spread out from his chest like icy fingers as images of Anna Belle sped across his mind like a movie.

In college, her hair flowing and eyes flashing against Death Valley stadium lights as the Tigers won the national championship. The warmth of her body against his as she hugged him in her excitement.

Her fingertips grazing his cheek as he cried at his father's funeral. The surprising strength of her small stature as she held him up at the grave.

Her unmistakable beauty in her wedding dress as she said her vows to him in the cathedral.

The hardness of her eyes when she told him she was filing for divorce.

"Grayson?" Brandon's voice cut through the memories.

He looked to his friend. "She's always extremely careful about her allergy. She steered far away from anything that could remotely have cherries or cherry juice or even be cross-contaminated with them. She was almost paranoid about it." Privately of course. Not many outside her tight circle of family and friends knew of the allergy.

Brandon nodded. "So we've been told."

"But either way, she always carries her EpiPen. In her purse. In her car. In her office. Everywhere." The woman nearly mortgaged their house with how many she bought and stowed everywhere.

Brandon nodded again. "We've opened an investigation into the circumstances surrounding her death."

Wait, what? "Do you suspect foul play?" That would be the only thing that made sense. Anna Belle would never be so reckless with her allergy.

Then again, who would want to hurt her?

"Why don't you tell us where you've been the past several days?" Danielle interrupted, crossing her arms.

Ahh. Yes. Reality crashed into his racing mind. An ex-husband would definitely be of interest when his wife died in such an unusual manner. Ex-wife. "I went out of town. To St. Francisville."

"What were you doing there?" Danielle's body stood as rigid as her tone.

"Playing golf."

"Where?" She stared straight at him.

Grayson tightened his jaw. She might just be doing her job, but she didn't have to have such an attitude.

"The Bluffs. And before you ask, I stayed at the lodge there on Thompson Creek."

Brandon sat on the very edge of the couch, writing in a small notebook balanced on his knee. "When did you leave town?"

"Wednesday. About eleven that morning."

"You've been gone, what, five days?" Danielle's eyes were still narrowed. "That's quite a long weekend golf trip."

Grayson didn't reply because there wasn't a question. He knew how this played out. He'd consulted enough.

"Were you playing in a tournament or with a group?" Brandon's pen hovered over the notebook.

"Not a tournament. I played Thursday with some friends of mine from medical school. We had an 8:00 a.m. tee time."

Brandon scribbled. "Their names?"

"Skipper Bertrand, Tom Bridges, Robert Bertram, and Donny Olson."

"What time did you finish up?" Brandon asked.

Grayson lifted a shoulder. "About noon or so."

"And after you finished the round?" Brandon's gaze held an unspoken apology.

"We grabbed lunch at the club."

"All of you?" Danielle interrupted.

"Yes. All of us."

"Then what?" Brandon asked.

Grayson shifted in his recliner. "I went back to my room at the lodge and fell asleep in front of the television." He cut his stare to Danielle. "*Tombstone*, starring Val Kilmer and Kurt Russell, and I don't remember what channel."

Brandon tapped his pen against the notebook. "Do you remember what time you left the club?"

Grayson's mind wouldn't function right. "I'd guess about one or so."

"And you went to your room and watched television? Fell asleep watching a movie, you say?" If Danielle tried to hide her disdain, she failed miserably.

"Yes. I woke up about six and took a shower."

"Why? What did you do that night?" Danielle asked.

Grayson ran a hand down his face. "I met my friends at the Francis Southern Table. Our reservations were for seven."

"How long were you there?" Her tone matched her facial expression.

"I'm not sure. When we finished eating, we left. I got back to the lodge about eight thirtyish."

"Why didn't you answer my calls?" Brandon asked. "I left you a voice mail."

"I lost my cell phone in Thompson Creek." For the first time in a really long time, he wished he'd had his phone.

"When did you lose it?" Brandon asked.

"Thursday morning. First hole." Grayson shook his head "I figured that was a sign of how I'd be playing that day, but I actually shot two under." Seemed lame now, considering Anna Belle was dead.

"So you were *asleep* from about one until six, alone in your hotel room?" Danielle took a step around the couch, still staring him down.

Grayson nodded. "I was dozing in front of the TV. I don't know what else to tell you. That's what I was doing."

Brandon shot his partner a hard stare. "What about Friday? Did you play with your group again?"

Grayson shook his head. "Only Tom and I played."

"All day?" Danielle pressed.

Grayson shrugged. "Basically a repeat of Thursday. I got up and ate breakfast in the club, then met Tom at eight for a round."

"Did you have lunch at the club when you were done?" Brandon asked. "Or go to a restaurant?"

"The club." Now even Brandon was pushing the envelope.

Grayson shook his head. Enough. He'd been a consultant for the police department, had worked with Brandon many times, for pity's sake. "What happened with Anna Belle, Brandon? She'd always been so careful about her allergy. She saw it as a weakness in herself and hated it. She let very few people even know about it."

"We can't really comment on an open investigation—"

"We're still working on gathering all the facts." Brandon cut off his partner.

Grayson's throat tightened like concrete filled his mouth, and his memory raced through police procedure. Notification. That's what they were doing here, but as an ex, he wasn't legally considered her next of kin.

Anna Belle had alienated her mother, the only living relative she'd had, but Grayson had liked her the few times he met her. She still lived in a double wide in Breaux Bridge, about two hours away. He looked at Brandon. "Have you called her mom? Do you want me to?"

"Her next of kin has been notified." Danielle shifted her weight from one foot to the other.

"Her mother is staying at the Darkwater Inn," Brandon offered.

Danielle took a couple of steps toward him. "Did anybody see you at all Thursday afternoon in St. Francisville?"

"I don't know."

"What about the rest of the weekend? What did you do?" Danielle pressed.

He opened his mouth to answer that he'd slept in, then went and toured the USS *Kidd*, but clamped his mouth shut in that split second before he spoke. The clouds of shock in his mind cleared just enough. He cut his eyes to Brandon. "When did Anna Belle die?"

Brandon and Danielle looked at one another. A volume of unspoken words passed between them.

Finally, Brandon turned to him. "Thursday afternoon."

Grayson shook his head. "That can't be. She was scheduled to be involved with a corporate game with her company at a rented house all day Thursday, Friday, and Saturday. It was a controlled environment."

Danielle nodded. "She died during the course of the game, Mr. Thibodeaux." She paused, letting her words sink in. "The game *you* custom designed for her to participate in."

Just when he thought it couldn't get any worse.

"You need to come to the station with us and answer some questions." Danielle put her hands on her hips. The leather of her holster creaked. "About that game."

"Have you already spoken to my business partner? Colton York? He handled the contract with Deets PR." Grayson tightened his jaw.

He'd told Colton that they shouldn't have taken the job. Even worse, Colton and the Deets PR contract didn't allow for the players to fully know they were involved in a game, so they were playing in the dark.

Brandon gave a little nod. "He gave us some basic information and is going to speak with us again. But he said you were the actual creator of the game."

Grayson paused. While he knew he didn't have to go anywhere to answer any questions, he wanted to help Brandon in the investigation. But not tonight.

"I'm happy to assist you in your investigation, but I think it best I wait to answer any questions until I can adjust from the initial shock." Right now, he needed to process.

Brandon nodded, even though Danielle looked ready to spit nails.

"How about I come in Tuesday morning about nine, and we can talk then?" Grayson stood and led the way to the front door. He needed time to process everything.

"Sure." Brandon hesitated at the door. "I'm sorry, man. See you Tuesday." He headed out, Danielle not saying a word as she followed.

Grayson moved his truck to let them out, then grabbed his duffel and clubs and brought them into the house. He made it as far as the dining room before he dropped them on the floor, the thud of his clubs against the hardwoods echoing in his head. He gripped the back of a chair, steadying himself against actuality.

Anna Belle—dead.

The room seemed to be spinning, but Grayson recognized his mind was trying to accept she was gone while his emotions spun off in varying directions. His psychologist's mind attempted to categorize what he thought. To characterize his emotions. The shock and disbelief, then the uncertainty of what he even felt. All normal reactions but nonetheless destabilizing. He forced himself to head to his bedroom.

He could almost see her here, in the room once called theirs. Her long, blond hair splayed across the pillows as she slept, looking more like a porcelain doll than a young woman. Curled up in the chair in the corner with a book, her feet covered in fuzzy socks on the ottoman. Bouncing on the bed and yelling at the TV as LSU lost against Alabama—again. Running across the room in her fleece pajamas after turning off the light to jump on the bed and under the covers, unnerved from watching a scary movie.

Cherished memories assaulted him. The gentle love they shared early in their marriage. Laughter and midnight picnics in bed. The whispers of encouragement. The tenderness of her fingertips on his cheek. Sharing secrets. Making plans. Holding on to each other through the pounding of multiple hurricanes. The sweet kisses and passionate embraces. The loving until the sun rose over the crescent city.

But it all changed. Oh, did it change.

What was once passion mutated into heated exchanges. His trust lost in her betrayal. His honesty discarded with her lies. Lashes meant to cut. Words used as soul stealers. Accusations. Lies. Her deception challenging the boundaries of his forgiveness.

Now she was gone forever.

Order your copy of *STRATAGEM* today to continue reading!

ENJOY A SAMPLE FROM BAYOU JUSTICE...

Prologue: 1955

Overgrown and untamed, the Louisiana bayou swallowed Jimmy Jones into its swampy depths. Cypress branches slapped his face as he slowed from his dead-out run to a sprint. Gasping as if the air had been vacuumed from his lungs, he stopped and squatted behind a cluster of wild palmettos, listening . . . waiting. Only the blood pounding in his ears registered. He panted and willed his breathing capacity to increase before his next running jag. He had to keep moving, had to get away.

Men's voices erupted from behind him. He jumped, then raced in the opposite direction of their whoops and hollers. His leg muscles burned as the mushy bayou sucked at his feet, as if he ran in quicksand. Swerving left, he ducked under a low-hanging limb. Spanish moss stuck in his hair. He jerked the stringy lichen free and tossed them aside, his feet continuing to make tracks away from the hunters.

Faster and faster he ran, in spite of nature's obstacles blocking his escape route. Mustiness with the underlining sweet aroma of onion flowers filled Jimmy's nostrils—or could that be the stench of his fear? From the closeness of the shouts, he gauged the two men followed right on his heels, gaining on him. If he could just make it to the road...

"There he is. Get him!"

Jimmy wove to the right, then leapt over two fallen oaks. He landed with a thud. The sound of bone snapping overpowered the thudding in his ears. Jolts of pain shot up his right leg from his ankle. No time to check.

Keep running or die.

"I see him. Got him between the crosshairs."

"Don't kill him. It's no fun hanging a dead man."

Hearing the ominous words, Jimmy bolted to his feet. His right ankle gave, but his spirit refused to buckle. He had no other option but to run.

The roar of a bullet discharging resonated a split second before Jimmy's left thigh burned hot. He fell to his knees and then toppled face-first into the cool mud, cool despite the summer heat in the bayou. Digging his hands into the mushy soil, he tried to lift his upper body. Fire licked the muscles in his thigh. Despite being shot, he had to keep running.

"Got him. Told ya."

Too late to get away, the men's voices spoke mere feet above him. Jimmy shifted and turned over. The two men had dispensed with their white sheets—their faces now contorted into sneers. They couldn't be more than twenty-one or two, but hatred, raw and unabashed, flickered in their eyes. Mosquitoes buzzed about, seduced by the sweat dripping into Jimmy's eyes. He wiped his face with his shoulder. The butt of a shotgun made direct contact on the side of his head. Pain vibrated down to his neck and spine. White dots danced in front of his eyes before his vision blurred.

"We'd better hurry and haul him up. Gotta be done before anybody wanders out this-a-way."

The men yanked Jimmy to his feet, half pushing, half dragging him along the root-littered ground. Each movement sent spirals of pain and nausea throughout his body. The sweet hint of ripe hackberries hung in the thick air, making his stomach churn even more.

He opened his eyes, squinting at the backwoods men who shoved him to the ground at the base of a large live oak tree. The setting sun's rays blinded what little he could see. Closing his eyes, he rested his head against the bark.

A strong tug on his hair jolted his head upright. He snapped his eyes open. Rough rope scraped against his throat.

"Get that noose on there nice and tight."

Jimmy's blood thrummed through his veins. Why had he even come to the bayou? Hadn't he been warned, told over and over again how things still were down in the South?

A jerk, then the rope around his neck tightened. He gulped in oxygen. Another jerk, and he sailed above the ground. Struggling with what remained of his energy, he kicked and twisted. Only air skittered beneath his dangling feet.

The men's vile laughter reached his ears. Too late to turn back time. Too late to do things over.

Eyes too swollen to push out the burning tears, Jimmy squinted as a flash of light danced before his face. He pinched his eyes closed and hung his head.

He could only pray that one day, there would be justice in this bayou.

Today wasn't that day.

CHAPTER ONE

Humidity, the South's great oppressor, seized the Louisiana bayou firmly by the throat. Late afternoon heat washed through the air in waves, turning and mixing to make the region downright sticky. CoCo LeBlanc wiped her brow and squinted, scanning the grassy shores. A living bulk shifted on the lush embankment, then the alligator stretched its mouth, his jagged teeth glistening in the late afternoon sun. Moodoo appeared healthy. CoCo stared, smiling at the twelve-foot reptile. She let out a long sigh. It'd been a rough couple of weeks, nursing the prehistoric beast back from the brink of death. Stupid poachers—would they never learn they couldn't hunt alligators anytime they got the notion? If she ever caught them. . .

Enjoy a sample from Bayou Justice...

Moodoo waddled along the banks, then surged his large body into the bayou. CoCo marked his location on her tracking sheet and then fired up the airboat's engine. She settled into the single seat before turning the steering wheel to head back to the house. Picking up speed, the airboat skimmed over murky bayou. Drops of water jetted up, spraying CoCo's face and arms. She leaned closer to the edge of the boat, welcoming the cool mist. July in Lagniappe meant misery, no matter how you chopped it.

She banked the airboat and tied off on the knotty root of a live oak tree that had survived for several centuries. Stepping to the ground, she let the air pockets bubble up around her feet before striding toward the house with sure steps. Her hair plastered to the nape of her neck, and her thin cotton tank-top clung to her back. Too bad her tan-lines were so messed up because she couldn't wear the same style shirt to work everyday.

A man's angry voice burst through the cicadas' chirped song. "You get out, or I'll have the sheriff force you out."

"You get on, now, Beau Trahan. Before I put a *gris gris* on you," her grandmother replied, her voice quivering.

CoCo recognized that tone, and quickened her pace. What now? She rounded the corner of the old plantation home to find Mr. Beau and Grandmere facing off on the veranda. She took the stairs two at a time—the wood creaking in protest. "What's going on here?"

The businessman in slacks and shirt, complete with power-red tie, faced her and glared. "Your grandmother seems to think she's above the law. As usual."

"Get off my land, you old goat." Grandmere's deep green eyes narrowed to slits and she took a step in his direction.

"It's not your land, *vielle*." He wagged his finger in front of Grandmere's face.

Not a good move on his part to call her an old woman, not good at all. CoCo shifted between the dueling elders, popping her hands on her hips. "What's this all about, Grandmere?" She turned to her grandmother but kept track of Mr. Beau from the corner of her eye.

"He says he owns this house." Her grandmother waved a crumpled piece of paper. "Says he's evicting us. Just threats. All little men like him can do is threaten."

"Read the notice, you bat. Marcel signed this land over to me years ago when he couldn't pay his gambling debt. It's all legal—I drew up the papers myself." Beau Trahan, tall and distinguished as a retired politician should look, crossed his arms over his puffed-up chest.

Sounded like something her late grandfather would have done.

CoCo and her sisters had moved in with their grandparents thirteen years ago when their parents had died in a car accident. Grandpere died five years ago, after CoCo had returned to Lagniappe from college. The last years of his life had been littered with gambling and depression.

CoCo pried the paper from her grandmother's fist and scanned the eviction notice, chewing her bottom lip. Thirty days, that's all they had to save their home. She squared her shoulders and set her jaw, piercing him with her stare. "You've served your notice, Mr. Trahan. I'll contact my attorney immediately, and he'll get back to you regarding this matter."

"Not going to do you any good, young lady. The law's on my side." He directed his words to CoCo, but his eyes remained locked on Grandmere. Even in the stifling heat, not a single strand of gray hair moved out of place.

"The spirits are on mine." Grandmere wore that hazy expression she got when riled to the point of pulling out her voodoo paraphernalia.

Oh, no, not the spirits again. CoCo let out a deep sigh and gripped her grandmother's shoulder, digging her fingers into Grandmere's bony frame. "Please leave, Mr. Trahan."

"Thirty days, Marie. That's it. And only because the law stipulates I have to give you that much time." Beau spun around and stomped to his pristine red Cadillac. He slammed the door, revved the engine, then peeled out down the dirt and gravel driveway.

CoCo waited until the rooster tails of dust disappeared before turning back to her grandmother. "Did Grandpere sign over the deed to this house?"

Grandmere's eyebrows shot up over her fading green eyes. "Not that he ever told me. Beau Trahan, that *cooyon* is only trying to cause trouble, *ma chère*. I'll handle him." Her arthritic-gnarled hands grabbed the handle of the screen door.

Shoving her foot against the base of the door, CoCo tapped her grandmother's shoulder. The blue veins were apparent under Grandmere's thin skin. "No voodoo, Grandmere. I mean it."

"Just because you've turned your back on the old ways, doesn't mean the rest of us have." Grandmere shot a look that could freeze fireballs, her jade eyes turning into icicles. "You'll see. You were wrong to drop your training, CoCo. You're a natural."

Biting her tongue, CoCo moved her foot and let her grandmother enter. The argument stayed as constant as the bayou's summers. Ever since she'd come to Christ two years ago, she'd walked away cold from voodoo, black magic, and all that her grandmother had been teaching her. Why couldn't—no, wouldn't—her family open their eyes and see the truth? Didn't they realize their eternal lives were at stake?

A breeze stirred the hot air, teasing the edges of the eviction notice. CoCo shook off her guilty conscience and marched inside the house. She'd deal with her family's salvation later. Right now, she had to find an attorney. Preferably a great one.

For a moment she considered calling her middle sister, Alyssa, up in Shreveport. Just as suddenly as the thought scampered across her mind, she disregarded the idea. Alyssa wasn't interested in the pressing issues happening in Lagniappe. As usual, the responsibility fell to CoCo.

The kitchen had always before been a place of soothing with its bright yellow paint on the walls and cabinets, adding a sunny glow to the room. Despite the lack of updated appliances, the kitchen welcomed. She glanced at the clock—4:10, she needed to hurry before businesses closed for the day. She grabbed the Vermilion parish phone book, dropped into the kitchen chair, and flipped through the business pages. Not much choice of attorneys. All the last names looked familiar, but none of the first names rang any bells. CoCo closed her eyes and jabbed her finger on the middle of the page.

Trahan Law Firm

Oh, but no. This wouldn't do.

Lord, could You give me a little direction here? She flipped to the other side of the page and repeated her random selection process.

Dwayne Williams, Attorney

That sounded promising. A whole lot better than anything to do with a Trahan. She pushed back her chair and lifted the cordless phone off the counter. Punching with more force than necessary, CoCo dialed the number listed in the phone book.

On the second ring, a chipper female voice answered. "Law Offices of Dwayne Williams, how may I help you?"

"Hello. My name is CoCo LeBlanc and I need to speak with an attorney as soon as possible." She chewed the inside of her mouth.

"Yes, ma'am. Just a moment, and I'll connect you with Mr. Williams."

Elevator music sounded over the line. Pretty slick, getting to talk to a lawyer on the first call. Maybe because it was so close to quitting time?

"Dwayne Williams." His voice sounded deep, full of timbre.

"Mr. Williams, my name is CoCo LeBlanc, and I need a lawyer. A man, Beau Trahan, has just served my grandmother, and me, with an eviction notice on our home."

"Did you say Beau Trahan?"

"Yes." She pushed the bangs from her forehead. "Is that a problem?" Great, leave it to her to pick out an attorney who probably sat in Mr. Beau's back politician pocket.

"No, not at all." The sound of papers crinkling rustled in the background. "I can work you in tomorrow morning at nine to discuss your case. Is that a good time for you?"

Fast appointment, too. "That'll be perfect. I'll see you then." She hung up the phone, staring at it, hard and long. Jumbled thoughts bounced off the edges of her mind as she worried her bottom lip.

Did she dare call him? It'd been two years since they'd spoken. Did she want to open up all that hurt and anger again? Yet, maybe he could talk some sense into his grandfather.

Jerking the phone up again before she could change her mind, she punched the number she knew by heart, still knew as well as her own. Would Luc Trahan answer?

～

Luc Trahan strode up and down the length of the front porch, glancing down the long driveway lined with oak trees and then back to the wood planks beneath him.

"You're going to wear out the veranda if you don't stop pacing," Felicia said.

He glanced at his younger sister, sitting properly in her wheelchair. "I'm just ready to get this over with."

"He's gonna blow, you know that, yes?"

"I do. That's why I need to get it over with as soon as he gets here." Luc turned and began the next lap. How could he break the news gently to his grandfather? He shook his head. There was no easy way. Felicia had hit the nail on the head—Beau Trahan would blow a gasket when Luc told him that he had no intentions of taking over the managerial reins of D'Queue Casino. Luc enjoyed his job as a freelance consultant for an accounting firm and had no desire to go elsewhere.

"Luc, look at me." His sister's soft voice never failed to calm him.

He did. Her big blue eyes twisted his heart.

"You're doing the right thing, no matter what Grandfather and Mom think."

"I know. I just hate to disappoint either of them." He dropped onto the porch swing adjacent to her wheelchair. "He wants this so badly for me."

"It's not what you want. It goes against everything you believe in."

"And Mom..."

Felicia smiled. "Oh, she'll moan and grumble, only because she's scared of him." She touched the back of his hand, caressing reassurance into his very being. "He isn't going to kick us out like Mom thinks he will."

"What if he does?" His gaze rested on her sweet face.

So sweet, so gentle, so unfair cerebral palsy had attacked her frail body. At only twenty-eight years old, she was confined to a wheelchair, one leg too weak for her to even walk across the room. Would Grandfather kick them out of the house if Luc didn't abide by his wishes? That could never happen—Felicia needed the stability of their home and the care their grandfather's money provided.

"Stop worrying so much, you." She gave his hand a final squeeze before dropping her own back in her lap. "He's threatened Mom with that for years now, yet he's never given us the boot. He's all talk."

"I wish I could be as sure. This just might be what calls his bluff."

Felicia flashed her full-tooth smile. "With all his ranting and raving over me and Frank, he still didn't follow through on his threats. We'll be fine." She stared out into the yard. "When did he say he would be here?"

"He told Mom he was on his way when he called about ten minutes ago."

His cell phone rang, the chords to Dixie playing loud and clear. He snapped if off his belt, flipped it open, and pressed it to his ear. "Hello."

"Luc."

Just his name—that's all it took for his heart to stutter. Her sultry voice always did make his pulse race. His memory slammed the image of her curly black hair, dark eyes with specks of green dancing around the irises, and tanned face to the forefront of his mind. Her strong French heritage had blessed her appearance, that much was certain.

He swallowed back the emotions clogging his throat. "CoCo."

"Your grandfather just left here." Her breathing came across the line as ragged, hitching.

"What was he doing at your place?" Luc shook his head at Felicia's inquiring stare. What could the old man be up to now?

"Serving us an eviction notice." His ex-fiancée's voice quivered. He recognized that trait—she barely had control over her emotions.

"An eviction notice? What're you talking about?" Luc stood and paced again.

"Just what I said. He hand-delivered an eviction notice to Grandmere today, right before I got home from work."

His gut clenched. Work. Her work. He gritted his teeth. The memory of yet another reason they broke up slammed into his mind.

"Luc, are you listening?"

"Yeah. I just don't understand."

"Neither do I." Her throaty sigh over the line tightened the knot holding his stomach hostage. "I wanted you to know what he's up to, and to tell you that I have a meeting with an attorney first thing in the morning."

Lawyers, already? What exactly had his grandfather done? He ran a hand over his hair. "I'm sure it's just a misunderstanding."

"I don't know what's gotten into him, but I'm not going to battle him without legal counsel."

No, CoCo wouldn't back down from any fight. He knew that all-too-well. Her personality wouldn't let her roll over and play dead.

"So, why are you calling me?"

"I don't really know." Her voice changed, moving into the confrontational tone he also recognized. "I thought you should be aware. I'm not going to lie down and take your grandfather's bullying. I intend to fight him with everything I can."

"Curses, *cunjas*, and hexes, CoCo?" He could have bitten off his tongue for letting that slip out. The pain was still raw, even after two years of not being together.

She snorted. "Some things never change. I made a mistake in calling you, Luc. You're too much like the old man to see reason."

Ouch, that stung. "I'm sor—"

"Consider yourself warned. My family will fight you Trahans."

The disconnecting click cut loud in his ear. He held it a minute longer, not wanting to believe she'd hung up on him. Even when he'd ended their relationship and walked away, he'd never hung up on her.

Lord, why can't I control my tongue?

"Was that CoCo?"

He placed the phone back on his belt clip and stared at his sister. "Yeah."

She practically bounced in her chair. "What'd she want?" Hope of his and CoCo's reconciliation glimmered in her eyes.

He hated to disappoint her, but any hope of that just went down like the setting sun. Just as it had when his father had died, and he'd realized he couldn't marry CoCo LeBlanc. "To let me know Grandfather served her with an eviction notice."

Felicia's eyes, already round, grew as large as Confederate coins. "What? When?"

"Just now, apparently."

She covered her mouth with her hand. "Oh, no. What's Grandfather thinking?"

A rumble on the road caused them both to stare at the driveway. Sure enough, their grandfather's Caddy sped along the dirt road.

"I don't know. I'm guessing we're about to find out."

Grandfather slammed the door of his precious car, ran a hand over his thinning hair, and then strode up the stairs. A smile danced on his face, a rare sight. "Luc, Felicia." He gave them a brief nod, not breaking stride as he headed for the door.

Lord, I don't know what to say. I can't antagonize him, yet I can't help him either without knowing what's going on.

"Grandfather," Luc began, staring down at the porch. His grandfather's shoes didn't even have a coat of dust covering them. Dirt ran in fear from Beau Trahan.

"Yes?" His grandfather glanced over his shoulder. "What is it, boy?"

"I just got a call from CoCo LeBlanc. Want to tell me what's going on?"

Chuckling, Grandfather let his hand fall from the door handle and then moved to sit on the porch swing. "Little lady already called you, huh? Trying to sweet talk you into getting me to change my mind, I guess." He laughed and slapped his thigh. "Hope you told her you weren't buying into her feminine wiles again."

Luc shifted his weight from one foot to the other, despising himself for feeling like a disobedient teenager. "What're you doing?"

"Demanding what's mine, of course." His grandfather's eyes set hard in his chiseled face.

"An eviction notice on the LeBlanc's property?" Luc shook his head. "What's up with that?"

"Marcel LeBlanc signed that deed over to me years ago to cover a gambling debt to the casino. I've been really nice, not making them move. Now that I'm retiring, letting you step into my shoes, I have to move out of the penthouse. Since I don't want to make your momma and sister here move out, I'm claiming my property."

Guilt nudged against Luc's chest, but he picked his battles one at a time. "You can't just evict them, Grandfather. Where will they go? Their family's lived in that house since before the Civil War."

"Not my problem, son." His grandfather studied him. "You aren't still sweet on that little swamp witch, are you?"

"I just don't think it's right to evict them."

His grandfather shook his head as he pushed to his feet. "You're too soft, Luc. You'll have to toughen up to be manager at the casino."

Luc leaned against the porch rail. Maybe he appeared casual, even though his insides turned as mushy as quicksand. *Dear God, help me make him understand.*

Felicia gave a slight tilt of her head. "I need to get inside. It's too hot out here." She pushed the control on the automatic wheelchair. Luc moved and opened the door for her. She gave him an encouraging smile as she rolled into the house. He let the screen door bang behind her.

His grandfather hit him with a hard glare, his hazel eyes not dimmed by the years. "You got something else to say to me?"

"About being too soft to be casino manager..."

Grandfather let out a loud laugh. "Don't you worry, son. I'll help thicken up your skin."

He took a deep breath. "It's not that I don't think I can do it. I just don't want the job."

"What?" His grandfather's eyes bugged bigger than a bullfrog's.

"I don't believe in gambling, Grandfather. You know that. I never said I wanted to follow in your footsteps." Luc let out a slow breath. "I love being a consultant, and don't want to change jobs."

His grandfather jumped to his feet. "I'm not believing this. After all my hard work, the years I put in there to get you in position to take over, I can't—"

"I never said I wanted you to do any of that. You just assumed. I'm perfectly content where I am."

The shout Grandfather emitted made Luc jump. "I don't care what you want. You'll take over at the casino, and that's final."

Luc drew up to his full six-foot-three, towering a good four inches over his grandfather, and stared into the old man's eyes. "No, I won't. I'm staying as a freelance consultant."

"You will or else." Grandfather stood toe-to-toe with him.

"Or else what?"

"Or else I'll not only kick you all out in the street, but I'll also publicly disown you so you'll be dead in this town."

ABOUT THE AUTHOR

Best-selling author of more than thirty novels, ROBIN CAROLL writes Southern stories of mystery and suspense, with a hint of romance to entertain readers. Her books have been recognized in several awards, including the Carol Award, HOLT Medallion, Daphne du Maurier, RT Reviewer's Choice Award, and more. Robin serves the writing community as Executive/Conference Director for ACFW.

For More Information
www.robincaroll.com